CONTENTS

CAST OF CHARACTERS

(in the order of their appearance)

Roderick Alleyn		*Of the Criminal Investigation Department, Scotland Yard*
Susan Max		*Character Woman*
Hailey Hambledon		*Leading Man*
Courtney Broadhead		*Second Juvenile*
St John Ackroyd		*Comedian*
Carolyn Dacres		*Leading Lady*
Alfred Meyer	*Of the Carolyn Dacres Comedy Company*	*Her husband: Proprietor and Managing Director of Incorporated Playhouses Ltd*
Valerie Gaynes		*A Beginner*
George Mason		*Meyer's partner: Business Manager, Incorporated Playhouses Ltd*
Ted Gascoigne		*Stage Manager*
Francis Liversidge		*First Juvenile*
Brandon Vernon		*Character Man*
Fred	*Of the Stage Staff*	*Head Mechanist*
Bert		*Stage-hand*
Bob Parsons		*A dresser*
Gordon Palmer		*A bear-cub*
Geoffrey Weston		*His Leader*
Dr Rangi Te Pokiha		*A Maori physician*
Detective-Sergeant Wade		
Detective-Inspector Packer	*Of the New Zealand Police Force*	
Detective-Sergeant Cass		
Superintendent Nixon		
Singleton		*Stage door keeper at the Royal*

FOREWORD

Although I agree with those critics who condemn the building of imaginary towns in actual countries I must confess that there is no Middleton in the North Island of New Zealand, nor is 'Middleton' a pseudonym for any actual city. The largest town in New Zealand is no bigger than, let us say, Southampton. If I had taken the Dacres Comedy Company to Auckland or Wellington, Messrs Wade, Packer, and Cass, to say nothing of Dr Rangi Te Pokiha, might have been mistaken for portraits or caricatures of actual persons. By building Middleton in the open country somewhere south of Ohakune, I avoid this possibility, and, with a clear conscience, can make the usual statement that:

All the characters in this story are purely imaginary and bear no relation to any actual person.

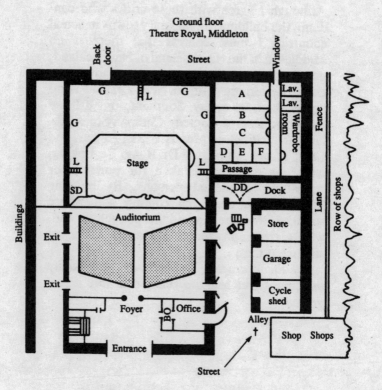

Ground floor
Theatre Royal, Middleton

Street

Back door

Window

G   L   G

G

G

L   L

Stage

SD

Auditorium

Exit

Exit

Foyer   BO   Office

Entrance

A

B

C

D   E   F

Passage

Lav.

Lav.

Wardrobe room

Fence

DD   Dock

Cs

Store

Garage

Cycle shed

Lane

Row of shops

Alley

†

Shop   Shops

Street

Buildings

Dressing rooms

A – Liversidge, Vernon, Broadhead
B – Valerie Gaynes
C – St. John Ackroyd
D – Carolyn Dacres
E – Hailey Hambledon
F – Susan Max

Key

L – Ladders
DD – Double doors
SD – Stage door
BO – Box office
Cs – Cases
G – Grid

CHAPTER 1

Prologue in a Train

The clop and roar of the train was an uneasy element somewhere at the back of the tall man's dreams. It would die away – die away and fantastic hurrying faces come up to claim his attention. He would think 'I am sure I am asleep. This is certainly a dream.' Then came a jolt as they roared, with a sudden increase of racket, over a bridge and through a cutting. The fantastic faces disappeared. He was cold and stiff. For the hundredth time he opened his eyes to see the dim carriage-lamps and the rows of faces with their murky high-lights and cadaverous shadows.

'Strange company I've got into,' he thought.

Opposite him was the leading man, large, kindly, swaying slightly with the movement of the long narrow-gauge carriage, politely resigned to discomfort. The bundle of rugs in the next seat to the tall man was Miss Susan Max, the character woman. An old trouper, Susan, with years of jolting night journeys behind her, first in this country, then Australia, and then up and down the provinces in England, until finally she made a comfortable niche for herself with Incorporated Playhouses in the West End. Twenty years ago she had joined an English touring company in Wellington. Now, for the first time, she revisited New Zealand. She stared, with unblinking eyes, at the dim reflections in the window-pane. The opposite seat to Susan's was empty. In the next block George Mason, the manager, a dyspeptic, resigned-looking man, played an endless game of two-handed whist with Ted Gascoigne, the stage-manager.

And there, nodding like a mandarin beside old Brandon Vernon, was little Ackroyd, the comedian, whose ill-temper was so much at variance with his funny face. Sitting in front of Mason, a pale young man fidgeted restlessly in his chair. This was Courtney Broadhead. 'Something the matter with that youth,' thought the tall man. 'Ever since Panama—' He caught the boy's eye and looked beyond him to where Mr Francis Liversidge, so much too beautifully dressed, allowed Miss Valerie Gaynes to adore him. Beyond them again to the far end of the long carriage were dim faces and huddled figures. The Carolyn Dacres English Comedy Company on tour in New Zealand.

He felt very much an outsider. There was something about these people that gave them a united front. Their very manner in this night train, rattling and roaring through a strange country, was different from the manner of other travellers. Dozing a little, he saw them in more antiquated trains, in stage-coaches, in wagons, afoot, wearing strange garments, carrying bundles, but always together. There they were, their heads bobbing in unison, going back and back.

A violent jerk woke him. The train had slowed down. He wiped the misty window-pane, shaded his eyes, and tried to look out into this new country. The moon had risen. He saw aching hills, stumps of burnt trees, some misty white flowering scrub, and a lonely road. It was very remote and strange. Away in front, the engine whistled. Trees, hills and road slid sideways and were gone. Three lamps travelled across the window-pane. They were off again.

He turned to see old Susan dab at her eyes with her handkerchief. She gave him a deprecatory smile.

'Those white trees are manuka bushes,' she said. 'They bloom at this time of the year. I had forgotten.'

There was a long silence. He looked from one dimly-lit slumping figure to another. At last be became aware of Hambledon's gaze, fixed on himself.

'Do you find us very queer cattle?' said Hambledon, with his air of secret enjoyment.

'Why do you ask that?' said the tall man quickly.

'I noticed you looking at us and wondered what were your thoughts. *Do* you think us queer cattle?'

In order not to disturb Susan Max and to make himself

heard above the racket of the train, he bent forward. So did the tall man. With their heads together under the murky lamp, they looked like conspirators.

'That would be an ungracious thought,' said the tall man, 'after your kindness.'

'Our kindness? Oh, you mean George Mason's offer of a seat in our carriage?'

'Yes. The alternative was a back-to-the-engine pew by a swinging door, among commercial travellers, and next a lavatory.'

Hambledon laughed silently.

'Ah well,' he said, 'even queer cattle may be preferable to all that.'

'But I didn't say I thought—'

'If you had it would not have been very strange. Actors are a rum lot.'

'The last man I heard say that was an actor – and a murderer,' said the tall man.

'Really?' Hambledon raised his head. 'You don't by any chance mean Felix Gardener?'

'I do. How did you guess—?'

'*Now* I know who you are. Of course! How stupid of me! I have seen your photograph any number of times in the papers. It's been worrying me.'

His companion looked at Susan Max. Her three chins were packed snugly down into her collar and her eyes were closed. Her whole person jogged rhythmically with the motion of the train.

'She knew me,' he said, 'but I asked her not to give me away. I'm on a holiday.'

'I should have guessed from your name of course. How inadequate one's memory is. And without your – your rank—'

'Exactly. They spelt me wrongly in the passenger list.'

'Well, this is very interesting. *I* shan't give you away.'

'Thank you. And at any rate we part company in Middleton. I'm staying for a few nights to see your show and look round, and then I go on to the South Island.'

'We may meet again,' said Hambledon.

'I hope so,' said his companion cordially.

They smiled tentatively at each other, and after an uncertain pause leant back again in their seats.

The train roared through a cutting and gathered speed. 'Rackety-plan, rackety-plan,' it said, faster and faster, as though out of patience with its journey. The guard came through and turned down the lamps. Now the white faces of the travellers looked more cadaverous than ever. The carriage was filled with tobacco smoke. Everything felt grimy and stale. The shrill laughter of Miss Valerie Gaynes, in ecstasy over a witticism of Mr Liversidge's, rose above the din. She stood up, a little dishevelled in her expensive fur coat, and began to walk down the carriage. She swayed, clutched the backs of seats, stumbled and fell half across George Mason's knees. He gave her a disinterested squeeze, and made a knowing grimace at Gasgoigne who said something about: 'If you *will* go native.' Miss Gaynes yelped and got up. As she passed Hambledon and the tall man she paused and said:

'I'm going to my sleeper. They call it "de luxe". My God, what a train!'

She staggered on. When she opened the door the iron clamour of their progress filled the carriage. Cold night air rushed in from outside bringing a taint of acrid smoke. She struggled with the door, trying to shut it behind her. They could see her through the glass panel, leaning against the wind. Hambledon got up and slammed the door and she disappeared.

'Have you taken a sleeper?' asked the tall man.

'No,' said Hambledon. 'I should not sleep and I should probably be sick.'

'That's how I feel about it, too.'

'Carolyn and Meyer have gone to theirs. They are the only other members of the company who have risked it. That young woman has just go to be expensive. Valerie, I mean.'

12

'I noticed that in the ship. Who is she? Any relation of old Pomfret Gaynes, the shipping man?'

'Daughter.' Hambledon leant forward again. 'Academy of Dramatic Art. Lord knows how big an allowance, an insatiable desire for the footlights and adores the word "actress" on her passport.'

'Is she a good actress?'

'Dire.'

'Then how—?'

'Pomfret,' said Hambledon, 'and push.'

'It seems a little unjust in an overcrowded profession.'

'That's how it goes,' said Hambledon with a shrug. 'The whole business is riddled with preferment nowadays. It's just one of those things.'

Susan Max's head lolled to one side. Hambledon took her travelling cushion and slipped it between her cheek and the wall. She was fast asleep.

'There's your real honest-to-God actress,' he said, leaning forward again. 'Her father was an actor-manager in Australia and started life as a child performer in *his* father's stock company. Susan has trouped for forty-five years. It's in her blood. She can play anything from grande dame to trollop, and play it well.'

'What about Miss Dacres? Or should I say Mrs Meyer? I never know with married stars.'

'She's Carolyn Dacres all the time. Except in hotel registers, of course. Carolyn is a great actress. Please don't think I'm using the word "great" carelessly. She is a great actress. Her father was a country parson, but there's a streak of the stage in her mother's family, I believe. Carolyn joined a touring company when she was seventeen. She was up and down the provinces for eight years before she got her chance in London. Then she never looked back.' Hambledon paused and glanced apologetically at his companion. 'In a moment you will accuse me of talking shop.'

'Why not? I like people to talk shop. I can never

13

understand the prejudice against it.'

'You don't do it, I notice.'

The tall man raised one eyebrow.

'I'm on a holiday. When did Miss Dacres marry Mr Alfred Meyer?'

'About ten years ago,' said Hambledon, shortly. He turned in his seat and looked down the carriage. The Carolyn Dacres Company had settled down for the night. George Mason and Gascoigne had given up their game of two-handed whist and had drawn their rugs up to their chins. The comedian had spread a sheet of newspaper over his head. Young Courtney Broadhead was awake, but Mr Liversidge's mouth was open and those rolls of flesh, so well disciplined by day, were now subtly predominant. Except for Broadhead they were all asleep. Hambledon looked at his watch.

'It's midnight,' he said.

Midnight. Outside their hurrying windows this strange country slept. Farm houses, lonely in the moonlight, sheep asleep or tearing with quick jerks at the short grass, those aching hills that ran in curves across the window-panes, and the white flowering trees that had made old Susan dab her eyes. They were all there, outside, but remote from the bucketing train with its commercial travellers, its tourists and its actors.

'The fascination of a train journey,' thought the tall man, 'lies in this remoteness of the country outside, and in the realisation that it is so close. At any station one may break the spell of the train and set foot on the earth. But as long as one stays in the train, the outside is a dream country. A dream country.' He closed his eyes again and presently was fast asleep and troubled by long dreams that were half broken by a sense of discomfort. When he woke again he felt cold and stiff. Hambledon, he saw, was still awake.

Their carriage seemed to be continually turning. His mind made a picture of a corkscrew with a gnat-sized train twisting industriously. He looked at his watch.

14

'Good lord,' he said. 'It's ten past two. I shall stay awake. It's a mistake to sleep in these chairs.'

'Ten past two,' said Hambledon. 'The time for indiscreet conversation. Are you sure you do not want to go to sleep?'

'Quite sure. What were we speaking of before I dozed off? Miss Dacres?'

'Yes. You asked about her marriage. It is difficult even to guess why she married Alfred Meyer. Not because he is the big noise in Incorporated Playhouses. Carolyn had no need of that sort of pull. She had arrived. Perhaps she married him because he was so essentially commonplace. As a kind of set-off to her own temperament. She has the true artistic temperament.'

The tall man winced. Hambledon had made use of a phrase that he detested.

'Don't misunderstand me,' Hambledon continued very earnestly. 'Alf is a good fellow. He's very much liked in the business. But – well, he has never been a romantic figure. He lives for the firm, you know. He and George Mason built it between them. I've played in I.P. productions for twelve years now. Eight pieces in all and in five of them I've played opposite Carolyn.'

He had the actor's habit of giving full dramatic value to everything he said. His beautiful voice, with its practised inflexions, suggested a romantic attachment.

'She's rather a wonderful person,' he said.

'He means that,' thought his companion. 'He is in love with her.'

His mind went back to the long voyage in the ship with Carolyn Dacres very much the star turn, but not, he had to admit, aggressively the great actress. She and her pale, plump, rather common, rather uninteresting husband, had sat in deck chairs, he with a portable typewriter on his knees and she with a book. Very often Hambledon had sat on the other side of her, also with a book. They had none of them joined in the all-night poker parties with young Courtney Broadhead, Liversidge and Valerie Gaynes.

15

Thinking of these three he turned to look up the dim carriage. There was young Broadhead, still awake, still staring at the blind window-pane with its blank reflections. As if conscious of the other's gaze he jerked his head uneasily and with an abrupt movement rose to his feet and came down the carriage. As he passed them he said:

'Fresh air. I'm going out to the platform.'

'Young ass,' said Hambledon when he had gone through the door. 'He's been losing his money. You can't indulge in those sorts of frills, on his salary.'

They both looked at the glass door. Broadhead's back was against it.

'I'm worried about that boy,' Hambledon went on. 'No business of mine, of course, but one doesn't like to see that kind of thing.'

'They were playing high, certainly.'

'A fiver to come in, last night, I believe. I looked into the smoke-room before I went to bed. Liversidge had won a packet. Courtney looked very sick. Early in the voyage I tried to tip him the wink, but he'd got in with that bear leader and his cub.'

'Weston and young Palmer, you mean?'

'Yes. They're on the train. The cub's likely to stick to our heels all through the tour, I'm afraid.'

'Stage-struck?'

'What they used to call "shook on the pros." He hangs round Carolyn, I suppose you've noticed. She tells me his father – he's a Sir Something Palmer and noisomely rich – has packed him off to New Zealand with Weston in the hope of teaching him sense. Weston's his cousin. The boy was sacked from his public school, I believe. Shipboard gossip.'

'It is strange,' said the tall man, 'how a certain type of Englishman still regards the Dominions either as a waste-paper basket or a purge.'

'You are not a colonial, surely?'

'Oh, no. I speak without prejudice. Hullo, I believe we're stopping.'

16

A far-away whistle was followed by the sound of banging doors and a voice that chanted something indistinguishable. These sounds grew louder. Presently the far door of their own carriage opened and the guard came down the corridor.

'Five minutes at Ohakune for refreshments,' he chanted, and went out at the near door. Broadhead moved aside for him.

'Refreshments!' said Hambledon. 'Good lord!'

'Oh, I don't know. A cup of coffee, perhaps. Anyway a gulp of fresh air.'

'Perhaps you're right. *What* did he say was the name of the station?'

'I don't know. It sounded like a rune or incantation.'

'Oh–ah–coo–nee,' said Susan Max, unexpectedly.

'Hullo, Susie, you've come up to breathe, have you?' asked Hambledon.

'I haven't been to sleep, dear,' said Susan. Not really asleep, you know.'

'I'd forgotten you were an Australian.'

'I am not an Australian. I was born in New Zealand. Australia is a four-day journey from—'

'I know, I know,' said Hambledon with a wink at the tall man.

'Well, it *is* provoking, dear,' said Miss Max huffily. 'We don't like to be called Australian. Not that I've anything against the Aussies. It's the ignorance.'

A chain of yellow lights travelled past their windows. The train stopped and uttered a long steamy sigh. All along the carriage came the sound of human beings yawning and shuffling.

'I wish my father had never met my mother,' grumbled the comedian.

'Come on,' said Hambledon to the tall man.

They went out through the door. Courtney Broadhead was standing on the narrow iron platform of their carriage. His overcoat collar was turned up and his hat jammed over

17

his eyes. He looked lost and miserable. The other two men stepped down on to the station platform. The cold night air smelt clean after the fug of the train. There was a tang in it, salutary and exciting.

'It smells like the inside of a flower shop,' said Hambledon. 'Moss, and cold wet earth, and something else. Are we very high up in the world, I wonder?'

'I think we must be. To me it smells like mountain air.'

'What about this coffee?'

They got two steaming china baths from the refreshment counter and took them out on to the platform.

'Hailey! Hailey!'

The window of one of the sleepers had been opened and through it appeared a head.

'Carolyn!' Hambledon walked swiftly to the window. 'Haven't you settled down yet? It's after half past two, do you know that?'

The murky lights from the station shone on that face, finding out the hollows round the eyes and under the cheek bones. The tall man had never been able to make up his mind about Carolyn Dacres's face. Was it beautiful? Was it faded? Was she as intelligent as her face seemed to promise? As he watched her he realised that she was agitated about something. She spoke quickly, and in an undertone. Hambledon stared at her in surprise and then said something. They both looked for a moment at the tall man. She seemed to hesitate.

'Stand clear, please.'

A bell jangled. He mounted the platform of his carriage where Courtney Broadhead still stood hunched up in his overcoat. The train gave one of those preparatory backward clanks. Hambledon, still carrying his cup, hurriedly mounted the far platform of the sleeper. They were drawn out of the station into the night. Courtney Broadhead, after a sidelong glance at the tall man, said something inaudible and returned to the carriage. The tall man remained outside. The stern of the sleeping-carriage in front swayed

18

and wagged, and the little iron bridge that connected the two platforms jerked backwards and forwards. Presently Hambledon came out of the sleeper and, holding to the iron rails, made towards him over the bridge. As soon as they were together he began to shout:

'. . . very upset . . . most extraordinary . . . wish you'd . . .'

The wind snatched his voice away.

'I can't hear you.'

'It's Meyer – I can't make it out. Come over here.'

He led the way across the little bridge and drew his companion into the entrance lobby of the next carriage.

'It's Meyer,' said Hambledon. 'He says someone tried to murder him.'

CHAPTER 2

Mr Meyer in Jeopardy

The tall man merely stared at Hambledon who came to the conclusion that his astonishing announcement had not been heard.

'Someone has tried to murder Alfred Meyer,' he bawled.

'All right,' said the tall man. He looked disgusted and faintly alarmed.

'Carolyn wants you to come along to their sleeper.'

'You haven't told her—?'

'No, no. But I wish you'd let me—'

The inside door of the little lobby burst open, smacking Hambledon in the rear. The pale face of Mr Alfred Meyer appeared round the side.

'Hailey – do come along. What are you – oh!' He glanced at the tall man.

'We are both coming,' said Hambledon.

They all lurched along the narrow corridor off which the two sleepers opened. They passed the first door and Meyer led them in at the second. The "de luxe" sleeper was a small cabin with two narrow bunks and a wash-basin. Carolyn Dacres, wearing some sort of gorgeous dressing-robe, sat on the bottom bunk. Her arms were clasped round her knees. Her long reddish-brown hair hung in a thick twist over her shoulder.

'Hullo!' she said, looking at the tall man. 'Hailey says he thinks you'd better hear all about it.'

'I'm sure you'd rather talk over whatever has happened among yourselves. I assure you I've no desire to butt in.'

'Look here,' said Hambledon, '*do* let me explain – about you, I mean.'

'Very well,' said the tall man, looking politely resigned.

'We all knew him as "Mr Allen" on board,' began Hambledon. 'That's what he was in the passenger list. It was only tonight, in the train, that I realised he was

20

Roderick Alleyn – E Y N – Chief Detective-Inspector, CID, and full musical honours with a salute of two sawn-off shotguns.'

'My God!' said Mr Meyer plaintively. It was his stock expression.

'Why –' said Carolyn Dacres, 'why then you're – yes, of course. "The Handsome Inspector." Don't you remember, Pooh? The Gardener case? Our photographs were side by side in the *Tatler* that week, Mr Alleyn.'

'The only occasion,' said Chief Detective-Inspector Alleyn, 'on which I have felt there was any compensation for newspaper publicity.'

'Any *compensation*,' broke in Mr Meyer. 'My God! Well now, as you are an expert, will you listen to this? Sit down for God's sake. Move up, Carol.'

Alleyn sat on a trunk, Hambledon on the floor, and Meyer plumped down beside his wife. His large face was very white and his fat hands shook slightly.

'I'm all upset,' he said.

'I'll try to explain,' said Miss Dacres. 'You see, Hailey darling – and Mr Alleyn – Alfie-Pooh sat up late. He had a lot of correspondence to get through, and he brought his typewriter in here. Some time before we got to the last station he thought he would go out to that shocking little platform for a breath of fresh air. Didn't you, darling?'

Mr Meyer nodded gloomily.

'We were at that time travelling up or down a thing that I think they call the corkscrew. The guard, who is an exceedingly nice man, and so, so well informed, told us all about it. It appears that this corkscrew—'

'Spiral,' corrected Mr Meyer.

'Yes, darling. This spiral is quite remarkable as railway lines go. One is continually catching one's own tail and the guard's wagon is quite often in front of the engine.'

'Really, Carolyn!' expostulated Hambledon.

'Something of the sort, darling. However, that is of no real importance as far as this story goes. The only thing we

21

must all remember is that when it is corkscrewing the train keeps on turning round and round.'

'What can you mean?'

'Cut out the comedy, Carolyn,' begged Mr Meyer. 'This is serious.'

'Darling, *of course* it is. You see, Mr Alleyn, Alfie went out on the little platform and stood there, and all the time the train kept turning corners very fast and it was all rather impressive. Alfie was very excited and thrilled with the view, although it was so dark he could not see much, except the other parts of the train corkscrewing above and below him. He heard a door bang, but he did not look round because he thought it was just someone going along the train. He was holding on very tight with both hands. Luckily. Because otherwise when this person pushed him he would have—'

'Here!' said Mr Meyer firmly. 'I'll tell them. I was on the platform facing outwards. I noticed the iron door to the steps was opened back and there was nothing between me and God knows all. It was blowing a gale. I kind of knew people were going past me on their way through the train, but I didn't look round. We came to one of these hairpin-bends and as we swung round someone kicked me on the behind. Hard. By God, I nearly went over. As nearly as damn it. I tell you I lurched out over the step. I grabbed at the door with my left hand, but I must have pulled it away from the catch on the wall as if I was going through and shutting it after me. See what I mean? I clutched the platform rail with my right hand – just caught it close to the iron stanchion by the steps. It seemed to last a lifetime, that hanging outwards. Then the train swung round the opposite way and I got back. Of course when I was all right again and turned round the man had gone. God, I'm all to pieces. Look in that case there, Hailey. There's a bottle of brandy.' He turned pale bulging eyes on Alleyn.

'What the hell do you make of that?'

'Extremely unpleasant,' said Alleyn.

'Unpleasant! Listen to him, will you!'

'My poor Alfie,' said his wife. 'You shall have quantities of brandy. Pour it out, Hailey. There are glasses there, too. We shall all have brandy while Mr Alleyn tells us who tried to assassinate my poor Pooh. Don't spill it, Hailey. There! Now, Mr Alleyn?'

She looked up with an air of encouragement at the chief inspector. 'Is she being deliberately funny?' Alleyn wondered. 'She's not really one of those vague women who sound like fools and are as deep as you make them. Or is she? No, no, she's making a little "cameo-part" of herself, for us to look at. Perhaps she has done it for so long that she can't stop.'

'What I want to know is, what do I do?' Meyer was saying.

'Stop the train and tell the guard?' suggested Carolyn, sipping her brandy. 'You pull the communication cord and pay five pounds and then some woman comes forward and says you attempted to—'

'Carolyn, do be quiet,' begged Hambledon, smiling at her. 'What do you think, Alleyn?'

'You are quite sure that you were deliberately kicked?' asked Alleyn. 'It wasn't someone staggering along the train who lost his balance and then his head, when he thought he'd sent you overboard?'

'I tell you I was kicked. I bet you anything you like I've got a black and blue behind.'

'Darling! We must put you in a cage and take you on tour.'

'What ought I to do, Alleyn?'

'My dear Mr Meyer, I – really I don't quite know. I suppose I ought to tell you to inform the guard, and telegraph the police from the next station. There are some very tight footballers farther along the train. I wonder—'

'Of *course*,' said Carolyn with enthusiasm. 'How brilliant of you, Mr Alleyn. It was a drunken footballer. I mean, it all fits in so splendidly, doesn't it? He would

23

know how to kick. Think of the All Blacks.'

Mr Meyer listened solemnly to this. Hambledon suddenly began to laugh. Alleyn hurriedly lit a cigarette.

'It's all very well for you to laugh,' said Mr Meyer. He felt his stern carefully, staring at Alleyn. 'I don't know about the police,' he said. 'That'd mean the Press, and we've never gone in for that sort of publicity. What do you think, Hailey? "Attempted Murder of Well-known Theatrical Manager." It's not too good. It isn't as if it had been Carolyn.'

'I should think not indeed,' agreed Hambledon with difficulty.

'So should I think not indeed,' said Carolyn.

'Mr Meyer,' said Alleyn, 'have you any enemies in your company?'

'Good God, no. We're a happy little family. I treat my people well and they respect me. There's never been a word.'

'You say that several people went past you while you were on the platform,' said Alleyn. 'Did you notice any of them in particular?'

'No. I stood with my back to the gangway.'

'Do you remember,' asked Alleyn after a pause, 'if there was anyone standing on the opposite platform, the one at this end of our carriage that was linked to yours by the iron bridge?'

'I don't think so. Not when I went out. Someone might have come out later. You know how it is – all dark and noisy and windy. I had my hat pulled down and my scarf up to my eyes. I simply stood with my back half turned to that platform looking out at the side.'

'How long was it before we got to the last station – Okahune?'

'I should think about half an hour.'

'What time was it,' Alleyn asked Hambledon, 'when I woke up and we began to talk? I looked at my watch, do you remember?'

'It was ten past two. Why?'

'Oh, nothing. We got to Okahune at two-forty-five.'

Hambledon glanced sharply at Alleyn. Carolyn yawned extensively and began to look pathetic.

'I'm sure you are longing for your beds,' said Alleyn. 'Come on, Hambledon.'

He got up and was about to say good night when there was a bang at the door.

'Mercy!' said Carolyn. 'What now? Surely they can't want to punch more holes in our tickets. Come in!' Valerie Gaynes burst into the little sleeper. She was dressed in a shiny trousered garment, covered with a brilliant robe, and looked like an advertisement for negligées in an expensive magazine. She made a little rush at Carolyn, waving her hands.

'I heard you talking and I simply *had* to come in. Please forgive me, darling Miss Dacres, but something rather awful has happened.'

'I know,' said Carolyn promptly, 'you have been kicked by a drunken footballer.'

Miss Gaynes stared at her.

'But why—? No. It's something rather awkward. I've – I've been robbed.'

'Robbed? Pooh darling, this is a most extraordinary train. Do you hear what she says?'

'Isn't it too frightful? You see, after I had gone to bed—'

'Valerie,' interrupted Carolyn. 'You do know Mr Alleyn, don't you? It appears he is a famous detective, so he will be able to recover your jewels when he has caught Pooh's murderer. Really, it is very lucky you decided to come to New Zealand, Mr Alleyn.'

'I am glad you think so,' said Alleyn tonelessly. 'I'd be extremely grateful,' he added, 'if you kept my occupation a secret. Life's not worth living if one's travelling companions know one is a CID man.'

'Of course we will. It will be so much easier for you to discover Valerie's jewels if you're incog., won't it?'

'It's not jewels, it's money,' began Miss Gaynes. 'It's quite a lot of money. You see, Daddy gave me some English notes to change when I got to New Zealand because of the exchange, and I kept some of them out for the ship, and gave some of them to the purser, and the night before we landed I got them from the purser and – and – they were all right, and I – I – '

'Have some brandy?' invited Carolyn suddenly.

'Thank you. Daddy will be simply livid about it. You see, I can't remember when I last noticed I still had them. It's all terribly confusing. I put them in a leather folder thing in my suit-case when I got them from the purser.'

'That was a damn' silly thing to do,' said Mr Meyer gloomily.

'I suppose it was, but I'm awful about money. *Such* a fool. And, you see, this morning, before I shut the suit-case, I felt the folder and it rustled, so I thought, well, that's all right. And then, just now, I couldn't sleep in this frightful train, so I thought I'd write a letter, and I got out the folder and it was full of paper.'

'What sort of paper?' asked Carolyn, sleepily.

'Well, that's what makes me wonder if it's just a low joke someone's played on me.'

'Why?' asked Alleyn.

'Oh!' said Miss Gaynes impatiently, 'you must be *too* pure and clean-minded at Scotland Yard.'

Hambledon murmured something to Alleyn who said: 'Oh, I see.'

'It was the brand they had in the ship. I noticed that. I call that pretty good, don't you? I mean, to notice that. Do you think I'd make a sleuthess, Mr Alleyn? No, but really, isn't it a bore? *What* ought I to do? Of course I've got a letter of credit for Middleton, but after all one doesn't like being burgled.'

'Did you look at your folder, or whatever it was, after breakfast this morning?' asked Meyer suddenly.

'Er – no. No, I'm sure I didn't. Why?'

'How much was in it?'

'I'm not sure. Let me think. I used four – no, five pounds for tips and then I paid Frankie ten that I lost at—'

She stopped short, and a kind of blankness came into her eyes.

'Oh, what's the use, anyway,' she said. 'I suppose it was about ninety pounds. It's gone. And that's that. I mustn't keep you up, darling Miss Dacres.'

She made for the door. Alleyn opened it.

'If you would like to let me see the leather case—' he said.

'Too sweet of you, but honestly I'm afraid the money's gone for good.'

'Well, I should let him see it,' said Carolyn, vaguely. 'He may be able to trace it directly to the murderous foot-baller.'

'*What* murderous footballer?'

'I'll tell you in the morning, Valerie. Good night, I'm so sorry about your money, but Mr Alleyn will find it for you as soon as he has time. We've all had quite enough excitement for one night. Let us curl up in our horrid little sleepers.'

'Good night,' said Miss Gaynes and went out.

Alleyn looked at Carolyn Dacres. She had shut her eyes as soon as Valerie Gaynes had gone. She now opened one of them. It was a large, carefully made-up eye, and it was fixed on Alleyn.

'Good night, Carol,' said Hambledon. ''Night, Alf. Hope you get some sleep. Not much of the night left for it. Don't worry too much about your adventure.'

'Sleep!' ejaculated Mr Meyer. 'Worry! We get to Middleton in an hour. Scarcely worth trying. I can't lie down with any hope of comfort and *you'd* worry if someone tried to kick you off a train on the top of a mountain.'

'I expect I should. Coming, Alleyn?'

'Yes. Good night, Miss Dacres.'

'Good night,' said Carolyn in her deepest voice.

'So long,' said Mr Meyer bitterly. 'Sorry you've been troubled.'

Hambledon had already gone out into the little corridor, and Alleyn was in the doorway, when Carolyn stopped him.

'Mr Alleyn!'

He turned back. There she was, still looking at him out of one eye, like some attractive, drowsy, but intelligent bird.

'Why didn't Valerie want you to see the leather writing-folder?' asked Carolyn.

'I don't know,' said Alleyn. 'Do you?'

'I can make a damn' good guess,' said Carolyn.

CHAPTER 3

Off-stage

The Dacres Company arrived at Middleton in time for breakfast. By ten o'clock the stage staff had taken possession of the Theatre Royal. To an actor on tour all theatres are very much alike. They may vary in size, in temperature, and in degree of comfort, but once the gas-jets are lit in the dressing-rooms, the grease-paints laid out in rows on the shelves, and the clothes hung up in sheets on the walls, all theatres are simply 'theatre'. The playhouse is the focus-point of the company. As soon as an actor has 'found a home', and, if possible, enjoyed a rest, he goes down to the theatre and looks to the tools of his trade. The stage-manager is there with his staff, cursing or praising the mechanical facilities behind the curtain. The familiar flats are trundled in, the working lights are on, the prompter's table stands down by the footlights and the sheeted stalls wait expectantly in the dark auditorium.

Soon the drone of the run-through-for-words begins. Mechanics peer from the flies and move, rubber-footed, about the stage. The theatre is alive, self-contained and warm with preparation.

The Royal, at Middleton, was a largish playhouse. It seated a thousand, had a full stage and a conservative but adequate system of lighting and of overhead galleries, grid, and ropes. Ted Gascoigne, who was used to the West End, sniffed a little at the old-fashioned lighting. They had brought a special switchboard and the electrician morosely instructed employees of the local power-board in its mysteries.

At ten o'clock Carolyn and her company were all asleep or breakfasting in their hotels. Carolyn, Valerie Gaynes, Liversidge, Mason and Hambledon stayed at the Middleton, the most expensive of these drear establishments. For the rest of the company, the splendour of their lodgings was in exact ratio to the amount of their salaries, from Courtney Broadhead at The Commercial down to Tommy Biggs, the least of the staff, at 'Mrs Harbottle, Good Beds'.

George Mason, the manager, had not gone to bed. He had shaved, bathed, and changed his clothes, and by ten o'clock, uneasy with chronic dyspepsia, sat in the office at The Royal talking to the 'advance', a representative of the Australian firm under whose auspices the company was on tour.

'It's going to be big, Mr Mason,' said the advance. 'We're booked out downstairs, and only fifty seats left in the circle. There's a queue for early-door tickets. I'm very pleased.'

'Good enough,' said Mason. 'Now listen.'

They talked. The telephone rang incessantly. Box-office officials came in, the local manager of the theatre, three slightly self-conscious reporters, and finally Mr Alfred Meyer, carrying a cushion. This he placed on the swivel chair, and then cautiously lowered himself on to it.

'Well, Alf,' said Mason.

''Morning, George,' said Mr Meyer.

Mason introduced the Australian advance, who instantly seized Mr Meyer's hand in a grip of iron and shook it with enthusiasm.

'I'm very glad to meet you, Mr Meyer.'

'How do you do?' said Mr Meyer. 'Good news for us, I hope?'

The reporters made tentative hovering movements.

'These gentlemen are from the Press,' said Mason. 'They'd like to have a little chat with you, Alf.'

Mr Meyer rolled his eyes round and became professionally cordial.

'Oh, yes, yes,' he said, 'certainly. Come over here, gentlemen, will you?'

The advance hurriedly placed three chairs in a semicircle close to Meyer, and joined Mason, who had withdrawn tactfully to the far end of the room.

The reporters cleared their throats and handled pads and pencils.

'Well now, what about it?' asked Mr Meyer helpfully.

'Er,' said the oldest of the reporters, 'just a few points that would interest our readers, Mr Meyer.'

He spoke in a soft gruff voice with a slight accent. He seemed a very wholesome and innocent young man.

'Certainly,' said Mr Meyer. 'By God, this is a wonderful country of yours . . .'

The reporters wrote busily the outlines for an article which would presently appear under the headline: 'Praise for New Zealand: An Enthusiastic Visitor.'

*   *   *

Two young men and a woman appeared in the office doorway. They were Australians who had travelled over to join the company for the second piece, and now reported for duty. Mason took them along to the stage-door, pointed out Gascoigne, who was in heated argument with the head mechanist, and left them to make themselves known.

The stock scene was being struck. The fluted columns and gilded walls of all stock scenes fell forward as softly as leaves, and were run off into the dock. An Adam drawing-room, painted by an artist, and in excellent condition, was shoved together like a gigantic house of cards and tightened at the corners. Flack, flack, went the toggles as the stagehands laced them over the wooden cleats.

'We don't want those borders,' said Gascoigne.

'Kill the borders, Bert,' said the head mechanist, loudly.

'Kill the borders,' repeated a voice up in the flies. The painted strips that masked the overhead jerked out of sight one by one.

'Now the ceiling cloth.'

Outside in the strange town a clock chimed and struck eleven. Members of the cast began to come in and look for their dressing-rooms. They were called for eleven-thirty.

31

Gascoigne saw the Australians and crossed the stage to speak to them. He began talking about their parts. He manner was pleasant and friendly, and the Australians, who were on the defensive about English importations, started to thaw. Gascoigne told them where they were to dress. He checked himself to shout:

'You'll have to clear, Fred; I want the stage in ten minutes.'

'I'm not ready for you, Mr Gascoigne.'

'By – you'll have to be ready. What's the matter with you?'

He walked back to the stage. From up above came the sound of sawing.

Gascoigne glared upwards.

'What are you *doing* up there?'

An indistinguishable mumbling answered him.

Gascoigne turned to the head mechanist.

'Well, you'll have to knock off in ten minutes, Fred. I've got a show to rehearse with people who haven't worked for four weeks. And we go up tonight. Tonight! Do you think we can work in a sawmill. What is he *doing*?'

'He's fixing the mast,' said the head mechanist. 'It's got to be done, Mr Gascoigne. This bloody stage isn't—'

He went off into mechanical details. The second act was staged on board a yacht. The setting was elaborate. The lower end of a mast with 'practical' rope ladders had to be fixed. This was all done from overhead. Gascoigne and the head mechanist stared up into the flies.

'We've flied the mast,' said the mechanist, 'and it's too long for this stage, see. Bert's fixing it. Have you got the weight on, Bert?'

As if in answer, a large black menace flashed between them. There was a nerve-shattering thud, a splintering of wood, and a cloud of dust. At their feet lay a long object rather like an outsize in sash-weights.

Gascoigne and the mechanist instantly flew into the most violent of rages. Their faces were sheet-white and their

32

knees shook. At the tops of their voices they apostrophised the hidden Bert, inviting him to come down and be half killed. Their oaths died away into a shocked silence. Mason had run round from the office, the company had hurried out of the dressing-rooms and were clustered in the entrances. The unfortunate Bert came down from the grid and stood gaping in horror at his handiwork.

'Gawdstreuth, Mr Gascoigne, I don't know how it happened. Gawdstreuth, Mr Gascoigne, I'm sorry. Gawdstreuth.'

'Shut your – face,' suggested the head mechanist, unprintably. 'Do you want to go to gaol for manslaughter?'

'Don't you know the first – rule about working in the flies? Don't you know—?'

Mason went back to the office. One by one the company returned to their dressing-rooms.

* * *

'And what,' said the oldest of the three reporters, 'is your opinion of our railroads, Mr Meyer? How do they compare with those in the Old Country?'

Mr Meyer shifted uncomfortably on his cushion and his hand stole round to his rear.

'I think they're marvellous,' he said.

* * *

Hailey Hambledon knocked on Carolyn's door.

'Are you ready, Carol? It's a quarter past.'

'Come in, darling.'

He went into the bedroom she shared with Meyer. It looked exactly like all their other bedrooms on tour. There was the wardrobe trunk, the brilliant drape on the bed, Carolyn's photos of Meyer, of herself, and of her father, the parson in Bucks. And there, on the dressing-table, was her complexion in its scarlet case. She was putting the final touches to her lovely face and nodded to him in the looking-glass.

'Good morning, Mrs Meyer,' said Hambledon and kissed her fingers with the same light gesture he had so often used on the stage.

'Good morning, Mr Hambledon.' They spoke with that unnatural and half-ironical gaiety that actors so often assume when greeting each other outside the theatre.

Carolyn turned back to her mirror.

'I'm getting very set-looking, Hailey. Older and older.'

'I don't think so.'

'Don't you? I expect you do, really. You think to yourself sometimes: "It won't be long before she is too old for such-and-such a part."'

'No. I love you. To me you do not change.'

'Darling! So sweet! Still, we do grow older.'

'Then why, why, why not make the most of what's left? Carol – do you really believe you love me?'

'You're going to have another attack. Don't.'

She got up and put on her hat, giving him a comically apprehensive look from under the brim. 'Come along now,' she said.

He shrugged his shoulders and opened the door for her. They went out, moving beautifully, with years of training behind their smallest gestures. It is this unconscious professionalism in the everday actions of actors that so often seems unreal to outsiders. When they are very young actors, it often is unreal, when they are older it is merely habit. They are indeed 'always acting', but not in the sense that their critics suggest.

Carolyn and Hambledon went down in the lift and through the lounge towards the street door. Here they ran into Chief Detective-Inspector Alleyn, who was also staying at the Middleton.

'Hullo!' said Carolyn. 'Have you been out already? You *are* an early one.'

'I've been for a tram ride up to the top of those hills. Do

34

you know, the town ends quite suddenly about four miles out, and you are on grassy hills with little bits of bush and the most enchanting view.'

'It sounds delicious,' said Carolyn vaguely.

'No,' said Alleyn, 'it's more exciting than that. How is your husband this morning?'

'Still very cross, poor sweet. And black and blue, actually, just as he prophesied. It *must* have been a footballer. Are you coming to the show tonight?'

'I want to, but, do you know, I can't get a seat.'

'Oh, nonsense. Alfie-Pooh will fix you up. Remind me to ask him, Hailey darling.'

'Right,' said Hambledon. 'We ought to get along, Carol.'

'Work, work, work,' said Carolyn, suddenly looking tragic. 'Goodbye, Mr Alleyn. Come round to my dressing-room after the show.'

'And to mine,' said Hambledon. 'I want to know what you think of the piece. So long.'

'Thank you so much. Goodbye,' said Alleyn.

'*Nice* man,' said Carolyn when they had gone a little way.

'Very nice indeed. Carol, you've got to listen to me, please. I've loved you with shameless constancy for – how long? Five years?'

'Surely a little longer than that, darling. I fancy it's six. It was during the run of *Scissors to Grind* at the Criterion. Don't you remember—'

'Very well – six. You say you're fond of me – love me –'

'Oughtn't we to cross over here?' interrupted Carolyn. 'Pooh said the theatre was down that street, surely. Oh, do be careful!' She gave a little scream. Hambledon, exasperated, had grasped her by the elbow and was hurrying her across a busy intersection.

'I'm coming to your dressing-room as soon as we get there,' he said angrily, 'and I'm going to have it out with you.'

'It would certainly be a better spot than the footpath,' agreed Carolyn. 'As my poor Pooh would say, there is a right and wrong kind of publicity.'

'For God's sake,' said Hambledon, between clenched teeth, 'stop talking to me about your husband.'

* * *

Before going to the theatre young Courtney Broadhead called in at the Middleton and asked for Mr Gordon Palmer. He was sent up to Mr Palmer's rooms, where he found that young man still in bed and rather white about the gills. His cousin and mentor, Geoffrey West, sat in an arm-chair by the window, and Mr Francis Liversidge lolled across the end of the bed smoking a cigarette. He, too, had dropped in to see Gordon on his way to rehearsal it seemed.

The cub, as Hambledon had called Gordon Palmer, was seventeen years old, dreadfully sophisticated, and entirely ignorant of everything outside the sphere of his sophistication. He had none of the awkwardness of youth and very little of its vitality, being restless rather than energetic, acquisitive rather than ambitious. He was good-looking in a raffish, tarnished sort of fashion. It was entirely in keeping with his character that he should have attached himself to the Dacres Comedy Company and, more particularly, to Carolyn Dacres herself. That Carolyn paid not the smallest attention to him made little difference. With Liversidge and Valerie he was a great success.

'Hullo, Court, my boy,' said Gordon. 'Treat me gently. I'm a wreck this morning. Met some ghastly people on that train last night. What a night! We played poker till – when was it, Geoffrey?'

'Until far too late,' said Weston calmly. 'You were a young fool.'

'He thinks he has to talk like that to me,' explained Gordon. 'He does it rather well, really. What's your news, Court?'

'I've come to pay my poker debts,' said Courtney. He drew out his wallet and took some notes from it. 'Yours is here too, Frankie.' He laughed unhappily. 'Take it while you can.'

'That's all fine and handy,' said Gordon carelessly. 'I'd forgotten all about it.'

*　　*　　*

Mr Liversidge poked his head in at the open office door. He did not come on until the second act, and had grown tired of hanging round the wings while Gascoigne thrashed out a scene between Valerie Gaynes, Ackroyd, and Hambledon. Mr Meyer was alone in the office.

'Good morning, sir,' said Liversidge.

''Morning, Mr Liversidge,' said Meyer, swinging round in his chair and staring owlishly at his first juvenile. 'Want to see me?'

'I've just heard of your experience on the train last night,' began Liversidge, 'and looked in to ask how you were. It's an outrageous business. I mean to say—!'

'Quite,' said Meyer shortly. 'Thanks very much.'

Liversidge airily advanced a little farther into the room.

'And poor Val, losing all her money. Quite a chapter of calamities.'

'It was,' said Mr Meyer.

'Quite a decent pub, the Middleton, isn't it, sir?'

'Quite,' said Mr Meyer again.

There was an uncomfortable pause.

'You seem to be in funds,' remarked Mr Meyer suddenly.

Liversidge laughed melodiously. 'I've been saving a bit lately. We had a long run in Town with the show, didn't we? A windfall this morning, too.' He gave Meyer a quick sidelong glance. 'Courtney paid up his poker debts. I didn't expect to see *that* again, I must say. Last night he was all down-stage and tragic.'

'Shut that door,' said Mr Meyer. 'I want to talk to you.'

*   *   *

Carolyn and Hambledon faced each other across the murky half-light of the star dressing-room. Already, most of the wicker baskets had been unpacked, and the grease-paints laid out on their trays. The room had a grey, cellar-like look about it and smelt of cosmetics. Hambledon switched on the light and it instantly became warm and intimate.

'Now, listen to me,' he said.

Carolyn sat on one of the wicker crates and gazed at him. He took a deep breath.

'You're as much in love with me as you ever will be with anyone. You don't love Alfred. Why you married him I don't believe even God knows, and I'm damn' certain you don't. I don't ask you to live with me on the quiet, with everyone knowing perfectly well what's happening. That sort of arrangement would be intolerable to both of us. I do ask you to come away with me at the end of this tour and let Alfred divorce you. Either that, or tell him how things are between us and give him the chance of arranging it the other way.'

'Darling, we've had this out so often before.'

'I know we have but I'm at the end of my tether. I can't go on seeing you every day, working with you, being treated as though I was – what? A cross between a tame cat and a schoolboy. I'm forty-nine, Carol, and I – I'm starved. Why won't you do this for both of us?'

'Because I'm a Catholic.'

'You're not a good Catholic. I sometimes think you don't care tuppence about your religion. How long is it since you've been to church or confession or whatever it is? Ages. Then why stick at this?'

'It's my Church sticking to me. Bits of it always stick. I'd feel I was wallowing in sin, darling, truthfully I would.'

'Well, wallow. You'd get used to it.'

'Oh, Hailey!' She broke out into soft laughter, but warm soft laughter that ran like gold through every part she played.

'Don't!' said Hambledon. 'Don't!'

'I'm so sorry, Hailey. I am a pig. I do adore you, but, darling, I can't – simply can't live in sin with you. Living in sin. Living in sin,' chanted Carolyn dreamily.

'You're hopeless,' said Hambledon. 'Hopeless!'

'Miss Dacres, please,' called a voice in the passage.

'Here!'

'We're just coming to your entrance, please, Mr Gascoigne says.'

'I'll be there,' said Carolyn. 'Thank you.'

She got up at once.

'You're on in a minute, darling,' she said to Hambledon.

'I suppose,' said Hambledon with a violence that in spite of himself was half whimsically-rueful, 'I suppose I'll have to wait for Alf to die of a fatty heart. Would you marry me then, Carol?'

'What is it they all say in this country? "*Too right.*" *Too right* I would, darling. But, poor Pooh! A fatty heart! Too unkind.' She slipped through the door.

A moment or two later he heard her voice, pitched and telling, as she spoke her opening line.

'"Darling, what do you think! He's asked me to marry him!"' And then those peals of soft warm laughter.

CHAPTER 4

First Appearance of the Tiki

The curtain rose for the fourth time. Carolyn Dacres, standing in the centre of the players, bowed to the stalls, to the circle and, with the friendly special smile, to the gallery. One thousand pairs of hands were struck together over and over again, making a sound like hail on an iron roof. New Zealand audiences are not given to cheering. If they are pleased they sit still and clap exhaustively. They did so now, on the third and final performance of Ladies of Leisure. Carolyn bowed and bowed with an air of enchanted deprecation. She turned to Hailey Hambledon, smiling. He stepped out of the arc and came down to the footlights. He assumed the solemnly earnest expression of all leading actors who are about to make a speech. The thousand pairs of hands redoubled their activities. Hambledon smiled warningly. The clapping died away.

'Ladies and gentlemen,' began Hambledon reverently, 'Miss Dacres has asked me to try and express something of our' – he looked up to the gallery – 'our gratitude, for the wonderful reception you have given the first play of our short' – he looked into the stalls – 'our all *too* short season in your beautiful city.' He paused. Another tentative outbreak from the audience. 'This is our first visit to New Zealand, and Middleton is the first town we have played. Our season in this lovely country of yours is, of necessity, a brief one. We go on to – to –' he paused and turned helplessly to his company. 'Wellington,' said Carolyn. 'To Wellington, on Friday. Tomorrow, Wednesday and Thursday we play *The Jack Pot*, a comedy which we had the honour of presenting at the Criterion Theatre in London. Most of the original cast is still with us, and, in addition, three well-known Australian artists have joined us for this piece. May I also say that we have among us a New Zealand actress who returns to her native country after a distinguished career on the London stage – Miss Susan Max.' He turned to old Susan, who gave him a startled look of gratitude. The audience applauded vociferously. Old Susan, with shining eyes, bowed to the house and then, charmingly, to Hambledon.

'Miss Dacres, the company, and I, are greatly moved by the marvellous welcome you have given us. I – I may be giving away a secret, but I am going to tell you that today is her birthday.' He held up his hand. 'This is her first visit to Middleton; I feel we cannot do better than wish her many happy returns. Thank you all very much.'

Another storm of hail, a deep curtsy from Carolyn. Hambledon glanced up into the OP corner, and the curtain came down.

'And God forbid that I should ever come back,' muttered little Ackroyd disagreeably.

Susan Max, who was next to him, ruffled like an indignant hen.

'You'd rather have the provinces, I suppose, Mr Ackroyd,' she said briskly.

Old Brandon Vernon chuckled deeply. Ackroyd raised his comic eyebrows and inclined his head several times. 'Ho-ho. Ho-*ho*!' he sneered. 'We're all touchy and upstage about our native land, are we!'

Susan plodded off to her dressing-room. In the passage she ran into Hailey Hambledon.

'Thank you, dear,' said Susan. 'I didn't expect it, but it meant a lot.'

'That's all right, Susie,' said Hambledon. 'Go and make yourself lovely for the party.'

Carolyn's birthday was to be celebrated. Out on the stage the hands put up a trestle-table and covered it with a white cloth. Flowers were massed down the centre. Glasses, plates, and quantities of food were arrayed on lines that followed some impossible standard set by a Hollywood super-spectacle, tempered by the facilities

41

offered by the Middleton Hotel, which had undertaken the catering. Mr Meyer had spent a good deal of thought and more money on this party. It was, he said, to be a party suitable to his wife's position as the foremost English comedienne, and it had been planned with one eye on the Press and half the other on the box-office. The *pièce de résistance* was to be in the nature of a surprise for Carolyn and the guests, though one by one, he had taken the members of his company into his confidence. He had brought from England a jeroboam of champagne – a fabulous, a monstrous bottle of a famous vintage. All the afternoon, Ted Gascoigne and the stage hands had laboured under Mr Meyer's guidance and with excited suggestions from George Mason. The giant bottle was suspended in the flies with a counterweight across the pulley. A crimson cord from the counterweight came down to the stage and was anchored to the table. At the climax of her party, Carolyn was to cut this cord. The counterweight would then rise and the jeroboam slowly descend into a nest of maiden-hair fern and exotic flowers, that was to be held, by Mr Meyer himself, in the centre of the table. He had made them rehearse it twelve times that day and was in a fever of excitement that the performance should go without a hitch. Now he kept darting on to the stage and gazing anxiously up into the flies, where the jeroboam hung, invisible, awaiting its big entrance. The shaded lamps used on the stage were switched on. With the heavy curtain for the fourth wall, the carpet and the hangings on the set, it was intimate and pleasant.

A little group of guests came in from the stage-door. A large vermilion-faced, pleasant-looking man, who was a station-holder twenty miles out in the country. His wife, broad, a little weather-beaten, well dressed, but not very smart. Their daughter, who was extremely smart, and their son, an early print of his father. They had called on Carolyn, who had instantly asked them to her party, forgotten she had done so, and neglected to warn anybody

42

of their arrival. Gascoigne, who received them, looked nonplussed for a moment, and then, knowing his Carolyn, guessed what had happened. They were followed by Gordon Palmer, registering familiarity with backstage, and his cousin, Geoffrey Weston.

'Hullo, George,' said Gordon. 'Perfectly marvellous. Great fun. Carolyn was too thrilling, wasn't she? I must see her. Where is she?'

'Miss Dacres is changing,' said Ted Gascoigne, who had dealt with generations of Gordon Palmers.

'But I simply can't wait another *second*,' protested Gordon in a high-pitched voice.

'Afraid you'll have to,' said Gascoigne. 'May I introduce Mr Gordon Palmer, Mr Weston, Mrs – mumble-mumble.'

'Forrest,' said the broad lady cheerfully. With the pathetic faith of most colonial ladies in the essential niceness of all young Englishmen, she instantly made friendly advances. Her husband and son looked guarded and her daughter alert.

More guests arrived, among them a big brown man with a very beautiful voice – Dr Rangi Te Pokiha, a Maori physician, who was staying at the Middleton.

Alleyn came in with Mason and Alfred Meyer, who had given him a box, and greeted him, after a final glance at the supper-table. They made a curious contrast. The famous Mr Meyer, short, pasty, plump, exuded box-office and front-of-the-house from every pearl button in his white waistcoat. The famous policeman, six inches taller, might have been a diplomat. 'Magnificent appearance,' Meyer had said to Carolyn. 'He'd have done damn' well if he'd taken to "the business".'

One by one the members of the company came out from their dressing-rooms. Most actors have an entirely separate manner for occasions when they mix with outsiders. This separate manner is not so much an affectation as a *persona*, a mask used for this particular appearance. They wish to show how like other people they are. It is an innocent form

43

of snobbishness. You have only to see them when the last guest has gone to realise how complete a disguise the *persona* may be.

Tonight they were all being very grown-up. Alfred Meyer introduced everybody, carefully. He introduced the New Zealanders to each other, the proprietor and proprietress of the Middleton to the station-holder and his family, who of course knew them perfectly well *de haut en bas*.

Carolyn was the last to appear.

'Where's my wife?' asked Meyer of everybody at large. 'It's ten to. Time she was making an entrance.'

'Where's Carolyn?' complained Gordon Palmer loudly.

'Where's *Madame?*' shouted George Mason jovially.

Led by Meyer, they went to find out.

Alleyn, who, with Mason, had joined Hambledon, wondered if she was instinctively or intentionally delaying her entrance. His previous experience of leading ladies had been a solitary professional one, and he had very nearly lost his heart. He wondered if by any chance he was going to do so again.

At last a terrific rumpus broke out in the passage that led to the dressing-rooms. Carolyn's golden laugh. Carolyn saying 'O-o-oh!' like a sort of musical train whistle. Carolyn sweeping along with three men in her wake. The double doors of the stage-set were thrown open by little Ackroyd, who announced like a serio-comic butler:

'Enter *Madame!*'

Carolyn curtsying to the floor and rising like a moth to greet guest after guest. She had indeed made an entrance, but she had done it so terrifically, so deliberately, with a kind of twinkle in her eye, that Alleyn found himself uncritical and caught up in the warmth of her famous 'personality'. When at last she saw him, and he awaited that moment impatiently, she came towards him with both hands outstretched and eyes like stars. Alleyn rose to the occasion, bent his long back, and kissed each of the hands. The Forrest family goggled at this performance, and Miss

Forrest looked more alert than ever.

'A-a-ah!' said Carolyn with another of her melodious hoots. 'My distinguished friend. The famous—'

'No, no!' exclaimed Alleyn hastily.

'Why not! I insist on everybody knowing I've got a lion at my party.'

She spoke in her most ringing stage voice. Everybody turned to listen to her. In desperation Alleyn hurriedly lugged a small packet out of of his pocket and, with another bow, put it into her hands. 'I'm making a walloping great fool of myself,' he thought.

'A birthday card,' he said. 'I hope you'll allow me—'

Carolyn, who had already received an enormous number of expensive presents, instantly gazed about her with an air of flabbergasted delight that suggested the joy of a street waif receiving a five-pound note.

'It's for *me!*' she cried. 'For *me,* for *me,* for *me.*' She looked brilliantly at Alleyn and at her guests. 'You'll all have to wait. It must be opened now. Quick! Quick!' She wriggled her fingers and tore at the paper with excited squeaks.

'Good lord,' thought Alleyn, 'how does she get away with it? In any other woman it would be nauseating.'

His gift was at last freed from its wrappings. A small green object appeared. The surface was rounded and graven into the semblance of a squat figure with an enormous lolling head and curved arms and legs. The face was much formalised, but it had a certain expression of grinning malevolence. Carolyn gazed at it in delighted bewilderment.

'But what is it? It's jade. It's wonderful – but—?'

'It's greenstone,' said Alleyn.

'It is a tiki, Miss Dacres,' said a deep voice. The Maori, Dr Rangi Te Pokiha, came forward, smiling.

Carolyn turned to him.

'A tiki?'

'Yes. And a very beautiful one, if I may say so.' He glanced at Alleyn.

'Dr Te Pokiha was good enough to find it for me,' explained Alleyn.

'I want to know about – all about it,' insisted Carolyn.

Te Pokiha began to explain. He was gravely explicit, and the Forrests looked embarrassed. The tiki is a Maori symbol. It brings good fortune to its possessor. It represents a human embryo and is the symbol of fecundity. In the course of a conversation with Te Pokiha at the hotel Alleyn had learned that he had this tiki to dispose of for a *pakeha* – a white man – who was hard-up. Te Pokiha had said that if it had been his own possession he would never have parted with it, but the *pakeha was* very hard-up. The tiki was deposited at the museum where the curator would vouch for its authenticity. Alleyn, on an impulse, had gone to look at it and had bought it. On another impulse he had decided to give it to Carolyn. She was enthralled by this story, and swept about showing the tiki to everybody. Gordon Palmer, who had sent up half a florist's shop, glowered sulkily at Alleyn out of the corners of his eyes. Meyer, obviously delighted with Alleyn's gift to his wife, took the tiki to a lamp to examine it more closely.

'It's lucky, is it?' he asked eagerly.

'Well you heard what he said, governor,' said old Brandon Vernon. 'A symbol of fertility, wasn't it? If you call that luck!'

Meyer hastily put the tiki down, crossed his thumbs and began to bow to it.

'O tiki-tiki be good to little Alfie,' he chanted. 'No funny business, now, no funny business.'

Ackroyd said something in an undertone. There was a guffaw from one or two of the men. Ackroyd, with a smirk, took the tiki from Meyer. Old Vernon and Mason joined the group.

Their faces coarsened into half-smiles. The tiki went from hand to hand, and there were many loud gusts of laughter. Alleyn looked at Te Pokiha who walked across to him.

'I half regret my impulse,' said Alleyn quietly.

'Oh,' said Te Pokiha pleasantly, 'it seems amusing to them naturally.' He paused and then added: 'So may my great grandparents have laughed over the first crucifix they saw.'

Carolyn began to relate the story of Meyer's adventure on the train. Everybody turned to listen to her. The laughter changed its quality and became gay and then helpless. Meyer allowed himself to be her foil, protesting comically.

She suddenly commanded everyone to supper. There were place-cards on the table. Alleyn found himself on Carolyn's right with Mrs Forrest, for whom a place had been hurriedly made, on his other side.

Carolyn and Meyer sat opposite each other halfway down the long trestle-table. The nest of maiden-hair fern and exotic flowers was between them, and the long red cord ran down to Carolyn's right and was fastened under the ledge of the table. She instantly asked what it was there for, and little Meyer's fat white face became pink with conspiracy and excitement.

It was really a very large party. Twelve members of the company, as many more guests, and the large staff, whom Carolyn had insisted on having and who sat at a separate table, dressed in their best suits and staring self-consciously at each other. Candles had been lit all down the length of the tables and the lamps turned out. It was all very gay and festive.

When they were settled Meyer, beaming complacently, rose and looked round the table.

'Ladies and gentlemen,' said Meyer, 'I suppose this is quite the wrong place for a speech, but we can't have anything to drink till I've made it, so I don't need to apologise.'

'Certainly not' – from Mason.

'In a minute or two I shall ask you to drink the health of the loveliest woman and the greatest actress of the century – my wife.'

'Golly!' thought Alleyn. Cheers from everybody.

'But before you do this we've got to find something for you to drink it in. There doesn't appear to be anything on the table,' said Meyer, with elaborate nonchalance, 'but we are told that the gods will provide so I propose to leave it to them. Our stage-manager tells me that something may happen if this red cord here is cut. I shall therefore ask my wife to cut it. She will find a pair of shears by her plate.'

'Darling!' said Carolyn. '*What* is all this? Too exciting. I shan't cause it to rain fizz, shall I? Like Moses. Or was it Moses?'

She picked up the enormous scissors. Alfred Meyer bent his fat form over the table and stretched out his short arms to the nest of fern. A fraction of a second before Carolyn closed the blades of the scissors over the cord, her husband touched a hidden switch. Tiny red and green lights sprang up beneath the fern and flowers, into which the jeroboam was to fall and over which Meyer was bending.

Everyone had stopped talking. Alleyn, in the sudden silence, received a curious impression of eager dimly-lit faces that peered, of a beautiful woman standing with one arm raised, holding the scissors as a lovely Atropos might hold aloft her shears, of a fat white-waistcoated man like a Blampied caricature, bent over the table, and of a red cord that vanished upwards into the dark. Suddenly he felt intolerably oppressed, aware of a suspense out of all proportion to the moment. So strong was this impression that he half rose from his chair.

But at that moment Carolyn cut through the cord.

Something enormous that flashed down among them, jolting the table. Valerie Gaynes screaming. Broken glass and the smell of champagne. Champagne flowing over the white cloth. A thing like an enormous billiard ball embedded in the fern. Red in the champagne. And Valerie Gaynes, screaming, screaming. Carolyn, her arm still raised, looking down. Himself, his voice, telling them to go away, telling Hambledon to take Carolyn away.

'Take her away, take her away.'

And Hambledon: 'Come away. Carolyn, come away.'

CHAPTER 5

Intermezzo

'No, don't move him,' said Alleyn.

He laid a hand on Hambledon's arm. Dr Te Pokiha, his bronze fingers still touching the top of Meyer's head, looked fixedly at Alleyn.

'Why not?' asked Hambledon.

George Mason raised his head. Ever since they had got rid of the others Mason had sat at the end of the long table with his face buried in his arms. Ted Gascoigne stood beside Mason. He repeated over and over again:

'It was as safe as houses. Someone's monkeyed with it. We rehearsed it twelve times this morning. I tell you there's been some funny business, George. My God, there's been some funny business.'

'Why not?' repeated Hambledon. 'Why not move him?'

'Because,' said Alleyn, 'Mr Gascoigne may be right.'

George Mason spoke for the first time.

'But who'd want to hurt him? Old Alf! He hasn't an enemy in the world.' He turned a woebegone face to Te Pokiha.

'You're sure, Doctor, he's – he's – gone?'

'You can see for yourself, Mr Mason,' said Te Pokiha; 'the neck is broken.'

'I don't want to,' said Mason, looking sick.

'What ought we to do?' asked Gascoigne. They all turned to Alleyn. 'Do I exude CID?' wondered Alleyn to himself, 'or has Hambledon blown the gaff?'

'I'm afraid you must ring up the nearest police station,' he said aloud. There was an instant outcry from Gascoigne and Mason.

'Good God, the police!'

'What the hell!'

' . . . but it was an accident!'

'That'd be finish!'

'I'm afraid Mr Alleyn's right,' said Te Pokiha; 'it is a matter for the police. If you like I'll ring up. I know the superintendent in Middleton.'

'While you're about it,' said Mason with desperate irony, 'you might ring up a shipping office. As far as this tour's concerned—'

'Finish!' said Gascoigne.

'We've got to do something about it, Ted,' said Hambledon quietly.

'We built it up between us,' said Mason suddenly. 'When I first met Alf he was advancing a No. 4 company in St Helens. I was selling tickets for the worst show in England. We never looked back. We've never had a nasty word, never. And look at the business we've built up.' His lips trembled. 'By God, if someone's killed him – you're right, Hailey. I'm – I'm all anyhow – you fix it, Ted. I'm all anyhow.'

Dr Te Pokiha looked at him.

'How about joining the others, Mr Mason? Perhaps a whisky would be a good idea. Your office—?'

Mason got to his feet and came down to the centre of the table. He looked at what was left of Alfred Meyer's head, buried among the fern and broken fairy lights, wet with champagne and with blood. The two fat white hands still grasped the edges of the nest.

'God!' said Mason. 'Do we have to leave him like that?'

'It will only be for a little while,' said Alleyn gently. 'I should let Dr Te Pokiha take you to the office.'

'Alf,' murmured Mason. 'Old Alf!' He stood there, his lips shaking, his face ugly with suppressed emotion. Alleyn, who was accustomed to scenes of this sort, was conscious of his familiar daemon which took little at face value, and observed so much. The daemon prompted him to notice how unembarrassed Gascoigne and Hambledon were by Mason's emotion, how they had assumed so easily a mood of sorrowful correctness, almost as if they had rehearsed the damn' scene, and the daemon.

They got Mason away. Te Pokiha went with him and said he would ring up the police. The unfortunate Bert, the stage-hand who had rigged the tackle under Meyer's and Gascoigne's directions, was hanging about in the wings and now came on the stage. He began to explain the mechanics of the champagne stunt to Alleyn.

'It was like this 'ere. We fixed the rope over the pulley, see, and on one end we fixed the bloody bottle and on the other end we hooked the bloody weight. The weight was one of them corner weights we used for the bloody funnels.'

'Ease up on the language, Bert,' suggested Gascoigne moodily.

'Good-oh, Mr Gascoigne. And the weight was not so heavy as the bottle, see. And we took a lead with a red cord from just above the weight, see, and fixed it to the table. So when the cord was cut she came down gradual like, seeing she was that much heavier than the weight. The weight and the bottle hung half-way between the pulley and the table, see, so when she came down, the weight went up to the pulley. It was hooked into a ring in the rope. We cut out the lights and used candles so's nothing would be noticed. We tried her out till we was sick and tired of her and she worked corker every time. She worked good-oh, didn't she, Mr Gascoigne?'

'Yes,' said Gascoigne. 'That's what I say. There's been some funny business.'

'That's right,' agreed Bert heavily. 'There bloody well must of.'

'I'm just going aloft to take a look,' said Gascoigne.

'Just a moment,' interrupted Alleyn. He took a note-book and pencil from his pocket. 'Don't you think perhaps we had better not go up just yet, Mr Gascoigne? If there has been any interference, the police ought to be the first on the spot, oughtn't they?'

'I think I'll go and see how Carolyn is,' said Hambledon suddenly.

'They're all in their dressing-rooms,' said Gascoigne.

Hambeldon went away. Alleyn completed a little sketch in his notebook and showed it to Gascoigne and Bert.

'Was it like that?'

'That's right, mister,' said Bert, 'you got it. That's how it was. And when she cut the bloody cord, see . . . ' he rambled on.

Alleyn looked at the jeroboam. It had been cased in a sort of net which closed in at the neck, and was securely wired to the rope.

'Wonder why the cork blew out,' murmured Alleyn.

'The wire was loosened a bit before it came down,' said Gascoigne. 'He – the governor himself – he went aloft after the show specially to do it. He didn't want a stage-wait after it came down. He said the wire would still hold the cork.'

'And it did till the jolt – yes. What about the counter-weight, Mr Gascoigne? That would have to be detached before the champagne was poured out.'

'Bert was to go up at once and take it off.'

'I orfered to stay up there, like,' said Bert. 'But 'e says "No,", 'e says, "you can see the show and then go up. I'll watch it." Gawd, Mr Gascoigne—'

Alleyn slipped away through the wings. Off-stage it was very dark and smelt of theatre. He walked along the wall until he came to the foot of an iron ladder. He was reminded most vividly of his only other experience behind the scenes. 'Is my mere presence in the stalls,' he thought crossly, 'a cue for homicide? May I not visit the antipodes without elderly theatre magnates having their heads bashed in by jeroboams of champagne before my very eyes? And the answer being "No" to each of these questions, can I not get away quickly without nosing into the why and wherefore?'

He put on his gloves and began to climb the ladder. 'Again the answer is "No." The truth of the matter is I'm an incurable nosy parker. Detect I must, if I can.' He reached the first gallery, and peered about him, using his electric torch, and then went on up the ladder. 'I wonder how she's

53

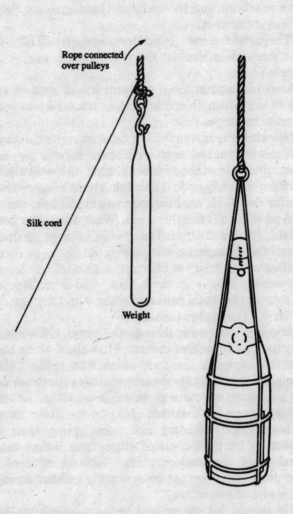

Rope connected over pulleys

Silk cord

Weight

54

taking it? And Hambledon. Will they marry each other in due course, provided – After all, she may not be in love with Hambledon. Ah, here we are.'

He paused at the top gallery and switched on his torch.

Close beside him a batten, slung on ropes, ran across from his gallery to the opposite one. Across the batten hung a pulley and over the pulley was a rope. Looking down the far length of the rope, he saw it run away in sharp perspective from dark into light. He had a bird's-eye view of the lamplit set, the tops of the wings, the flat white strip of table; and there, at the end of the rope in the middle of the table, a flattened object, rather like a beetle with a white head and paws. That was Alfred Meyer. The other end of the rope, terminating in an iron hook, was against the pulley. The hook had been secured to a ring in the end of the rope, and the red cord which Carolyn had cut was also tied to the ring. The cut end of the cord dangled in mid-air. On the hook he should have found the counterweight.

But there was no counterweight.

He looked again at the pulley. It was as he had thought. A loop of thin cord had been passed round the near end of the batten and tied to the gallery. It had served to pull the batten eighteen inches to one side. So that when the bottle dropped it was slightly to the right of the centre of the table.

'Stap me and sink me!' said Alleyn and returned to the stage. He found Ted Gascoigne by the stage-door. With him were two large dark men, wearing overcoats, scarves, and black felt hats; a police officer, and a short pink-faced person who was obviously the divisional surgeon. 'Do they call them divisional surgeons in this country?' wondered Alleyn.

They were some time at the stage-door. Gascoigne talked very fast and most confusedly. At last he took them on to the stage, where they were joined by Te Pokiha. From the wings Alleyn watched them make their examination. It gave him a curious feeling to look on while other men did his own job. They examined the end of the rope which was still knotted into the net enclosing the bottle, and the piece of red-bound wire cord that lay on the table. Gascoigne explained the mechanism of the descending jeroboam. They peered up into the grid. Gascoigne pointed out the other end of the red cord.

'When Miss Dacres cut it, it shot up,' he explained.

'Yes,' said the detective. 'Ye-ees. That's right. Ye-ees.'

'Out comes the old notebook,' said Alleyn to himself.

'Hullo,' said a voice at his elbow. It was Hambledon.

'Carolyn wants to see you,' he whispered. 'What's happening out there?'

'Police doing their stuff. Wants to see me, does she?'

'Yes, come on.'

He led the way into the usual dark wooden passage. The star dressing-room was the first on the left. Hambledon knocked on the door, opened it, and led the way in. Carolyn sat at her dressing-table. She still wore the black lace dress she had put on for the party. Her hair was pushed back from her face as though she had sat with her head in her hands. Old Susan Max was with her. Susan sat comfortably in an arm-chair, radiating solid sense, but her eyes were anxious. They brightened when she saw Alleyn.

'Here he is, dear,' she said.

Carolyn turned her head slowly.

'Hullo,' she said.

'Hullo,' said Alleyn. 'Hambledon says you want me.'

'Yes, I do.' Her hands were trembling violently. She pressed them together between her knees.

'I just thought I'd like you here,' said Carolyn. 'I've killed him, haven't I?'

'No!' said Hambledon violently.

'My dear!' said Susan.

'Well, I have. I cut the cord. That was what did it, wasn't it?' She still looked at Alleyn.

56

'Yes,' said Alleyn in a very matter-of-fact voice, 'that was what set the thing off. But you didn't rig the apparatus, did you?'

'No. I didn't know anything about it. It was a surprise.'

She caught her breath and a strange sound, something like laughter, came from her lips. Susan and Hambledon looked panicky.

'Oh!' cried Carolyn. 'Oh! Oh!'

'Don't!' said Alleyn. 'Hysterics are a bad way of letting things go. You feel awful afterwards.'

She raised one of her hands and bit on it. Alleyn picked up a bottle of smelling-salts from the dressing-table and held it under her nose.

'Sniff hard,' he said.

Carolyn sniffed and gasped. Tears poured out of her eyes.

'That's better. You're crying black tears. I thought that stuff was waterproof. Look at yourself.'

She gazed helplessly at him and then turned to the glass. Susan gently wiped away the black tears.

'You're a queer one,' sobbed Carolyn.

'I know I am,' agreed Alleyn. 'It's a pose, really. Would you drink a little brandy if Hambledon got it for you?'

'No.'

'Yes, you would.' He looked good-humouredly at Hambledon, who was standing by her chair. 'Can you?' asked Alleyn.

'Yes – yes, I'll get it.' He hurried away.

Alleyn sat on one of the wicker baskets and spoke to old Susan.

'Well, Miss Max, our meetings are to be fraught with drama, it seems.'

'Ah,' said Susan with a sort of grunt.

'What do you mean?' asked Carolyn. She turned to the mirror and, very shakily, dabbed at her face with a powder-puff.

'Mr Alleyn and I have met before, dear,' explained

57

Susan. 'Over that dreadful business with Felix Gardener, you know.'

'Yes. We spoke about it that night on the train.' Carolyn paused, and then she began to speak rapidly, urgently and with more command over her voice.

'That's why I wanted to see you. That night on the train. You remember what – he – said. Someone had tried to kill him. Have you thought of that?'

'I have,' said Alleyn.

'Well then – I want you to tell me, please, is this anything to do with it? Has someone – the same someone – done tonight what they failed to do on the train? Mr Alleyn – has someone murdered my husband?'

Alleyn was silent.

'Please answer me.'

'That's a question for the police, you know.'

'But I want *you* to tell me what you think. I must know what you think.' She leant towards him. 'You're not on duty. You're in a strange country, like all of us, and far away from your job. Don't be official, please don't. Tell me what you think!'

'Very well,' said Alleyn after a pause. 'I think someone has interfered with the tackle that was rigged up for – for the stunt with the champagne, you know.'

'And that means murder?'

'If I am right – yes. It looks like it!'

'Shall you speak to the police? They are there now, aren't they?'

'Yes. They are out there.'

'Well?'

'I regard myself as a layman, Miss Dacres. I shall certainly not butt in.' His voice was not final. He seemed to have left something unsaid. Carolyn looked fixedly at him and then turned to old Susan.

'Susie, darling, I want to talk to Mr Alleyn. Do you mind? You've been an angel. Thank you so much. Come back soon.'

When Susan had gone Carolyn leant forward and touched Alleyn's hand.

'Listen,' she said, 'do you feel friendly towards me? You do, don't you?

'Quite friendly.'

'I want you for my friend. You don't believe I could do anything very bad, do you? Or let anything very bad be done without making some effort to stop it?'

"What is in your mind?' he asked. 'What are you trying to say?'

'If I should want your help – yes, that's it – would you give it me?'

Her hand was still on his. She had patched up the stains made by her tears and her face looked beautiful again. He had seen her lean forward like that on the stage; it was a very characteristic gesture. Her eyes seemed to cry out to him.

'If I can be of any help,' said Alleyn very formally, 'of course I shall be only too glad—'

'No, no, no. That's not a bit of good. Sticking out all your prickles like that,' said Carolyn, with something of her old vigour. 'I want a real answer.'

'But, don't you see, you say too much and too little. What sort of help do you want from me?'

'I don't know, I don't know.'

'Come,' said Alleyn, 'I'll promise to stay in Middleton a little longer. When do you go on to Wellington?'

'When? We were to open there next week, but now – I don't know.'

'Listen to me. I give you one piece of advice. Don't try and keep anything in the dark, no matter what it is. Those fellows out there will want to talk to you. They'll have to ask you all sorts of questions. Answer them truthfully, no matter what it means, no matter how painful it may be, no matter where you think their questions are leading you. Promise me that and I'll pledge you my help, for what it's worth.'

Carolyn still leant towards him, still looked straight at him. But he felt her withdrawal as certainly as though it had been physical.

'Well?' he asked. 'Is it a bargain?'

But before she could answer him Hailey Hambledon came back with the brandy.

'The detectives want us all to wait in the wardrobe-room,' he said. 'I don't know about you, Alleyn.'

'You haven't given me away to anyone, have you?' asked Alleyn.

'No, no. Only we three realise you're a detective.'

'Please let it stay like that, will you?' asked Alleyn. 'I'm most anxious that it should be so.'

'I'll promise you *that*,' said Carolyn.

Their eyes met.

'Thank you,' said Alleyn quietly. 'I'll join you later.'

CHAPTER 6

Second Appearance of the Tiki

'Who's that?' demanded the largest of the three detectives. 'Just a minute there, please.' He was on the stage and had caught sight of Alleyn through the open door of the prompt entrance.

'It's me,' said Alleyn in a mild voice and walked through. The detective, Te Pokiha, and the police doctor, were all standing by the table.

'Who's this gentleman, Mr Gascoigne?' continued the detective.

'Er – it's – er – Mr Alleyn, Inspector.'

'Member of the company?'

'No,' said Alleyn, 'just a friend.'

'I thought I said no one was to come out here. What were you doing, sir? Didn't you understand—?'

'I just thought—' began Alleyn with that particular air of hurt innocence that always annoyed him when he met it in his official capacity. 'I just thought—'

'I'll have your full name and address, if *you* please,' interrupted the inspector, and opened his notebook. 'Allan, you said. First name?'

'Roderick.'

'How do you spell—?' The inspector stopped short and stared at Alleyn.

'A-l-l-e-y-n, Inspector.'

'Good God!'

'New Scotland Yard, London,' added Alleyn apologetically.

'By cripes, sir, I'm sorry. We'd heard you were – we didn't know – I mean –'

'I shall call at headquarters when I get to Wellington,' said Alleyn. 'I've got a letter somewhere from your chief. Should have answered it. Very dilatory of me.'

'I'm very, very sorry, sir. We thought you were in Auckland. We've been expecting you, of course.'

'I changed my plans,' said Alleyn. 'All my fault, Inspector—?'

'Wade, sir,' said the inspector, scarlet in the face.

'How do you do?' said Alleyn cheerfully, and held out his hand.

'I'm very very pleased to meet you, Chief Inspector,' said Inspector Wade, shaking it relentlessly. 'Very very pleased. We had word that you were on your way, and as a matter of fact, Superintendent Nixon was going to look in at the Middleton as soon as you came down. Yes, that's right. The super was going to call. We've all been trained on your book.[1] 'It's – it's a great honour to meet the author.'

'That's very nice of you,' said Alleyn, easing his fingers a little. 'I should have called at your headquarters on my arrival, but you know how it is in a new place. One puts off these things.' He glanced through the wings on to the stage.

'That's right. And now we meet on the job as you might say. Ye-ees.'

'Not *my* job, thank the Lord,' said Alleyn, 'and, look here. I want to hide my job under a bushel. So – if you don't mind – just don't mention it to any of these people.'

'Certainly, sir. I hope you'll let the boys here meet you. They'd be very very pleased, I know.'

'So should I – delighted. Just tip them the wink, if you don't mind, to forget about the CID. And as I'm a layman, I suppose you want to ask me a few questions, Inspector?'

The New Zealander's large healthy face again turned red.

'Well now, sir, that makes me feel a bit foolish but – well – yes, we've got to do the usual, you know.'

'Of course you have,' said Alleyn very charmingly.

[1]*Principles and Practice of Criminal Investigation,* by Roderick Alleyn, MA (Oxon), CID. (Sable & Murgatroyd, 2ls.)

'Nasty business, isn't it? I shall be most interested to see something of your methods if you will allow me.'

'It's very fine of you to put it that way, sir. To be quite frank I was wondering if you would give us an account of what took place before the accident. You were in the party, I understand.'

'A statement in my own words, Inspector?' asked Alleyn, twinkling.

'That's right,' agreed Wade with a roar of laughter, which he instantly quelled. His two subordinates, hearing this unseemly noise, strolled up and were introduced. Detective-Sergeants Cass and Packer. They shook Alleyn's hand and stared profoundly at the floor. Alleyn gave a short but extremely workmanlike account of the tragedy.

'By cripes!' said Inspector Wade with great feeling. 'It's not often we get it like that. Now, about the way this champagne business was fixed. You say you made a sketch of it, sir?'

Alleyn showed him the sketch.

'Ought to have worked OK,' said Wade. 'I'll go up and have a look-see.'

'You'll find it rather different, now,' said Alleyn. 'I ventured to have a glance up there myself. I do hope you don't mind, Inspector: It was damned officious, I know, but I didn't get off the ladder and I'm sure I've done no harm.'

'That's quite all right, sir,' said Wade heartily. 'No objections here. We don't have Scotland Yard alongside us every day. You say it's different from your sketch?'

'Yes. May I come up with you?'

'Too right. You boys fix up down here. Get the photographs through and the body shifted to the mortuary. You'd better ring the station for more men. Get a statement from the stage-manager and the bloke that rigged this tackle. You can take that on, Cass. And Packer, you get statements from the rest of the crowd. Are they all in the wardrobe-room?'

'I think they will be there by now,' said Alleyn. 'The guests have gone, with the exception of a Mr Gordon Palmer and his cousin Mr Weston who, I believe, are still here. Mr George Mason, the business manager, has a list of the names and addresses. The guests simply came behind the scenes for the party and are casual acquaintances of the company. Mr Palmer and his cousin came out in the same ship as the company. I – I suggested that perhaps they might be of use. They were,' said Alleyn dryly, 'delighted to remain.'

'Good-oh,' said Wade. 'Get to it, you boys. Are you ready, Mr Alleyn?'

He led the way up the iron ladder. When he reached the first gallery he paused and switched on his torch.

'Not much light up there,' he grunted.

'Wait a moment,' called Alleyn from below. 'There's a light-border. I'll see if I can find the switch.'

He climbed up to the electrician's perch and, after one or two experiments, switched on the overhead lights. A flood of golden warmth poured down through the dark strips of canvas.

'Good-oh,' said Wade.

'It is extraordinary,' thought Alleyn, 'how ubiquitous they make that remark. It expresses anything from acquiescence to approbation.'

He mounted the iron ladder.

'Well now, sir,' said Wade, 'it all looks much the same as your sketch to me. Where's the difference?'

'Look at the rope by the pulley,' suggested Alleyn, climbing steadily. 'Look at the end where the counterweight should be attached. Look—'

He had reached the second platform where Wade sat, dangling his legs. He turned on the ladder and surveyed the tackle.

'Hell's gaiters!' said Alleyn very loudly. 'They've put 'em back again.'

A long silence followed. Alleyn suddenly began to chuckle.

'One in the eye for me,' he said, 'and a very pretty one, too. All the same it's too damn' clever by half. Look here, Inspector, when I came up here twenty minutes ago the counterweight was *not* attached to the rope over there, and the pulley *had* been moved eighteen inches this way by a loop of cord.'

'Is that so?' said Wade solemnly. After another pause he glanced at Alleyn apologetically. It'd be very dark then, sir. No lights at all, I take it. I suppose—'

'I'll go into the box and swear my socks off and my soul pink,' said Alleyn. 'And I had a torch, what's more. No – it's been put right again. It must have been done while I was in the dressing-room. By George, I wonder if the fellow was up here on the platform when I came up the ladder. You had just got to the theatre when I went down.'

'D'you mean,' asked Wade, 'd'you mean to tell me that this gear was all different when we came in and someone's changed it round since? We'd have known something about that, Mr Alleyn.'

'My dear chap, but would you? Look here, kick me out. I've no business to gate-crash on your job, Inspector. It's insufferable. Just take my statement in the ordinary way and I'll push off. Lord knows, I didn't mean to buck round doing the CID official.'

Wade, whose manner up to now had been a curious mixture of deference, awkwardness, and a somewhat forced geniality, now thawed completely.

'Look, sir,' he said, 'you don't need to make any apologies. I reckon I know a gentleman when I meet one. We've read about your work out here, and if you like to interest yourself – well, we'll be only too pleased. Now! Only too pleased.'

'Extraordinary nice of you,' said Alleyn. 'Thank you so much for those few nuts and so on. All right. Didn't you stay by the stage-door for a bit, when you came in?'

Yes, that's right, we did. Mr Gascoigne met us there and started some long story. We didn't know what was up.

Simply got the message, there'd been an accident at the theatre. It took me a minute or two to get the rights of it and another minute or two to find out where the body was. You know how they are.'

'Exactly. Well now, while that was going on, I fancy our gentleman was up here and very busy. He came up under cover of all the hoo-hah on the stage some time after the event. He was just going to put things straight, when he heard me climbin' up de golden stair, as you might say. That must have given him a queasy turn. He took cover somewhere up here in the dark and as soon as I went down again he did what he had to do. Then, when you were safely on the stage and shut off by the walls of scenery, down he came pussy-foot, by the back-stage ladder, and mixed himself up with the crowd. Conjecture, perhaps—'

'I've just been reading your views on conjecture, sir,' said Wade.

'For the Lord's sake, Wade, don't bring my own burblings up against me, or I shall look the most unutterable ass. Conjecture or not, I think you'll find traces of this performance if you look round up here.'

'Come on, then, sir. Let's go to it.'

'Right you are. Tread warily, I would. Damn – it's slatted.'

The gallery turned out to be a narrow stretch of steel-slatted platform extending from the prompt corner to the back wall, round the back wall, and along the opposite side to the OP corner. It was guarded by a rail to which the ropes that raised the scenic clothes were made fast. They began to work their way round, hugging the wall and taking long steps on the tips of their toes.

'There's plenty of dust in these regions,' said Alleyn. 'I had a case that hung on just such another spot. Hung, by the way, is the right word. The homicide swung his victim from the grid.'

'You mean the Gardener case, sir? I've read about that.'

'Bless me, Inspector, if you're not better up in my cases

than I am myself. Stop a moment.'

They had moved out of the area of light, and switched on their torches. Alleyn swung his towards the rail.

'Here, you see, we are opposite the pulley. Now when I came up here before, a piece of cord had been passed round the batten on which the pulley is rigged. That beam, there. The rope to the beam stopped it from slipping and it was made fast to this cleat on the rail here. The effect was to drag the pulley eighteen inches or so this way.'

'What for, though?' asked Wade.

'In order that the jeroboam of fizz should fall, not into the nest of ferns and fairy lights, but on to the naked pate of poor Alfred Meyer.'

'Geeze!'

'And here, I think, I very much suspect, is the piece of cord. Neatly rolled round the cleat. Clever fellow, this. Keeps his head. What? Shall we move on?'

'I'll collect that cord on the way back,' grunted Wade. 'On you go, sir. After you.'

'There are any number of footprints on these damn' slats. The stage hands have been all over the place, of course.'

'Not much chance of anything there,' agreed Wade, 'but we'll have to see. If you're right, sir, the suspect's prints will be on top.'

'So they will. Here's the back wall. Another ladder here you notice. I daren't look down, I'm terrified of heights. Round we go. This, no doubt, is where he crouched with blazing eyes and bared molars while I climbed the ladder. Dramatic, ain't it? Also remarkably grubby. Bang goes the old boiled shirt. Hullo! Another ladder going down to the back of the stage. That'll be the one he used, I should think. Turn the corner gently. Now we're on the last lap.'

'And there's the pulley again.'

They had worked round to the OP gallery and were close by the pulley which hung within easy reach from its batten.

'Yes,' said Alleyn, 'and there hangs the counterweight

on the hook. I understand the weight is one of the sort that is used in the second act, to lead the ship's funnel down to the right spot. They've got several of them. Look. There is the funnel with the weight on it, just above our heads. And here, along the side, are several spare weights. Different sizes. You'll notice that the ring at the top of the hook would serve as a chock and prevent the rope whizzing through the pulley when the weight was removed. The weight hung exactly half-way, so there would be no slack rope on the table. '

'And you say there was no weight on this rope when you looked up here before?'

'There was no weight. The rope with the cut end of red cord simply hung in the pulley.'

He flashed his light on the beam. You'll notice the whole thing is within arm's length of the gallery. The table was placed well over to the side for that reason.'

'Well, I'll test the lantern for prints,' said Wade, 'but it's a bit hopeless. Anyway he'd use gloves. Don't you reckon it's a mistake sir, the way they've advertised the fingerprint system? Any fool crook knows better than to forget his gloves, these days.'

'There are times,' said Alleyn, 'when I could wish the penny Press-lords in the nethermost hell. Yet they have their uses, they have their uses. Nay, I can gleek on occasion.' Sensing Wade's bewilderment he added hurriedly: 'You're right, Inspector, but of course they have to come out in evidence. Prints, I mean. I grow confused. It must be the smell of fizz.'

'It was certainly a high-class way of murdering anybody,' said Wade dryly. 'Dong him one with a gallon of champagne. Good-oh!'

'I doubt if I shall enjoy even the soundest vintage years for some time to come,' said Alleyn. 'The whole place reeks of it. You can even smell it up here. Great hopping fleas!'

'What's wrong, sir?'

Alleyn was staring from the counterweight on the rope to those on the platform.

'My dear Wade, we have come within an ace of making the most frightful fools of ourselves. Look at that weight.'

'I am,' said Wade.

'Well, my dear chap, what's keeping it there?'

'The weight of the – Cripey, sir, the cork blew out and half the champagne with it. That weight ought to be on the stage. It ought to be heavier than the half-empty bottle.'

'Exactly. Therefore it is *very much* lighter than the full bottle. Therefore it is not the weight they rehearsed with. And what's more, the original weight must have hung hard by the lower gallery, half-way down to the stage, within easy reach. He didn't come up here for the first visit. He did his stuff from the lower gallery.'

'You're right, sir. And if you hadn't come up the first time, it would have looked more like an accident and less like homicide.'

Alleyn pulled in the rope and grasped it above the weight.

'Nothing like heavy enough,' he said. 'It must have been one of the big ones. Well – that's that. Are we staying aloft, Inspector?'

'I think we'll go down now, sir. I'll send Cass up to collect the stuff here. It'll need careful handling, and I think had better be done by daylight. I'll leave a man here, of course. Ye-es.'

Footsteps sounded on the stage below, and voices. They looked down and had a bird's eye view of a little procession. The police constable, whom Wade had left mounting guard over Meyer's body, opened the door in the box set. Through it came Dr Tancred, Dr Te Pokiha, and two men with a stretcher. The stretcher was laid on the stage. Tancred looked up into the grid, his hand over his eyes.

'You up there, Inspector?' he called.

'Here I am, Doctor.'

'All right if we move the body?'

'Has Cass got his photos OK?'

'Yes.'

'Good-oh, then, Doctor.'

They lifted the terrible head. Tancred and Te Pokiha examined it again. It lolled back and seemed to stare up to where the two men watched from above. Pieces of fern were stuck on the face, and it was cut with glass from the broken lights. Te Pokiha brushed the fern away. They hauled the body up from the chair. It seemed to be very heavy. At last they got it on the stretcher and covered it.

'All right,' said Tancred.

They carried Meyer away, the policeman holding the door open. Te Pokiha remained behind.

'Well, we may as well go down,' said Wade.

Alleyn did not answer. Wade turned to look at him. He was in the act of stooping. His long fingers reached for something that lay between two of the steel slats at his feet. His fingers edged at this little object, coaxed it up, and grasped it. He straightened, glanced down beneath him to where Te Pokiha stood, and then made a slight gesture of warning.

'What's up?' asked Wade softly.

Alleyn stretched out his hand into the light. On the palm lay a small green object of a singular shape. Its head lolled over to one side and it seemed to be grinning.

'Are you coming down?' called Te Pokiha from the stage.

CHAPTER 7

Wardrobe-room Muster

'It's a tiki,' said Wade.

'Yes. May be of some importance. Wait a moment.'

Alleyn pulled a handkerchief from his pocket, dropped the tiki on it and folded it over carefully.

'There you are, Inspector. I'll give you the history when we get down. In the meantime, if I may make a suggestion, keep it under your hat.'

They climbed down the OP ladder to the stage. Te Pokiha waited for them.

'If you've no further use for me, Mr Wade, I think I'll clear out,' he said. 'It's one o'clock.'

'Right-oh, then, Doctor,' agreed Wade. 'We'll want you for the inquest.'

'I suppose so.' He turned to Alleyn. 'I had no idea you were the famous Roderick Alleyn,' he said in his warm voice. 'It's strange that this should be your introduction to New Zealand. I have read—'

'Have you?' said Alleyn quickly. 'I'm supposed to be on a holiday for my health. And by the way, I particularly *don't* want my identity made public. As far as this affair goes, I'm a layman, Dr Te Pokiha. Inspector Wade very kindly allowed me to have a look at the pulley up there.'

'Has it been interfered with?' asked Te Pokiha.

'We're going to make a thorough examination by daylight, Doctor,' said Wade. 'I'll just see these other people now.'

Te Pokiha's dark eyes gleamed in his dark face.

'I'll wish you good night, then. Good night, Mr Alleyn. You seemed to be interested in my people. If you would care to come and see me while you are here—'

71

'I should be delighted,' said Alleyn cordially.

'Dinner tomorrow? Splendid. It's not far out. Twenty miles. I'll call for you at six.'

Alleyn shook the thin brown hand that Te Pokiha extended, and watched the Maori go out.

'Very, very fine fellow, Rangi Te Pokiha,' said Wade. 'Fine athlete, and brainy, too. Best type of Maori.'

'I met him at the hotel,' said Alleyn, 'and found him very interesting. There is no colour prejudice in this country, apparently.'

'Well, not in the way there is in India, for instance. Mind, there are Maoris and Maoris. Te Pokiha's high caste. His mother was a princess and his father a fine old chief. The doctor's had an English college education – he's ninety per cent civilised. All the same, sir, there's the odd ten per cent. It's there, no matter how civilised they are. See him when he goes into one of the back-country pas and you'll find a difference. See him when he goes crook! By gee, I did once, when he gave evidence on a case of – well, it was an unsavoury case and the doctor felt strongly about it. His eyes fairly flashed. He looked as if he might go off at the deep end and dance a haka in court.'

'A haka?'

'War-dance. They pull faces and yell. Great affair, it is. Well now, what about this tiki, Mr Alleyn?'

'Ah, yes.' Alleyn lowered his voice. 'Dr Te Pokiha put me in the way of buying that tiki. I gave it to Miss Carolyn Dacres as a birthday present tonight.'

'To the Dacres woman?' asked Wade, suddenly looking very sharp. 'You did? Is that so?'

'She is not "the Dacres woman" so far, you know,' said Alleyn. 'The tiki passed from hand to hand. It may be of interest to find out where it fetched up.'

'Of interest! I should say so. I'll see these people now. Cass!'

Detective-Sergeant Cass opened the door in the set and looked in.

72

'I'm going to the office, Cass. Send these people along one by one. You haven't left them alone, I hope?'

'No, sir. We've got them all together in one room now. Packer's in there.'

'All right.' He turned to Alleyn. 'Are you sticking to it a while longer, Mr Alleyn?'

'I think I'll wander in and join the party for a bit, if you've no objections.'

'That's quite all right, sir, that's quite all right. You just please yourself,' said Wade in his heartiest voice. Alleyn knew that the inspector was at once relieved to think that he would be left alone for examination of the others, and slightly disappointed at losing his chance of exhibiting his ability before the representative of Scotland Yard.

'I suppose,' thought Alleyn, 'I must give him an inferiority complex. He feels I'm criticising him all the time. If I don't remember to be frightfully hearty and friendly, he'll think I'm all English and superior. I know he will. I would myself, I suppose, in his shoes. He's been damn' pleasant and generous, too, and he's a very decent fellow. Dear me, how difficult it all is.'

He found his way along the dressing-room passage and, guided by the murmur of voices, knocked at the last door. It was opened by Detective-Sergeant Packer, who came half through the door. He was a fine specimen, was Packer; tall, magnificently built, with a good head on him. When he saw Alleyn he came to attention.

'Sergeant Packer,' said Alleyn, 'your inspector tells me I may come in here if I behave nicely. That all right?'

'Certainly, Chief Inspector,' said Packer smartly.

Alleyn looked at him.

'We shan't bother about the "Chief Inspector",' he murmured. 'Can you come outside for a second?'

Packer at once stepped out and closed the door.

'Look here,' said Alleyn, 'do those people in there realise I'm from the Yard?'

'I don't think they do, sir. I heard them mention your

73

name, but they didn't seem to know.'

'Good. Leave 'em in outer darkness. Just any old Allen. I asked Inspector Wade to warn you, but I suppose he hasn't had a chance. Miss Dacres, Miss Max, and Mr Hambledon know, but they'll keep quiet, I hope. Understand?'

'Yes, sir.'

'Splendid. Then just let me loose among 'em, Packer. I'll do no harm, I promise you.'

'Harm, sir? I should say *not*. If you'll excuse me mentioning it, sir, I've just read—'

'Have you? I'll give you a copy for yourself. Now usher me in. And chidingly, Packer. Be severe with me.'

Detective-Sergeant Packer was a young officer. He looked at the tall figure of Chief Inspector Alleyn and developed instant and acute hero-worship. 'He looks like one of those swells in the English flicks,' he afterwards confided to his girl, 'and he talks with a corker sort of voice. Not queeny, but just corker. I reckon he's all right. Gosh, I reckon he's a humdinger.'

Under a fearful oath of secrecy, long after there was any need for discretion, Packer described to his best girl the scene in the wardrobe-room.

'He said to me, kind of laughing – and he's got a corking sort of laugh – he said: "Be severe with me, Packer." So I opened the door and, as he walked through, I said: "Move along in there, if *you* please, sir. And kindly obey instructions." Very stiff. And he walked in and he said, "Frightfully sorry, officer," in a real dude voice. "Frightfullah sorrah, officahh" – only it sounded decent the way he said it. Not unnatural. Just English. "Frightfulla sorra –" I can't seem to get it.'

'And then what?' asked Packer's best girl.

'Well, and then he walked in. And I stayed on the outside of the door. He didn't tell me to, but I reckoned if I stayed out he'd get them to talk. I left the door a crack open and I walked noisily away and then quietly back again. I dunno what old Sam Wade would 'uv said if he'd come along. He'd 'uv gone horribly crook at me for not staying inside. Well, as soon as the Chief walks in they all start in squealing. "Oh, Mr Alleyn, what's happening? Oh, Mr Alleyn, what's the matter?" The girl Gaynes – Valerie Gaynes. You know—'

'She's the one that wore that corking dress in the play. I think she's lovely.'

'She makes me tired. She started squealing about the disgraceful way she'd been treated, and how she'd write to her old man and complain, and how they'd never dream of shutting her up like this in England, and how she reckoned the police in this country didn't know the way to behave. Give you a pain in the neck, dinkum, she would. Well, as I was telling you—'

Packer told his girl many times of this scene.

The fact of the matter was that Alleyn got an unpleasant shock when he walked into the wardrobe-room. He suddenly remembered that, during that night in the train Carolyn had told Valerie Gaynes he was a CID official, and here was Valerie Gaynes rushing at him with complaints about the New Zealand police, about the way she was being treated. Any moment she might give the show away. He glanced at Carolyn. She called Miss Gaynes, murmured something in her ear, and drew her down beside her.

'Oh!' said Valerie Gaynes flatly. 'Well, I think—'

'Of course you do,' said Carolyn quickly, 'but if you could manage not to *talk* quite so much, darling, it would be such a good idea.'

'But, Miss Dacres—'

'Yes, darling, but do you know, I think if I were you, I should just go all muted – like you did over your money, do you remember, when Mr Alleyn offered to look at your notecase.'

Valerie Gaynes suddenly sat down.

'That's right, darling,' said Carolyn jerkily. 'Come and sit down, Mr Alleyn. It seems we are all to be shut up in

75

here while they find out whether my poor Pooh was – whether it was all an accident or not.'

Her voice was pitched a note too high and her hands moved restlessly in her lap.

'That's the idea, I believe,' said Alleyn.

'What are they *doing* out there?' asked little Ackroyd peevishly.

'How much longer—?'

'Mr Alleyn, can you tell us—?'

They all began again.

'I know no more than you do,' said Alleyn, at last. 'I believe they propose to interview us all, singly. I've just had my dose. I got ticked off for loitering.'

'What did they ask you?' demanded young Palmer.

'My name and address,' said Alleyn shortly. He dragged forward a small packing-case, sat on it, and surveyed the company.

The wardrobe-room at the Royal was simply a very large dressing-room, occupied by the chorus when musical-comedy companies visited Middleton. The Dacres Company used it to store the wardrobes for their second and third productions. An ironing-table stood at one end, an odd length of stage-cloth carpeted the floor, and a number of chairs, covered with dustcloths, were ranged round the walls. It served the company as a sort of common-room – an improvised version of the old-fashioned green-room. Carolyn tried to create something of the long-vanished atmosphere of the actor-manager's touring company. She was old enough to have served her apprenticeship in one of the last of these schools and remembered well the homely, knit-together feeling of back-stage, the feeling that the troupe was a little world of its own, moving compactly about a larger world. With Meyer's help she had tried, so far as she was able, to keep the same players about her for all her productions. She used to beg Meyer to look for what she called useful actors and actresses, by which she meant adaptable people who could pour themselves into the

76

mould of a part and who did not depend upon individual tricks. 'Give me actors, Pooh darling, not types.' Perhaps that was why, with the exception of Valerie Gaynes and Courtney Broadhead, none of her company was very young. Valerie she had suffered only after a struggle, and, she confided in Hambledon, because she was afraid they might all begin to think she was jealous of young and good-looking women. Courtney came of an old acting family and took his work seriously. The rest – Ackroyd, Gascoigne, Liversidge, Vernon, Hambledon and Susan Max, were all over forty. They were, as Hambledon would have said, 'old troupers', used to each other's ways, and to the sound of each other's voices. There is a kind of fortuitous intimacy among the members of such companies. It would be difficult to say how well they really know each other, but they often speak of themselves as 'a happy family'. As he looked from one face to another Alleyn was aware of this corporate feeling in the Dacres Company. 'How are they taking it?' he wondered. He asked himself the inevitable question: 'Which? Which of these?' And one by one he watched them.

Hambledon had moved away from Carolyn and sat opposite her and beside George Mason. They were both very pale and silent. Mason's undistinguished face was blotched, as if he had been crying. He looked apprehensive and miserable and rather ill. Hambledon's magnificent head was bent forward. He held one long-fingered hand over his eyes, as though the light bothered him. Old Brandon Vernon sat with his arms folded and his heavy eyebrows drawn down. He had the peculiar raffish look of a certain type of elderly actor. His face was pale, as if it had taken on the texture of grease-paint, his mobile mouth seemed always about to widen into a sardonic grin; his eyes, lack-lustre, had an impertinent look. There were traces of No 9 in the hair on his temples and his chin was bluish. He played polished old men-of-the-world with great skill. When Alleyn came in Vernon was deep in conversation with little

Ackroyd, with whom he seemed to be annoyed. Ackroyd, whose amusing face was so untrustworthy a guide to his character, listened irritably. He grimaced and fidgeted, glanced under his eyelids at Carolyn.

Next to Ackroyd sat Liversidge, with an empty chair beside him. Valerie Gaynes had moved out of it when Carolyn called her. Alleyn was a little surprised to see how shaken Liversidge seemed to be. His too full, too obviously handsome face was very white. He was unable to sit still, and when he lit one cigarette from the butt of another his hands shook so much that he could scarcely control them.

Young Courtney Broadhead, on the other hand, looked solemn, but much less unhappy than he had appeared to be that night in the train. 'They have changed their roles,' thought Alleyn. For in the train Broadhead had stood huddled in his overcoat on the little iron platform, speaking to nobody; while Liversidge had shouted and shown himself off. Alleyn's thoughts returned persistently to the night in the train.

Ted Gascoigne had joined young Gordon Palmer and his cousin, Geoffrey Weston. The stage-manager was describing the mechanism of the pulley and the bottle. Gordon listened avidly, bit his nails, and asked innumerable questions. Weston said very little.

The stage-hands stood in an awkward and silent group at the far end of the room.

Alleyn had not been long in the room before he realised that the members of the company felt themselves constrained and embarrassed by the presence of Carolyn, and perhaps of Hambledon. Through their conversation ran a chain of sidelong glances, of half-spoken phrases. This, he told himself, was natural enough, since they must assume that they were in the presence of grief and there is nothing more embarrassing than other people's sorrow. 'But not to these people,' thought Alleyn, 'since they have histrionic precedents for dealing with sorrow. They are embarrassed for some other reason.'

Under cover of the general conversation he turned to Carolyn and said quietly: 'I am plagued with a horrible feeling that you may think I have brought misfortune to you.'

'You?' She looked at him in bewilderment. 'How should I think that?'

'By my gift.'

'You mean – the green figurine – the tiki?'

She glanced swiftly at Hambledon and away again.

'I wish you would return it to me and let me replace it by another gift,' said Alleyn.

Carolyn looked fixedly at him. Her hand went to her breast.

'What do you mean, Mr Alleyn?' she asked hurriedly.

'Is it in your bag?'

'I – yes. No.' She opened her bag and turned it out on her lap. 'No. Of course it's not. I haven't had it since – since before supper. Somebody took it from me – they were all looking at it. I remember distinctly that I did not have it.'

'May I ask who has it now?'

'Of course – if you want to.'

Alleyn raised his voice.

'Who's got Miss Dacres's tiki, please? She would like to have it.'

Dead silenece. He looked from one figure to another. They all looked bewildered and a little scandalised, as though Carolyn, by asking for her little tiki, had stepped outside the correct rendering of her part of tragic wife.

'It must be on the stage,' said Courtney Broadhead.

'Sure none of you has it?' pursued Alleyn.

The men felt in their pockets.

'I remember handing it on to you,' said Brandon Vernon to Ackroyd.

'Somebody took it from me,' said Ackroyd. 'You did, Frankie.'

'I?' said Liversidge. 'Did I? I haven't got it now. As a

matter of fact, I think I gave it to—' He hesitated and glanced at Carolyn.

'Yes?' asked Alleyn.

' – to Mr Meyer,' said Liversidge uncomfortably.

'Oh!' Carolyn drew in her breath swiftly. Old Susan looked directly at Alleyn with a curious expression that he could not read. Suddenly Valerie Gaynes cried out:

'It's unlucky – I thought at the time it looked unlucky. Something seemed to tell me. I've got a queer intuition about things—'

'I am quite sure,' said Carolyn steadily, 'that my tiki is not unlucky. And I know Alfie hadn't got it when we sat down to supper.'

'How do you know that, Miss Dacres?' asked Alleyn.

'Because he asked me for it. He wanted to look at it again. And I hadn't got it either.'

'But I say—'

Alleyn turned swiftly. Young Gordon Palmer stood with his mouth half open and a curiously startled look on his face.

'Yes, Mr Palmer?' asked Alleyn.

'Oh, nothing.' And at that moment Packer opened the door and said:

'Inspector Wade would like to speak to Mrs Meyer, please.'

'I'm coming,' said Carolyn. Her long graceful stride took her quickly to the door. Hambledon got there before her.

'May I take Miss Dacres to the office?' he asked. 'I'll come straight back.'

'Well, sir—' said Packer uncomfortably. He looked for a fraction of a second at Alleyn, who gave him the ghost of a nod.

'I'll just inquire,' said Packer. He went outside and closed the door. They could hear him talking to Sergeant Cass. He returned in a moment.

'If you would care to go along with Sergeant Cass and Mrs Mey – beg pardon – Miss Dacres, sir, that'll be all right. Sergeant Cass will come back with you.'

Alleyn strolled over to the door.

'I really cannot understand, officer,' he said, 'why I should be kept hanging about here. I've nothing whatever to do with this miserable business.' He added swiftly, under his breath: 'Keep Mr Hambledon talking outside the door if he returns.' And to Hambledon: 'Stay outside if you can.'

Hambledon stared, but Packer said loudly:

'Now that'll be quite enough from you, Mr Alleyn. We're only doing our duty, as you ought to realise. You go back to your chair, if you please, sir. Everything will be quite all right.'

'Oh, excellent Packer!' thought Alleyn and returned churlishly to his upturned case.

Carolyn and Hambledon went out with Packer, who shut the door.

At once the others seemed to relax. There was a slight movement from all of them. Courtney Broadhead said:

'I simply can't take it in. It's so horrible. So horrible.'

'That is how *you* feel about it, is it?' said Liversidge.

'I should think that's how everybody feels about it,' said old Susan Max. 'It's been a terrible experience. I shan't forget it in a hurry.'

'He looked so awful.' Valerie Gaynes's voice rose hysterically. 'I'll see it all my life. I'll be haunted by it. His head – all that mess!'

'My God!' choked George Mason suddenly, 'I've got to get out of this. I'm going to be sick. Here – let me out.'

He rushed to the door, his handkerchief clapped to his mouth, and his eyes rolling lamentably. 'Get me out!'

Packer opened the door, cast one glance at Mason's face, and let him through. Unpleasant noises were followed by the bang of a door.

'He's been slowly turning green ever since we came in here,' said Ackroyd. 'Damned unpleasant sight, it was. Why the devil does *he* have to turn queasy?'

'It's his stomach, dear,' said Susan. 'George suffers from dyspepsia, Mr Alleyn. Martyr to it.'

'You had to finish him off, Val,' Brandon Vernon

pointed out, 'by talking about the mess. Why did you have to bring that up?'

'Don't talk about bringing things up, for God's sake,' complained Liversidge.

'You look as if you were going on for Hamlet senior yourself, Frankie,' sneered Ackroyd.

'Oh, shut up,' said Liversidge violently.

'Well, nobody could feel iller than I do. I feel terrible,' said Valerie. 'Do you know that? I feel terrible.'

Nobody paid the slightest attention.

'What'll happen to the Firm?' asked Ackroyd of no one in particular. They all stirred uneasily. Gascoigne paused in his dissertation on counterweights and swung round.

'The Firm?' he said. 'The Firm will go on.'

'Do you mean Incorporated Playhouses?' asked Gordon Palmer eagerly.

'No,' snapped Ackroyd rudely, 'he means Wirth's Circus.'

'We always call Incorporated Playhouses "the Firm",' explained Susan good-naturedly.

'The great firm of Inky-P,' rumbled old Vernon.

'It was founded and built up by Mr Meyer, wasn't it?' asked Alleyn. 'He was actually the only begetter?'

'He and George Mason,' said Gascoigne. 'They made it together. George was a damn' good actor in his day – character, you know – never played straight parts. The governor met him somewhere and they doubled up. Yes, they started forty years ago as Mason & Meyer's Dramas Limited. A lot of omies the others were then, doing umpty-shows in the smalls.'

'That leaves me gaping,' said Alleyn apologetically. 'What is an "omie", Miss Max, and how does one recognise an "umpty-show"?'

'Ted means they were bad actors doing worse shows in one-eyed towns up and down the provinces,' said Susan.

'Yes,' continued Gascoigne, 'and today it's the biggest theatre combine in Europe. Wonderful achievement.'

'It'll be "George Mason" only now,' said Liversidge suddenly.

There was an uncomfortable silence.

'Yes,' said little Ackroyd. He looked under his lashes at Gascoigne. 'George will be a very wealthy man.'

At once Alleyn sensed a feeling of panic, of protest. Susan Max, who obviously disliked Ackroyd, planted her fat little hands on her knees and squared her shoulders.

'George Mason,' she said loudly, 'would rather be back advancing "The Worst Woman in London" than have this happen.'

'*Certainly.*' Gascoigne backed her up emphatically. 'I've stage-managed for the Firm for twenty-five years and it's been a happy little family for every day of it. Every day of it. Big as they are, they've gone on taking a personal interest. They run their own shows. Of course, this is just a holiday – but look at the way they've kept with the crowd. Mr Meyer was down in the office every morning and, make no mistake, he came down to work. He was *honest,* and by God, you can't say that for many of 'em. He and George were the whitest men in management.'

'Ah!' said Susan, ruffling her plumage, and looking with approval at Gascoigne.

'Well,' rumbled old Vernon, 'I've no quarrel with Inky P, and I hope to God George keeps me with him.'

'All right, all right,' protested Ackroyd. 'I'm not saying George isn't the curly-headed boy, am I, even if he hasn't always been quite quite?'

'What d'you mean by that?' demanded Vernon.

'I seem to remember hearing something about a company left stranded in America in the good old days,' said Ackroyd. 'Just one of those stories, you know, just one of those stories.'

'Then why repeat it?' snapped Vernon.

'Hear, hear,' said Gascoigne.

'Oh, dear, dear, *how* I do get myself in wrong, don't I?' cooed Ackroyd. He turned to Gascoigne. 'You keep on yammering about this bloody champagne stunt, Ted. You say it was fool-proof, accident-proof, all the rest of it.

Well – if it was, somebody's murdered Alfred Meyer. Now!'

Valerie Gaynes screamed and rushed across the room to the empty chair by Liversidge.

'Frankie!' she sobbed. 'Frankie! Not that! It's not true what they're saying – not true.'

'There, kiddy, there there!' crooned Mr Liversidge, stroking her arm and looking unpleasantly protective.

The door opened and George Mason returned. His round face was still very white.

'I'm very sorry, everyone,' he said simply, and returned to his seat.

'Better, Mr Mason?' asked Susan.

'Yes, thanks, Susie. Ashamed of myself. Where's Carolyn and Hailey?'

'Still out there.'

'While we're all together,' said Mason quietly, 'I'd just like to say that whatever happens I think I'd better call the company for midday tomorrow. I'll try and work out what's best to be done. Everyone on the stage at twelve, please, Mr Gascoigne.'

'Certainly, Mr Mason,' said Ted Gascoigne. 'Twelve o'clock tomorrow morning, please, ladies and gentlemen.'

Packer came in.

'The chief would like to see the stage staff.'

The little group at the far end of the room came forward and filed out through the door.

'Just a moment,' said Mason suddenly. 'Where are Miss Dacres and Mr Hambledon?'

'I think they've gone, sir.'

'Gone?'

'They've arrested them!' screamed Valerie Gaynes. 'My God, they've arrested them!'

'C – st!' said Mason savagely. 'Can no one keep that girl quiet!'

'They've just gone home, miss,' said Packer.

CHAPTER 8

Money

'The sooner you get down-stage and find yourself the better, young lady,' said Mason, when the staff had gone. 'What's the idea of all this tragedy stuff?'

'Oh, I can't help it,' wailed Valerie. 'I can't help it. I can't help it.'

'Nonsense,' said old Susan very loudly. 'Carolyn and Hailey arrested! The very idea!'

'I'm sorry. It was just him saying they'd gone. And it flashed through my mind – my poor tormented mind – how fond he is of her. I mean, we all know, and it was just—'

'Never mind, now,' interrupted Liversidge. 'Think of something else.'

'That's a suggestion,' said Alleyn cheerfully. 'Think of all the money you lost, Miss Gaynes. It's never turned up, I suppose?'

This had a salutary effect. Valerie stopped sobbing and caught her breath.

'No – I – no, it hasn't. But Mr Meyer was – awfully sweet. He – he advanced it to me – the same amount. And to think—'

'Really! Very kind of him.'

'Yes. He said he felt responsible, as I was under his wing. He said the Firm wouldn't let its people be out of pocket. And to think he's d—'

'D'you mean he gave it to you?' asked Ackroyd.

'Well – yes. He made me take it. I said it didn't matter – but he made me. And now he's lying there – mur—'

'That's just like him,' said Courtney Broadhead. 'He was wonderfully generous.'

'You've experienced his generosity, have you, Court?' asked Liversidge.

'Yes.' Broadhead looked straight at him. I have indeed.'

85

'Tell us about it, Court,' invited Gordon Palmer.

'Shut up, Gordon,' said Mr Weston, speaking for the first time since Alleyn had been in the room. 'Don't nosy-park.'

'Well,' said Liversidge, who seemed to have recovered a good deal of his composure. 'Well. It's nice to have an extra quid or two in your pocket. Thanks to you, Court, old boy, I've got one or two. I'll take you on again at Two's Wild whenever you like.'

'You were lucky at poker, were you, Mr Liversidge?' asked Alleyn lightly.

'I was. And poor old Court couldn't hold a court card.' He laughed.

'Must you?' said little Ackroyd. 'Oh, must you?'

'I think it's awful to make jokes,' began Valerie, 'when you think—'

'We're making epitaphs,' said Gordon Palmer. 'Or Court is, at any rate.' He glanced defiantly at Weston, and then turned to Broadhead. 'I've got a particular reason for asking it.'

'What is it?' said Broadhead.

'It's this. Where did you get the money to pay your poker debts?'

In the shocked silence that followed this amazing sentence Alleyn watched Liversidge. Liversidge himself watched Courtney Broadhead.

'I haven't the smallest objection to telling you,' said Broadhead. His face was scarlet, but he faced young Palmer collectedly. 'Mr Meyer lent it to me.'

'Oh,' said Gordon. He glanced sheepishly at Liversidge.

'Gordon!' Geoffrey Weston remarked dispassionately. 'You're a bounder.'

'"Carruthers, you cad, you have disgraced the old school tie,"' jeered Gordon. 'Really, Geoff, you're too superb.'

'You're asking for a hiding,' continued Mr Weston, 'and I've a damned good mind to give it you.'

'I shall run away. I run faster than you. Don't be a ninny, Geoff. I said I had a reason for asking my question. I had. A damn' good reason. The day we left the ship Courtney asked me if I'd mind waiting for my winnings till he began to draw his money. I said no, that was all right. He said he had been a fool and was in the soup. That night, in the train, Val found she'd been robbed of a hundred quid. The next day Courtney paid Frankie Liversidge and me every penny he owed us. He said afterwards he'd had a windfall. Now he says Mr Meyer lent him the cash. Well, that's very charming. Pity, in a way, that Mr Meyer isn't here to—'

'You damned little tripe-hound,' bawled Courtney Broadhead, and made for him.

'Broadhead!' Alleyn made them all jump. Courtney swung round angrily.

'I shouldn't, really,' said Alleyn.

'By God, no one's going to talk to me like—'

'If there's an explanation,' said Gordon Palmer, who looked frightened but obstinate, 'why don't you give it? You seem to be out for blood this evening, don't you?'

Courtney Broadhead made a wild swipe at him. Alleyn caught his arm, did something neat and quick with it, and held him.

'Do you want the sergeant outside to referee, you unspeakable donkey?' inquired Alleyn. 'Go back to your seat.'

To the intense astonishment of everybody Courtney went.

'Now,' said Alleyn to Gordon Palmer, 'you will listen to me, if you please. If you have any information that is relevant to this business, you will give it to the police.'

'I'm at liberty to say what I choose,' said Gordon, backing away.

'Shut up,' said Weston.

'If you go about making statements that may be criminally slanderous, you won't be at liberty to do anything at all for some considerable time,' Alleyn told him. 'Sit down and attend to your elders and betters, and don't be rude. You are a thoroughly tiresome and stupid young cub, and I see small hope of your growing up into anything that remotely resembles a human being.'

'Look here, who the hell—?'

'Shut up,' said Weston.

Gordon retired, muttering.

'I think,' said Liversidge, 'that if I were in your place, Court, old boy, I'd just explain quietly. You owe it to yourself, you know.'

'There's nothing more to say,' began Broadhead. 'I lost at poker and couldn't pay my debts. I went to Mr Meyer the morning we got here and told him about it. He was extraordinarily decent and advanced me the money. I was to pay it back out of my salary.'

'Well then, old boy,' said Liversidge, 'you've no need to worry. It'll all be on the books, won't it, Mr Mason? I suppose Mr Meyer told you about it?'

'I agree with Mr Alleyn,' said Mason quietly, 'that there is nothing to be gained by discussing this matter here.'

'It won't be on the books,' said Courtney Broadhead. 'It was a private loan.'

There was a long, uncomfortable silence.

'I don't understand,' said Valerie Gaynes suddenly. 'Of course, Court didn't take my money. What's my money got to do with it? It was stolen in the ship. Probably a steward took it.'

Her voice flattened. She looked at Liversidge and away again.

'I'm sure a steward took it, Frankie,' she said. It was almost as though she pleaded with him.

'I'll bet it was a steward,' said Liversidge very heartily indeed. He flashed an intolerably brilliant smile at Courtney Broadhead.

'Well,' said Susan Max roundly, 'it may have been a steward or it may have been the captain of the ship, but it wasn't Courtney Broadhead, and only a fool or a rogue would suggest that it was.'

'Quite a champion of – ah – good causes tonight, aren't

88

you, Susie?' said Liversidge winningly.

'For God's sake,' said George Mason, 'can't you cut out all this stuff about Miss Gaynes's money and Courtney's money. We're up against a terrible tragedy and, my God, you all start selling a lot of cross-talk. What's going to happen to the show? That's what I'd like to know. What's going to happen to the show?'

And as if he had indeed sounded the very bottom of their trouble they at once became silent and anxious.

'The show!' said Gordon Palmer shrilly. 'You are an extraordinary crowd. The show doesn't matter – what's going to happen to *us?*'

At this protest from outside they all seemed to draw together. They looked anxiously at each other, ignoring Gordon.

'You don't seem to realise a man's been murdered,' he went on. His voice, trying to be compelling and indignant, was boyishly lame.

'Shut up,' said Geoffrey Weston.

'I won't. There's poor Mr Meyer—' The voice wobbled uncertainly.

'If Alfred Meyer can think at all where he's gone,' said little George Mason surprisingly, 'he's thinking about the show. The Firm came first with Alfred – always.'

There was a short silence.

'I'm very sorry it happened, ladies and gentlemen,' added Mason, 'very sorry for your sakes, I mean. We've brought you all this way. I – I can assure you you'll be – looked after. My partner wouldn't have wanted it otherwise. We're old friends, all of us. I can't just sort things out in my own mind but – if I've got anything to do with it there'll be no difference.'

He looked solemnly at his company. There was a little stir among them as they were touched by his sudden assumption of formality, and by the illusion of security that his words had given to them. And, as he watched them, it seemed to Alleyn that of all things security is most desired by actors since it is the one boon that is never granted them. Even when they are in great demand and command absurdly large salaries, he reflected, few of them contrive to save much money. It is almost as though they were under the compulsion of some ancient rule of their guild, never to know security but often to desire it. And he fell to thinking of their strange life and of the inglorious and pathetic old age to which so many of them drifted.

Packer came in interrupting his thought.

The inspector, said Packer, would now speak to Mr Mason, if the latter was feeling better. Mr Mason turned pale, said he felt much better, and followed the sergeant out.

'I hope to God he meant what he said,' rumbled old Brandon Vernon. 'I've been so long with the Firm I've forgotten what other managements are like.'

Gradually they settled down to the actor's endless gossip about 'shop'. It was obvious that they were all shocked – some of them deeply moved perhaps – by Meyer's death. But they slipped into their habitual conversation quite unconsciously and soon were talking peacably enough. Courtney Broadhead had gone to the far end of the room and stayed there, glowering, till old Vernon strolled across and tried to talk him into a better humour. They all completely ignored Gordon Palmer who sulked in a corner with his silent bear-leader.

Presently Packer returned.

'Inspector Wade would like to speak to you now, Mr Alleyn,' said Packer.

Alleyn followed him into the dark passage.

'Mr Wade was wondering if you'd be glad of the chance to get out of there, sir,' murmured Packer.

'I see. Very thoughtful of him.'

'Goodnight, sir.'

'Goodnight, Packer. I'll see you again, I expect.'

'Good-oh, sir,' said Packer with enthusiasm.

Alleyn made his way to the office where he found Wade

seated at Alfred Meyer's desk with the colossal Cass in attendance.

'I thought perhaps you were getting a bit fed up in there, sir,' said Wade.

'It wasn't dull,' said Alleyn. 'The conversation took rather an interesting turn.'

'Yes?'

Alleyn related his experiences in the wardrobe-room.

'Oh,' said Wade, 'that's a bit of news, now, all that about Mr Courtney Broadhead and the Gaynes woman. We'll just get some notes on that, if we may, sir. Cass'll take it down in shorthand. Now, how does it go?'

'Briefly,' said Alleyn, 'like this. Liversidge, Miss Gaynes, young Gordon Palmer, his cousin, Geoffrey Weston, who seems to have strange ideas on the duties of a bear-leader, and Courtney Broadhead, all played poker for high stakes on the voyage out. Gordon Palmer and Liversidge were conspicuous winners, Broadhead a conspicuous loser. Some time between the last evening on board ship and the following evening on board the train, approximately a hundred pounds in notes was stolen from Miss Valerie Gaynes. The notes were in a leather writing-folder which she kept in a suitcase. In the train I noticed that Broadhead seemed greatly worried and I said so to Mr Hambledon. I had a seat in the company's carriage. Mr Broadhead spent a good deal of time on the platform. I can give you a more detailed, though incomplete, record of his movements, if you wish.'

'If you please, sir.'

'Well, here goes. I've a shocking memory, but it has retained one or two small items. At midnight the company, with the exception of Mr and Mrs Meyer – Miss Dacres you know – and Miss Gaynes, were in the carriage. The other three had gone to their sleepers. At about ten minutes past twelve, I went to sleep. I woke at two-ten. The company were as they had been before I dozed off. A few minutes later, Mr Broadhead went out on the platform. He was visible through the glass door. At two-forty-five we reached Ohakune.. Mr Hambledon and I went out and got coffee. Miss Dacres called us into her sleeper. We were met on the way by Mr Meyer who took us there. He said someone had tried to tip him overboard from the sleeper platform, about an hour before we got to Ohakune. He was not certain of the time. It may have been forty minutes or longer. If so this attempt was made while I was asleep. While Mr Meyer was relating his experience to us, Miss Gaynes came in and reported the loss of her money. When I offered to cast the eye at her ravished suitcase she was unflatteringly tepid and melted away.'

'Er,' said Cass.

'Yes?' asked Alleyn.

'That last sentence, sir – er – "when I offered to look" –'

'I phrased it badly,' said Alleyn. 'I offered to examine Miss Gaynes's leather folder. She declined, and shortly afterwards withdrew.'

'Thanks,' said Cass.

'Returning to the wardrobe-room. While I was there Mr Gordon Palmer remarked that Mr Courtney Broadhead had paid his poker debts the morning after our train journey. Mr Palmer told us that Mr Broadhead had previously asked for time in the settlement of these debts. Mr Palmer asked Mr Broadhead where he had raised the wind.'

'Obtained the requisite sum,' murmured Cass.

'Certainly, Cass. Mr Broadhead showed signs of the liveliest indignation and offered violence.'

'Did he strike Palmer?' asked Wade.

'No. I ventured to apply a back-arm bend. Mr Broadhead informed us that he had confided in the deceased, who had advanced him the money. Mr Palmer then remarked that it was unfortunate that Mr Meyer could not substantiate this statement. It was at this stage that the attempt at violence occurred. How's that for official language?'

'Pardon?'

'No matter. Now, look here, Inspector. I had the impression that young Palmer was not doing his nasty stuff quite off his own bat. I rather fancy someone had egged him on to bait Courtney Broadhead.'

'Do you, sir? Any idea who?'

'Mr Liversidge,' said Alleyn abstractedly, 'was *so* helpful and kind. He suggested that no doubt Mr Meyer had made a note of the loan and that this would clear the whole matter up.'

'Well, so it would, sir, wouldn't it?'

'Yes. Mr Broadhead explained that the loan was a personal matter and was not recorded on the books.'

'Is that so?' said Wade. He regarded Alleyn solemnly. 'Well now, sir, that's very interesting. You might look at it this way. A young fellow who hasn't got the cash to pay his debts suddenly pays them and when people get inquisitive he says he was given the money by someone who's just been murdered.'

'Yes, that's how Master Palmer put it,' said Alleyn.

'About the tiki,' said Wade after a pause. 'I asked the Dacres wom—Mrs Meyer where it was, and she said she gave it to someone before supper. Neither she nor Hambledon could remember anything about it according to themselves. Nor could Mr Mason. Now there's this Mason. I understand he comes in for the money. I suppose it's a big estate, but you never know with theatricals. We'll have to watch Mr Mason.'

'Yes,' agreed Alleyn. 'I watched him go green in the face just now. He got out just in time – only just.'

'He said something about that. When did it happen?'

'Just after I asked my question about the tiki.'

'Get this down,' said Wade to Cass.

Alleyn described Mr Mason's dilemma.

'So he went out, did he?' grunted Wade. 'I'll have something to say to young Packer about that. Too right, I will. Letting him out just because he kidded he felt crook. These blasted youngsters. It may have been one big bluff.

93

What if Mason was the one who had the tiki last and suddenly remembered it? Say he kidded he was crook so's he could see if he had it in his pockets? I'll talk to young Packer.'

'Er – yes. Quite so,' agreed Alleyn diffidently. 'But I assure you, Wade, the gentleman would most certainly have been ill where he stood if Packer had restrained him. Judging from the lamentable sounds that reached us, he got no farther than the passage. I don't think he escaped Packer's eye, you know.'

'You mean,' said Wade with scriptural accuracy, 'he vomited?'

'I do,' said Alleyn, 'and to some purpose.'

'Then he wasn't kidding he was crook?'

'He *may* be a crook, but why should he—'

'No, no. I mean, he wasn't making out he *felt* crook.'

'I – I beg your pardon. No. I should say definitely not.'

'Ugh!' grunted Wade.

'Of course,' said Alleyn mildly, 'he may have palmed a piece of soap and eaten it on the sly in order to make himself sick. But no – he didn't foam at the mouth.'

'I wonder what's the strength of this Firm of theirs – Incorporated Playhouses, or whatever they call it. Any idea, sir?'

'When Mason went out they all began talking about it. One of them – Ackroyd, I think – remarked that Mr Mason would be a very wealthy man.'

'Did he, though? Well – there's motive, sir.'

'Oh, rather. Money. The first motive, I always say,' agreed Alleyn.

'He's just gone – Mason, I mean. I asked him about this Incorporated Playhouses. He said, quite frank, that he'd be the whole works now Meyer was out of it. 'Course, he *would* be frank about that. We'd find out, anyway. He made no trouble about our looking at the books, either, though I must say he didn't seem too pleased when I sat down here and started going through the drawers.'

'That was Mr Meyer's desk, wasn't it?' asked Alleyn.

'Yes, that's right. I said: "This was deceased's private property, like, I suppose?" and he just nodded, and I must say he did look a bit sick. Kind of annoyed, too, as if he might go crook at me, any moment.'

'What, oh what,' wondered Alleyn, '*is* the fine shade of meaning attached to this word "crook"?' Aloud he asked:

'Have you been through the desk?'

'Not yet, sir. There's a whale of a lot of stuff. All very neat and business-like, though. He actually carted round the desk itself. Can you beat that? Couldn't do without it, Mason said. It's not much of an affair, either. Seems deceased had it for years and reckoned it brought him luck. Very superstitious gang, theatricals. It's a rickety old show too.'

Wade reached down to a lower drawer and pulled at the knob.

'A real old-timer,' he said and gave it a vigorous jerk. The drawer shot out suddenly. He looked down.

'Hul-lo!' said Wade. 'What's this? What's this!'

'It looks rather like a will,' said Alleyn.

CHAPTER 9

Courtney Broadhead's Scene

'By cripes, that's just what it is,' said Wade with the liveliest satisfaction.

He opened out his find and laid it on the desk. 'Quite short, too, it seems to be. Look here, sir.'

Alleyn read over his shoulder. Cass, with heavy nonchalance, moved a step or two nearer. A long silence followed, broken occasionally by a stertorous whispering noise made by Inspector Wade when he came upon a passage of involved legal phraseology. At last Alleyn straightened his long back and Wade brought his palm down with a slap on the open will.

'Money!' he said. 'We've got it here all right. Yee-ers. Notice the date? Two years ago. And three months. Seems Mr Mason is a principal legatee. Can you beat that? Meyer fixed the wife up with a whacking big lump sum and leaves the rest to his partner in – how does it go? – "in recognition of his lifelong devotion to the firm of Incorporated Playhouses and in memory of a friendship that only death can sever."'

'Pleasantly Victorian,' remarked Alleyn, 'and rather charming.'

'Well, they certainly hit the right note when they said Mason'd be a rich man,' said Wade.

'They did, didn't they?'

'Sixty thousand to the wife – and look at the residue. Forty thousand. Forty thousand, his share in the business, all to Mason. By gosh! Well, I'd better get on with the job, I suppose. I think we'll see this young Broadhead next. Looks to me as if there might be something in that, though it's too early to speculate. I reckon you'd say it's always too early to do that, wouldn't you, sir?'

'I say so, Mr Wade, but I do it just the same.'

Wade gave his great shout of laughter.

'It's human nature,' he said. 'Wondering! People spend half their time wondering about each other. That's what sells this detective fiction, I reckon.'

'I think you're right,' said Alleyn. 'It's what made policemen out of both of us, I wouldn't mind betting. Are you keen on your job, Wade?'

'Well now, that's a bit of a power, that is.' And Wade stared solemnly at Alleyn. 'Yes. Taking it all round, I'd say I was. Not but what it doesn't give you a pain in the neck sometimes. Making the usual inquiries. Following up information received. And the first two or three years are enough to break your heart, they're that slow. Police-constable duty, I mean. Of course, you didn't have any of that, sir.'

'Did I not?' asked Alleyn grimly.

'Why, I reckoned you'd be kind of—' He hesitated. 'You came at it from college, didn't you, sir? I mean you were kind of—'

'I went into the force before the days of Lord Trenchard's scheme. I came down from Oxford, and after three years soldiering, and a brief sojourn in the Foreign Office, signed on in the usual way and went on night duty in Poplar.'

'Is that so? Is that so?' Wade stared at Alleyn's fastidiously ironical face and looked as if he was trying to picture it beneath a helmet.

'How about Mr Broadhead?' said Alleyn.

'That's right. Get him, Cass.'

'Hadn't I better disappear?' suggested Alleyn when Cass had gone. 'It'll look a little odd if I don't.'

'I've been thinking about that, sir. Now, you say you don't want this crowd to know you're what you are. Well now, if you feel that way it's up to us to respect your wishes. It's just for you to say. And I'm very, very glad to have had your report on what you've heard. Still, it seems to me that with four of these theatricals knowing you're a Chief

Inspector from the Yard, it's not going to be a secret for long.'

'You're perfectly right,' groaned Alleyn.

'Well now, sir, what if I was to tell them who you are? Mind, if you want to keep out of it, you've only to say so and we'll respect your wishes, but if you're interested, we'd be only too pleased. I had a chat just now over the phone with the super, and I told him you were helping us anonymously, and he said he'd call on you in the morning, as maybe you'd be wanting to get home to bed shortly. He said we were to show you every courtesy, sir, and I'm sure we want to, but if you feel like sitting in official-like, well—' And here Inspector Wade, having wound himself up into a sort of struggling verbal cocoon, gave up the unequal contest and stared rather helplessly at Alleyn.

'My dear fellow,' said Alleyn quickly, 'of course I'll sit in if you'd like me to. It's extraordinarily nice of you to ask me. Tell them I'm a busy, by all means, if you think it'll serve any useful purpose. There comes young Broadhead now.'

Courtney Broadhead was ushered in by Cass. His face looked white and drawn in the harsh light shed by the office lamp. He stopped short just inside the door, stared unhappily at Wade, and then saw Alleyn.

'Hullo, Mr Alleyn,' he said. 'You still up?'

'Yes,' said Alleyn. 'This is Inspector Wade – Mr Courtney Broadhead.'

'Good evening, Mr Broadhead,' said Wade, with a kind of official heartiness. 'I'd just like a word with you, if you don't mind. You may be able to help us with one or two points.'

'Oh,' said Broadhead, still staring at Alleyn.

Wade glanced at the notes before him on Alfred Meyer's old desk.

'Now, Mr Broadhead, there are a few details I'd like to have from you about your journey down from Auckland in the Limited on Friday night.'

'Oh,' said Broadhead again. His mouth shaped itself into a curious half-smile and still he looked at Alleyn.

'I understand,' continued Wade, 'that up to a few minutes before the train reached Ohakune you were in the reserved carriage with the rest of the company. That is correct?'

'I think so. I really don't remember. You were in our carriage that night, weren't you, Mr Alleyn?'

'I was, yes,' said Alleyn.

Broadhead laughed unpleasantly.

'Perhaps you remember where I was before the train got to wherever-it-was.'

'I think I do.'

'Did you go out on the platform before the train reached Ohakune, Mr Broadhead?' asked Wade with rather unconvincing airiness.

'Believe I did. Ask Mr Alleyn.'

Wade looked blandly at Alleyn.

'I believe he did,' said Alleyn.

'At what time?' pursued Wade.

'Ask Mr Alleyn.'

'About two-thirty-five,' said Alleyn cheerfully.

'Wonderful memory you've got,' remarked Broadhead. 'Do they pay you for this?'

'Now, Mr Broadhead,' said Wade. 'Was Mr Meyer on the opposite platform to the one on which you stood? The sleeper-platform?'

'Doesn't Mr Alleyn know that too?' asked Broadhead.

'Chief Detective-Inspector Alleyn,' said Wade with a certain amount of relish, 'has been kind enough to make his own statement.'

Courtney Broadhead looked bewildered, then flabbergasted and then, strangely enough, relieved. Unexpectedly he burst out laughing.

'Oh, no!' he said. 'Not really. A genuine sleuth and in at the death! I got you wrong. I thought you were being the helpful little amateur. Sorry.' He examined Alleyn with interest. 'Good lord, you're the man with the marvellous press. The *Daily Sun* ran you in the Gardener case, didn't it?'

'Spare me,' said Alleyn.

'"The Handsome Sleuth or the Man Who Never Gives Up." I thought your name was spelt—'

'It is,' said Alleyn. 'The passenger list got it wrong.'

Broadhead was silent. He seemed to be turning over this new piece of information in his mind. Something of his former manner appeared when he spoke again.

'Are you interested professionally in this – this case?'

'We hope that the chief inspector,' said Wade, 'will very kindly give us the benefit of his advice.'

'Do you!' said Broadhead.

'Now about Mr Meyer on the sleeper-platform,' said Wade briskly. 'Was he there?'

'No. Not while I was outside.'

'You're sure about that?'

Cass glanced up from his notebook. Wade leant forward. Alleyn, who had an unlit cigarette between his lips, paused in the act of striking a match.

'Absolutely,' said Broadhead firmly.

Alleyn lit his cigarette.

'Yee-ers,' said Wade thoughtfully. He turned to Alleyn. 'I don't know if you'd care to put a question, sir?'

'Oh, thanks,' said Alleyn. 'Do you know I would, rather? Mr Broadhead, did you fall asleep in the carriage before we got to Ohakune?'

Broadhead stared.

'Yes. At least I dozed. Had a nightmare.'

'Any idea how long you were asleep?'

'No. Ten minutes perhaps. I don't know.'

'I was sound asleep myself. I remember noticing, just before I dozed off, that you and Mr Hambledon seemed to be the only other persons awake in the carriage.'

'I watched you fall asleep,' volunteered Broadhead. 'I remember that. You just shut your eyes and went still. The others all had their mouths open. I wondered if you were foxing.'

'Why?' said Alleyn sharply.

'I don't know. I thought you might be bored with the great HH.'

'With Hambledon? No. Did he go to sleep?'

'I don't think so. Wait a moment. The last thing I remember before I shut my own eyes was – was looking along the carriage towards the door. I thought they all looked half dead, swaying in their seats with their mouths open. I saw Hailey pick up a paper and hold it sideways to catch the light. His back was towards me, you know. I could see his arm and half the back of his head. That's the last thing I remember before I fell asleep.'

'And when you woke?'

'Nobody seemed to have moved. It was all rather unreal and smoky and noisy. Then you woke up and began to speak to Hambledon.'

'No one had moved,' murmured Alleyn to himself.

'At least—' Broadhead stopped short.

'Yes?'

'I've got a sort of hazy idea someone went down the corridor, past my chair. You know how one gets the impression of things when one dozes in a train. I might have dreamt it. No – I don't think I did. Someone went past. I think it half-woke me.'

'Do you mean that this person walked back from the direction of the platform at the head of the carriage, or towards it from the rear of the carriage?'

'Back. He was facing me. Probably been to the lav. at the rear of the sleeper.'

'He?'

'Yes. I think so. He must have sat down in one of the seats behind me.'

'He may have gone right through.'

'No. I remember waiting for the door to slam. It didn't. I went to sleep again.'

'Thank you,' said Alleyn. 'I've no other questions, Inspector Wade.'

'Good-oh, sir.' Wade turned to Broadhead. 'What did you do with Mrs Meyer's tiki?' he asked.

'What? Nothing. I never had it. Look here, what *is* all this about that damned little monster? You started it in the wardrobe-room, Mr Alleyn. What's the dazzling idea?'

'We simply want to trace the tiki, Mr Broadhead,' said Wade. 'Mrs Meyer has lost it.'

'She's also lost a husband,' said Broadhead tartly. 'I thought you were looking for a murderer, not a thief.'

'That's certainly—'

'What's more, I don't believe she cares tuppence whether the tiki's lost or found. What the hell are you driving at? Am I supposed to have pinched the filthy little object? I've had about as much as I can stand. You think I stole Val Gaynes's money, don't you? You think it's all a lie about Meyer lending me the cash. You think I'm a thief and a murderer—' His voice rose hysterically. Cass looked perturbed and moved a step or two nearer to Broadhead. Wade stood up hastily.

'Keep off,' shouted Broadhead; 'you can't arrest me – you can't—'

'My good ass,' advised Alleyn, 'don't put ideas in our heads and don't dramatise yourself. As you have suggested, this is a serious matter. Nobody's trying to arrest you. Inspector Wade has asked you a perfectly reasonable question. Why not answer it?'

'There now, Mr Broadhead,' said Wade, 'that's the way to look at it.'

'I suppose,' said Broadhead more quietly, 'you've heard all about the scene in the wardrobe-room. I suppose your distinguished colleague has told you what that little stinker Palmer said about me.'

'*And* all about your subsequent attempt upon the stinker,' murmured Alleyn. 'Yes.'

'Don't you think it was a pretty foul thing to sit there as if you were one of us, playing the spy, all agog to report to the police? Don't you? Don't you think it would have been the decent thing to say – to say –'

'To say,' suggested Alleyn helpfully: '"I'm a detective, so if one of you killed this very honest little gentleman whom you all profess to admire so much, don't do anything to give yourself away." No, Mr Broadhead.'

'My God, I was as fond of him as any of them. He was a damn' good friend to me.'

'Then,' said Alleyn, 'see if you can help Inspector Wade to trace the little greenstone tiki.'

'Oh, hell!' said Broadhead. 'All right! All right! Though what the suffering cats it's got to do with the case – All right. Go ahead.'

'Well, now,' said Wade. 'I understand you all took a look at this tiki before you sat down to supper. Did you handle it, Mr Broadhead?'

'Yes. I had it in my hand for a moment. Someone took it from me.'

'Who?'

'I think it was Frankie Liversidge. I'm not sure. It was passed round.'

'Yes. Now, Mr Broadhead, I want you to go back to the end of the performance, last night. Were you acting right up to the finish?'

'Acting!' said Broadhead distastefully. 'No, I wasn't "acting". I finished just before Miss Dacres's big scene.'

'What did you do then?'

'Stood in the wings for the company call at the curtain.'

'Then you *were* acting, as you might say,' insisted Wade crossly.

'If you call hanging about off-stage—'

'Let it go. After the play was over, what did you do?'

'Bolted to the dressing-room and took off my make-up.'

'Anyone with you?'

'Yes. Vernon and Frankie Liversidge.'

'All the time?'

'Vernon and I went back together. Frankie came in a minute or two later, I think. And Ackroyd joined us before we went along to the party.'

'All right. Now after the accident I understand that at the suggestion of Dr Te Pokiha and the chief inspector here you all went to your dressing-rooms and later to the wardrobe-room. Did you go directly to the wardrobe-room, Mr Broadhead?'

'No. I went into my dressing-room on the way.'

'What for?'

'To get my overcoat. I was shivering.'

'How long were you in the dressing-room?'

'About five minutes.'

'Five minutes to fetch a coat?'

'Well – Branny was there.'

'Who's he?'

'Brandon Vernon – the heavy. I told you we share the dressing-room. Branny had a flask there. We had a nip. Needed it. Frankie came in later and had one, too. Then we all went to the wardrobe-room.'

'To get to the dressing-room, you passed the iron ladder that goes up to the platform?'

'What platform?'

'I think it's called the grid,' said Alleyn diffidently. 'Or is it the flies?'

'Oh,' said Broadhead. 'Yes. I suppose we did. It's just by the dressing-room passage, isn't it?'

Wade shifted his position and became elaborately casual.

'You didn't happen to glance up towards the platform at all, I suppose?'

'Good lord, I don't know. Why should I?'

'You didn't get the impression anyone was up there?'

'I didn't get any impression at all.'

'Did you all leave the stage together – the whole company, I mean, and the guests?'

'Pretty well. Everyone was very quiet. The guests just

petered away as soon as they could. We stood for a moment by the entrance to the passage to let Miss Dacres go first. Then we followed.'

'All together?'

'We didn't make a football scrum of it,' said Broadhead crossly. 'It's a narrow passage.'

'When you got to the wardrobe-room, was everyone there?'

'I wasn't the last.'

'Who came in after you, Mr Broadhead?'

'Oh, lord!' said Broadhead again. 'Let's see. Well, Gascoigne was after me, and Mr Mason. Susan and Hailey Hambledon came in just before that, I think, with Miss Dacres. I'm not sure. No, by George, Mr Alleyn was last.'

'Quite right,' agreed Alleyn. 'I was a bad last.'

'Well,' said Wade, 'I think that'll be all, sir. If you've no objection, I'll get you to sign these notes later on when they've been put into longhand. We've got your address. Perhaps you'd look in some time tomorrow morning at the station.'

'Where is it?'

'Hill Street, Mr Broadhead. Top of Ruru Street. Anyone will direct you.'

'I suppose so. I could ask a policeman. At least he would know that.'

'Goodnight, Mr Broadhead,' said Wade coldly.

CHAPTER 10

The Case is Wide Open

'I wish I knew,' said Alleyn when Broadhead had gone, 'whether to give myself a kick in the neck or a slap on the back.'

'How's that, sir?' asked Wade.

'After the main body had retired to the dressing-rooms, Mr Mason, Mr Gascoigne, Dr Te Pokiha, the chief mechanist and I were left on the stage with the body. Until then I had imagined the whole show was simply a ghastly accident, but almost automatically I had suggested that none of the company left the theatre. The official mind must have functioned – reaction to sudden death or something. If I *had* suspected homicide, I should have done my best to keep them all on the stage. I don't think I would have succeeded without producing the Yard. But at that stage I didn't actually suspect, although I suppose I asked myself the routine question – "Homicide or Accident?" Well, as soon as we were alone the unhappy Bert gave tongue. He protested many times and with sanguinary monotony that there had been some funny business. So did Mr Gascoigne. They were all for going up aloft to take a look at the tackle. From being almost official I now became quite officious. I said: "No, no, gentlemen; we must must leave this for our wonderful police." "Scale not the heights," the old man said, and they heeded and gave over.'

'Quite right, too.'

'But was it? Suppose they had gone aloft? They would have found the tackle as it was when the bottle fell. They would have found it as I found it a few minutes later when I snooped up the ladder. Now what would have been the effect of this discovery on the murderer? If the murderer is not Mr Mason, or Mr Gascoigne, or Te Pokiha, or Bert, he would presumably have come out of his hole, found the stage empty, heard voices on the grid, and gone back into his hole. He would never have tidied up.'

'That's so. But we've got your evidence, anyway,' objected Wade.

'Yes, we have. We've caught him out in a bit of elaboration,' agreed Alleyn. 'If – if—' He rubbed his nose vexedly. 'I usually welcome elaborations. "Beware of fancy-touches" should be neatly printed and hung above every would-be murderer's cot. But this time I felt that, as far as we're concerned, there's a catch in it. Well, now, if our man is Te Pokiha, or Mason, or Gascoigne, or Bert, he would still have been unable to tidy up. By preventing the inspection of the tackle I made possible the alteration.'

'Well, sir, according to your way of looking at it, that's all to the good. The alteration was a blunder, as it turned out.'

'And we should never have found the tiki.'

'That's two blunders.'

'Is it?' said Alleyn. 'I've got my doubts about that.'

'I don't get you there, sir. Surely we ought to trace the tiki?'

'Oh, yes,' agreed Alleyn, screwing up one side of his face. 'We'll have to try. What did Hambledon and Mason have to say about it?'

'Oh, same story as young Broadhead. Mr Hambledon said he took it from Mrs Meyer soon after you gave it to her. He says he had a look at it and handed it onto someone else – thinks it was old Mr Vernon, but isn't sure. Mr Mason says he can't say who gave it to him, but he handled it and remembers giving it back to Mrs Meyer just before you all sat down to supper.'

'And Mrs Meyer?'

'Thinks she remembers he gave it to her and fancies she put it down on the table somewhere. There you are!'

'Yes,' said Alleyn, 'it's wide open.'

'Mrs Meyer—' began Wade and stopped abruptly.

'Look here, sir, what *do* I call the lady? Mrs Meyer or Miss Dacres?'

'Miss Dacres, I fancy.'

'Seems hardly nice in some ways. Well, then, Miss Dacres seemed a bit surprised when I asked her about the tiki. She gave me a look.'

'That's because I had already spoken to her about it.'

'Is that so? Did you get the same answer?'

'More or less. She looked in her bag and then said she didn't know what had become of it. All the same—'

'Well – there it is,' said Wade without noticing Alleyn's hesitation. 'Better get a move on, I suppose. Who'll we take next, sir?'

'If I might suggst, I think it would be as well to ask Gascoigne, the stage-manager, if he knows who was the last person, officially, to examine the apparatus.'

'Good enough,' said Wade, and sent for Gascoigne.

Gascoigne said that the last official inspection took place just before the end of the third act.

'Mr Meyer came round from the front of the house. He was as fussy about it as if it'd been a first night in town,' said Gascoigne. 'He asked me if everything was all right. I'd been up myself and seen it and we'd rehearsed it God knows how often. But to humour him I sent Bert up again and I'm blessed if the governor didn't climb up after Bert. It was then that he loosened the wire, I think. He was in a great flutter. By God, you'd almost think he knew something would happen. That was actually just before the last curtain. I remember they came down the ladder after we'd run down.'

'Which of them came first?'

'Bert. He came to me in the prompt-box and said it was all OK. Mr Meyer went off to the front of the house, I think.'

'And what did you do?'

'Me?' said Gascoigne, looking surprised. 'I got the staff to work setting the stage for the party. Bert and the local men did it.'

'Did you notice anyone go up the ladder after that?' asked Wade without hope.

'Of course I didn't. Wouldn't I be asking you to go after them if I had? Look here, Inspector, had that gear been interfered with? I'd like to go up and take a look at it.'

'You'd find no difference, Mr Gascoigne,' said Wade.

'But I tell you,' said Gascoigne violently, 'there must have been some funny business – there must have been.'

'Now listen, sir,' said Wade. 'When everybody left the stage at Chief Inspector Alleyn's suggestion—'

'What! Chief Inspector how much?' ejaculated Gascoigne.

Wade explained.

'Here!' said Gascoigne. 'Is there anything fishy about our company? Have you been tailing round after us, Mr Alleyn? What's the idea of all this?'

'I'm on a holiday,' explained Alleyn apologetically, 'and I've not been tailing anybody at all, Mr Gascoigne.'

'So you say,' muttered Gascoigne.

'It's true,' said Alleyn. 'S'welp me.'

'Now, Mr Gascoigne,' continued Wade doggedly, 'when they all left the stage after the accident, what did you do?'

'I stayed put. I wanted to go up and look at the gear, but Mr – Inspector – Alleyn said wait for the police. Why didn't you tell us who you were then?'

'It would have been in doubtful taste, don't you think?' asked Alleyn. 'You remained on the stage until the arrival of the police, I think?'

'Yes, I did,' said Gascoigne.

Wade glanced at Alleyn.

'Well, Mr Gascoigne, I think that's all I want to know just now. You're staying – where?'

'The Railway Hotel.'

'Good-oh, sir. Perhaps you'd look in at the station tomorrow. The inquest—' Wade shepherded Gascoigne out and came back looking worried.

'I reckon,' he said, 'we can cross him off unless there's

been any collusion. He met us at the door and you left him on the stage. He never had a chance to go up into the grid. Seems to me that the point we want to get at is what they all did when they left the stage. Isn't that right, sir?'

'I think so,' agreed Alleyn. 'Between the event and the time you and I went aloft, someone managed to climb one of the ladders and put things straight. It seems to me, Wade, that the most likely moment for this would be when they all left the stage. Off-stage it was quite dark. It would be a perfectly easy matter for one of them to slip aside behind the scenery, snoop round to the ladder at the back, and climb up. Whoever it was probably took off his or her shoes. Now, if this person went up during the time of the general exodus, he was probably hiding up there when I made my first visit. He'd want to get the job done as soon as possible and before the police arrived. It sounds more risky than it actually was. If he *had* been spotted he'd have said he was damn' well going to have a look at the gear and have made a song about its having been interfered with. We know Gascoigne could not have done this.'

'Nor Broadhead either, if Brandon Vernon agrees that they went together to the dressing-room,' said Wade.

'Right. Now let's look at the other half of the picture, shall we? The first visit, when the murderer cut the weight off the rope and moved the pulley. Again Broadhead says he and Vernon went together to the dressing-room, after the final curtain. That is, after Bert came down and reported the tackle all correct. If Vernon gives the same account, that lets both of them out. If Bert and his mates say Gascoigne was with them while they got ready for the party, that lets him out.'

'Looks as if it's a crack less wide open, sir, when you get at it like that. Now, when I talked to Mason, he said he was in the box-office during the last act. When the people began to come away, he went to his own office – this room we're in now – to have a word with the deceased. He says deceased left him here, saying he was going round to the stage.

110

Mason says he then made a note of the night's takings and did one or two jobs here. He went out once, ran along to tell the old chap who stage-door-keeps to show all the guests straight to the stage but to be sure and check up their names in order to keep off any hangers-on who hadn't been invited. I've spoken to old Singleton, the doorkeeper, and he remembers Mason running along the alley to give him this message. He says Mason came back here. So does Mason. The old chap stood by the stage-door looking after him. And to make it a bit tighter, the old bloke says he strolled along to the office a bit later to ask about something, and Mason was there at his desk. Dr Te Pokiha says he looked in before going to the party – he'd met Mason before – and stayed there yarning for a while, leaving Mason in the office. Now, Mr Alleyn, the only way Mason could have got behind the scenes without Singleton seeing him is by going through this door into the box-office, out at the front entrance where someone might have seen him, and round the block to the back of the theatre. The door at the back is locked on the inside. Even if he had the key he couldn't have done it in the time. He couldn't have got back before Singleton walked across, which he says was about five or six minutes later. That's that. Mason said he stayed on here – looking up his papers and so on – for a while – not long – and then joined the party. Singleton remembers Mason coming back and swears he didn't go behind the scenes until the last of the guests were in.'

'I was among the last of the guests,' said Alleyn, 'and I overtook Mr Mason at the stage-door.'

'Did you, sir? Did you, now! Well, I suppose you might say that's a pretty fair alibi for Mr Mason. Would he have time to go up aloft after he went in with you, now?'

'Plenty of time,' said Alleyn sadly, 'but he didn't do it. I remember perfectly well that he was on the stage all the time. He stood near me and I talked to him and to Hambledon.'

'That's what Hambledon said,' agreed Wade gloomily.

It's a blooming nark, dinkum it is. Still, there's better alibis than that have gone west before now, and I'm not going to forget this will. Mason's a whole lot better off by this murder.'

'Was he badly off before?' asked Alleyn lightly.

'That's what I reckon we'll have to find out, sir. Do you think the Yard—?'

'Oh, yes. They'll do it for you if it can be done. We call it making tactful inquiries. *Aren't* I glad I'm not there.'

'You're here, though,' said Wade, 'and I suppose they know it.'

'I don't like the way you said that, Inspector,' said Alleyn with a wry smile. 'And I know jolly well what you're thinking.'

Wade grinned sheepishly.

'Well, sir,' he said, 'it looks as if it's an English case more than a New Zillund one, now, doesn't it?'

'Wait and see,' said Alleyn. 'What about your tiki? And talking about the tiki, did you ask Mr Mason where he went with Dr Te Pokiha after the event? He was very much shaken and Te Pokiha took him off somewhere to give him a drink.'

'The doctor brought him here. There's a bottle of whisky and a couple of glasses in that cupboard there. I put 'em away to get Mason's prints. They seem to have taken it neat.'

'So Dr Te Pokiha felt a bit groggy, too,' said Alleyn. 'He seemed so very sedate and professional at the time. What happened when they'd had their neat whiskies?'

'The doctor rang us up and left Mason here with his grog, when we arrived. Mason says he was still here when we went past. I remember noticing that door was open on the alley-way and the lights in here were up. I fancy I caught sight of him. Anyway, the doorkeeper says he mooched along the yard after we'd come in, saw Mason in the office and talked to him. He says he went along as soon as he'd let us in and stayed until Mason went to the wardrobe-room. They walked along together.'

'That's right, too, sir,' said the silent Cass unexpectedly. 'I was just inside the stage-door when he came through. I sent him along. He was looking horribly crook.'

'Ill?' asked Alleyn cautiously.

'Too right, sir.'

'Crook or not,' said Wade, 'I'm not taking anything for gospel where Mr George Mason's concerned, by cripey I'm not. Now the D— Miss Dacres hasn't got even half an alibi for the first stunt – fixing the gear before the murder. She says she went to her dressing-room and was alone there till she came to the party.'

'What about her dresser?'

'Says she sent her off to doll herself up for the party. Now Miss Dacres *could* have slipped round to the ladder at the back, fixed the gear, and then gone to her room. When did she come in to the party, sir?'

'She came in last,' said Alleyn, and up through his mind welled the memory of Carolyn hooting melodiously as she came down the passage, of Ackroyd opening the door on to the stage, of Carolyn making her entrance, of himself going to meet her.

'Last!' exclaimed Wade. 'Last of the lot, and alone.'

'No. Not alone, Hailey Hambledon, Mr Mason and Mr Meyer went and fetched her.'

'That makes no odds,' said Wade.

'What about Mr Hambledon?' asked Alleyn.

'He says he left the stage with the others after the final curtain and went to his dressing-room. His dresser was there but he didn't want him and sent him away.'

'Yes. He was wearing a dinner-jacket. He'd only need to take his make-up off.'

'He could have gone up the first time, sir. As soon as the dresser had gone he could have slipped back to the stage and round to the ladder at the rear. It would have been after Mr Meyer and Bert okayed the gear.'

'How does he stand for the second visit? He stayed

113

behind with us – and the body – and left the stage while Gascoigne, Bert and I were still there. Said he was going to Miss Dacres's room. He was there when I arrived later on. He went out, at my suggestion, to get some brandy. I don't think he was away long enough to go up to the grid and get the brandy as well. *Might* have had time, I suppose, but it would have been damn' quick work.'

'As far as Mr Hambledon is concerned we haven't got a motive, sir, have we?'

Alleyn raised an eyebrow.

'I suppose you may say we haven't,' he said slowly.

'Is there anything—' began Wade.

'No, no. Nothing.'

A knock on the outside door heralded the entrance of Packer.

'Beg pardon, sir,' he said, 'but are you ready for another?'

'Yes – all right – all right,' said Wade impatiently. 'Send—'

'Beg pardon, sir, but Mr Ackroyd says could you see him next? He says there's something he'd like to tell you, particular.'

'Ackroyd? Which is he?'

'The comedian,' said Alleyn.

'Good-oh, then, Packer. Send him along.'

Packer went away with Cass.

'What's biting Mr Ackroyd, I wonder?' said Wade.

'I wonder,' murmured Alleyn.

'Is he one of their swell turns, sir? The funny man, is he?'

'Dreadfully funny,' said Alleyn.

'I haven't seen the show. I like a good laugh, but these stage plays seem kind of feeble-minded after the flicks, I reckon. Nothing but talk. I don't mind a bit of vordervil. Still, if it's funny—'

'Mr Ackroyd is a good comedian on the stage. I find him less entertaining when he's off it.'

'He looks a scream,' said Wade.

114

The scream appeared, ushered in by Cass.

Ackroyd was a dot of a man; beside the gigantic Cass he looked like a dwarf. 'And his face *is* funny,' thought Alleyn. 'That button of a nose was made to be painted red. He ought to be in pantomime rather than polite comedy. No, that's not fair – he's a really good actor. There are brains behind his work and that kind of humour that comes from inside – the Chaplin brand. But I don't think he's a very nice little man. Waspish.'

Ackroyd walked across to Inspector Wade with neat assurance. His stage mannerisms were faintly imposed on his everyday behaviour. One expected him to say something excruciatingly funny.

'I hope I don't intrude,' said Ackroyd.

'That's all right, sir,' said Wade heartily. 'Take a seat. You wanted to see me about something?'

'That's right. Mind, I don't want you to take too much notice of it. It's probably of no account. Still, I feel you ought to know about it. It's dead against the grain with me to butt in on other people's business, you know.'

'Lie,' thought Alleyn.

'We quite understand that, Mr Ackroyd,' said Wade.

'It's a confidential matter.' Ackroyd turned to Alleyn. 'No offence, you know, old boy.'

'None in the world,' said Alleyn cheerfully.

' – so if you wouldn't mind—'

'Mr Alleyn is a detective,' said Wade. 'He's in this case with us.'

'A detective?' shouted Ackroyd. 'By George, Meyer knew about it all the time, did he! Working for Meyer, were you?'

'I'm afraid I don't follow you, Mr Ackroyd. I am a policeman,' said Alleyn, 'not a private detective.'

'A Yard man?'

'Yes.'

'Then it couldn't have been him you were after.'

'Who d'you mean?' asked Wade.

'Why, Hambledon, of course,' said Ackroyd.

CHAPTER 11

St John Ackroyd and Susan Max

'Hambledon!' said Alleyn sharply. 'What the – I beg your pardon, Wade,' he added instantly. 'This is your show.'

'Go right ahead, sir.'

'Thank you so much.' Alleyn turned to Ackroyd. 'I must confess I'm curious to know why you thought I was interested in Mr Hambledon.'

'Don't mind me, old boy,' said Ackroyd easily. 'When the inspector here said you were a 'tec, I thought Alf Meyer had put you on to follow Hailey and the fair Carolyn. That's all. Quite natural, you know, under the circs.'

'I see,' said Alleyn, and was silent.

'It's like that, is it?' said Wade.

Ackroyd pulled a serio-comic face, thrusting his lower lip sideways with the tip of his tongue. 'Very much like it,' he said.

'Common little stinker,' thought Alleyn.

'D'you mean,' asked Wade, 'that she gave him cause for divorce?'

'That's my idea. No business of mine, mind.'

'Was it this you were wanting to tell me, Mr Ackroyd?'

'Oh God, no. At least, it's something to do with it. I was going to keep it under my hat, but Alf Meyer was a white man, and if he's been murdered—' He paused.

'That's right,' encouraged Wade. Alleyn was conscious of an illogical distaste for both of them.

'Well, it's like this,' said Ackroyd. 'The morning we got here I came down to the theatre. We had a call at ten-thirty. I got here early and went to my dressing-room. It's round the corner of the passage and up a right-angled one, so that actually it backs on to the star dressing-room. Well, in these wooden buildings of yours you can hear each other thinking. The walls are only thin partitions in this show. I

116

was getting my stuff out when I heard Hailey and the Great Actress talking in the star-room.'

'Mr Hambledon and Miss Dacres?'

'None other. Hailey was in the devil of a temper, trying to get her to say she'd levant with him at the end of this tour. Fact! And she said she wouldn't because she's a Catholic and doesn't believe in divorce. She was doing her "little devil" stuff. Seemed to be big with Hailey – he got all he-man and violent. Ttff! Then he said something like: "Would you marry me if Alf was dead?" And the Great Actress said she would. That took her off. She went out on the stage, and a minute later I heard her give her opening line.'

'Yes,' said Wade after a moment. 'Thanks, Mr Ackroyd. Doesn't sound exactly as if she was Hambledon's mistress, though, do you reckon?'

'God knows what she is. She'll be his wife before long, I don't mind betting you. Well, that's that. Probably nothing in it. I'll be off.'

'If you don't mind waiting a minute longer, sir, there are one or two formal questions.'

Wade asked Ackroyd what he did after the final curtain. He went straight to his dressing-room, it seemed. He was alone there until he came out for the party. He looked in at Liversidge's room and they then joined Vernon and Broadhead and went along to the party. After the catastrophe he left the stage with the others, went to his dressing-room, had a stiff nip and then joined the rest of the company in the wardrobe-room. On both these occasions he had repeatedly called out to the others from his own room. Asked about the train journey he said he slept solidly for at least an hour before they got to Ohakune, and had not the remotest idea who entered or left the carriage.

Cass took notes of this, as of all the former interviews. Ackroyd took it all very easily and gave some of his replies with an air of mock solemnity that the sergeant and Wade

117

found extremely diverting. When it was all over Ackroyd turned to Alleyn.

'And what, may one ask,' he said, 'is Scotland Yard's part in the proceedings?'

'Noises off, Mr Ackroyd,' replied Alleyn good-humouredly. 'I'm here by accident and the courtesy of Inspector Wade.'

'Funny me thinking you were a private sleuth. I say, old boy, you'll keep it under your hat won't you – about Hailey and the Dacres, you know. You're rather pally with them, I've noticed. That's what made me think you were watching them. Don't give me away, now, will you?'

'To Miss Dacres and Mr Hambledon? No,' said Alleyn bleakly.

Ackroyd walked over to the door.

'Of course,' he said, 'that fascinating blah stuff of hers goes down with the nit-wits. I've worked with her for six years and I know the lady. She's as hard as nails underneath. That's only my opinion, you know, for what it's worth. It's based on observation.'

'Was your suggestion about Mr Mason's past also based on observation?' asked Alleyn pleasantly.

'What's that, old boy? Oh George! No, I wasn't in the company he stranded in the States. I don't go out with bad shows.'

'But it's a true story?'

'Don't ask me. I was told it for gospel. You never know. But I get fed up with all this kow-towing to the Firm. Alf and George are no better than anybody else in management. Now Alf's gone I suppose all the spare spotlights will be trained on George. "Our Mr Mason." *And* of course on the Great Actress. By the way what's all the fuss about the little green whatsit you gave her?'

'Merely that it is lost and we should like to recover it.'

'Well if it's lost, she did the losing. She had it last.'

'Is that so!' exclaimed Wade.

'Certainly. Branny put it down on the table and she

118

picked it up and slipped it inside her dress. I'll swear to that in six different positions. Cheerio!'

And, like a good actor, on this effective line he made his exit.

'He's a hard case, that one,' said Wade appreciatively. 'I reckon he's a real shrewdy.'

'Yes,' agreed Alleyn, 'he's shrewd.'

'I'd like to know how much there is in that stuff about Hambledon. "Would you marry me if Alf was dead?" And she said she would. I'd like to know just how he said it. And, by gum, I'd like to know if there's a free passage from the top of Miss Dacres's dress downwards.'

'And I,' said Alleyn, 'would like to know when Miss Dacres found occasion to snub Mr Ackroyd, and why.'

'Hullo!' said Wade. 'Where d'you get that notion, sir?'

'From the funny gentleman's behaviour. He radiated a peculiar malevolence that I associate with snubs from the opposite sex.'

'Still, sir, he'd hardly want to involve her in a murder charge, now, would he? And that statement about the tiki – well.'

'It is Hambledon, I fancy, whom he would like to involve.'

Wade chewed this over, eyeing Alleyn with a sort of guarded curiosity.

'Well,' he said at last, 'We'd better get on. Let's see: there's that old lady, Miss Max, and Miss Gaynes, Mr Liversidge, Mr Weston, who's not a member of the company, his cousin, Young Palmer (ditto), and Mr Brandon Vernon. Suppose we see the old girl first, Cass.'

Cass went off.

'Miss Max is an old acquaintance of mine,' said Alleyn; 'she was in the Felix Gardener show.'

'Is that so, sir? Well, now, perhaps you would talk to her. I'd like to listen to your methods, sir. We've got our own little ideas here about interviews and it'd be very interesting to compare them.'

119

'Bless me, Wade, I'm afraid you won't find much to analyse in my remarks, especially to Miss Max. I'll talk to her if you like, only don't, for the Lord's sake, expect fireworks. Here she comes.'

In came old Susan Max. Her roundabout figure was neat in its velveteen evening dress. Her faded blonde hair had been carefully dressed for the party, her round honest face with its peculiar pallor, induced by years of grease-paint, had been delicately powdered but not made-up. She looked what she was, an actress of the old school. She waddled forward, her face lighting as she saw Alleyn.

'Well, Miss Max,' said Alleyn, pushing a chair up to the fire, 'I'm afraid you've had a long wait in the wardrobe-room. Sit down by the fire and cheer us up.'

'Me cheer you up,' said Susan. 'I like that.'

She gave a cackle of laughter, but when she looked up at him her faded blue eyes were anxious.

'I never thought we'd meet again – like this,' said old Susan.

'I know,' said Alleyn. 'It's strange, isn't it?'

'They'll be calling me a Jonah,' she said. The pudgy old hands moved restlessly in her lap.

'You a Jonah! Not a bit of it. You've met Inspector Wade, haven't you?'

Susan gave Wade a grand nod.

'He's asked me to have a talk with you about this beastly affair. Do the others still think I'm a harmless civilian?'

'Would you credit it, dear,' said Susan indignantly, 'that just before I came along here that girl blurted it all out!'

'Miss Valerie Gaynes?'

'Little idiot. I've no patience. Doing her emotional act all over the room. What business is it of hers?'

'None at all, I should have thought,' said Alleyn comfortably. 'Have a cigarette and tell me some scandal. How did she get her job?'

'Who? Gaynes? My dear, through influence, like every-body else nowadays. Her father's a lessor of our theatre in

Town. The girl knows nothing about the business. No poise. No charm. No personality. You were in front, weren't you? Well! What a *naughty* performance.'

'I wonder Miss Dacres puts up with it.'

'My dear, she has to. Some leading women don't mind poor supports, of course. Selfish. But Carolyn Dacres is an artist. Different type altogether,' said Susan, settling her chins.

'Anything between Liversidge and Valerie Gaynes?' asked Alleyn.

'Somebody ought to tell that girl to look after herself,' said Susan darkly. 'Not that they'd get any thanks for it. I've known Frankie Liversidge a good many years and I wouldn't care for any daughter of mine to be on those terms with him.'

'Anything in particular wrong with him?' asked Alleyn.

'Well, dear, he's not – not quite straight, shall we say, especially where women are concerned. But I mustn't sit here gossiping. It's all hours of the night as it is. What can I tell you?'

Alleyn asked her about her movements before and after the catastrophe. Like everyone else, she had spent the two significant periods in her dressing-room. At the end of the play she had gone straight there, removed her make-up and changed her dress. Miss Dacres's dresser had, at old Susan's invitation, also used the room to smarten herself up for the party.

'She's a nice woman – been with Miss Dacres for years, and she helped me with my change. The dress I wear in the last act is a beast to get out of. I was only just ready when the last of the guests arrived.'

After the catastrophe Susan had gone to the door of the star-room with Carolyn Dacres and had offered to go in with her.

'She said she'd rather be by herself, so I went on to my own room, dear. Minna – the dresser, you know – came in a little later. Miss Dacres had sent her away too. After a little while Minna said she couldn't bear to think of her there alone so she went back, and in a minute or two she came for me. The poor child – I mean Miss Dacres, for to me she *seems* a child – had thought she would like my company. She was sitting there quite quietly, staring in front of her. Shock. Couldn't talk about it or weep or do anything to ease her mind. Then she suddenly said she'd like to see you. Hailey Hambleon had come in and went to fetch you.'

'How long had he been there, Miss Max?'

'Let me see. He came in soon after I did. About ten minutes, I should say.'

'Ah,' said Alleyn with a sort of satisfied grunt. After a moment he leant forward.

'What sort of a fellow was Alfred Meyer?' he asked.

'One of the very best,' said Susan energetically. 'The right type of manager, and there aren't many of them left in the business. Always the same to everybody. Devoted to her.'

Alleyn remembered the pale commonplace little man, who had been so quiet in the ship and so frightened on the train.

'And she to him?' he asked.

Old Susan glanced at Cass and Wade.

'Very,' she said dryly.

'We've got to learn the truth, you know,' said Alleyn gently. 'We'll have to pry and pry. It's one of the most revolting aspects of a murder-case, and the victim is sometimes the greatest sufferer.'

'Then it is murder?'

'I'm afraid so.'

There was a long silence.

'Well,' said old Susan at last, 'it's no good making mysteries where there are none. She *was* very fond of Meyer. Not perhaps in a romantic fashion, exactly. He wasn't a figure for romance. But she was fond of him. You might say she felt safe with him.'

'And Hambledon?' asked Alleyn quietly.

Susan squared her fat shoulders and stared straight in front of her.

'If you mean anything scandalous, my dear, there's not a word of truth in it. Not a morsel. Mind, I don't say Hailey isn't devoted to her. He is, and has been for years, and he makes no bones about it. I've been with the Firm off and on for a long time and I know. But there's been no funny business between them, and don't let anybody tell you there has.'

'They've been trying,' said Alleyn. Susan suddenly slapped her hands on her lap.

'Ackroyd!' she cried.

'It was, but don't say so.'

'I'll be bound. Little beast. He's never forgiven her – never.'

'For what?'

'It was when he rejoined us for the revival of *Our Best Intentions* – a year ago it was. He's the type that always hangs round the leading woman and tries to go big with the management. You can smell 'em a mile off. Well, he tried it on with Carolyn Dacres and believe me it took him right off,' said Susan, becoming technical. 'As soon as the funny business started she was *well* up-stage and Mr Ackroyd made a quiet exit with no rounds of applause. He's a spiteful little beast and he's never forgiven her or Hailey. Hailey actually spoke to him about it, you know. I believe George Mason did, too. He's never forgotten it. You heard how he spoke about George tonight. Dragging in that American business.'

'Nothing in it?'

'My dear,' said Susan resignedly, 'I dare say something did happen. I rather think it did, but if we knew all the circumstances I've no doubt we'd find faults on both sides. George Mason started in a small way and he's not the only one, by a long chalk, that's got an incident of that sort to live down. My advice to you is, forget all about it. Whatever happened in the early days, he's an honest man

123

now. I've worked for him for a good many years and you can take my word for it. And what's more I wouldn't say the same for Ackroyd.'

'I see,' said Alleyn.

'Anything more?' asked Susan.

'I don't think so. Thank you so much. Perhaps Inspector Wade—'

'No thanks, sir, no thanks,' said Wade, getting up from the desk where he had sat in silence. 'Unless – the train –'

'Miss Max sat opposite me. She slept all the time, I fancy.'

'The train!' ejaculated Susan.

Alleyn explained.

'Yes,' said Susan, 'I was asleep. Do you mean you think that business on the train had something to do with this?'

'Who can tell?' murmured Alleyn vaguely. 'You're longing to get home to your bed, aren't you?'

'Well, I am.'

She hitched herself off the chair and waddled to the door. Alleyn opened it. She stood, a roundabout and lonely little figure, looking up at him very earnestly.

'In that other case in London someone nearly killed you by dropping a chandelier from the grid, didn't they?'

'So they did.'

'You don't think it's – it's given anyone an idea?'

Alleyn stared at her.

'I wonder,' he said.

CHAPTER 12

Liversidge Fluffs his Lines

'What was she driving at?' asked Wade when Susan had gone.

'Oh – the Gardener case. A neurotic property-man dumped half a ton of candelabra on the stage in a childish attempt to distract my attention. Later on he became victim No. 2, poor booby. Knew too much. It all came out in the evidence. I imagine they take a lot of trouble when men are working aloft. I remember the stage-manager told me the hands always have their tools tied to their wrists, in case of accidents.'

'Well, sir, you got some nice little bits out of the old lady. Of course her being a friend made a difference.'

'Of course,' agreed Alleyn cordially.

'Do you reckon there's anything in this story of Ackroyd's about Mason stranding a company in America?'

'I am inclined to agree with Miss Max's opinion of Ackroyd as a witness, but we'd better look into Mr Mason's history, of course. I'll get them to do that at the Yard.'

'Ackroyd means Mason walked out and left his company cold?'

'Yes. Not an unusual proceeding with small companies, I fancy, in the old days. A dirty trick, of course.'

'Too right – and if he's that sort – still, it doesn't mean every manager that strands a company would do in his partner.'

'Indeed not. The routes of touring companies would have been strewn with managerial corpses, I'm afraid.'

'There's the motive, though. You can't get away from that, sir,' persisted Wade.

'Oh, rather not. There's also the perfectly good alibi.'

'Don't I know it? Oh, well, Miss Max seems OK as far as the two important times are concerned.'

'What's happened to the dresser?' asked Alleyn.

'Oh, I saw her and the two Australians in the company and most of the staff soon after we got here. We just took statements and let them go. We've got their addresses. They're out of the picture as you might say. The Australians have only just joined the company and the stage-hands are local men with good characters.'

'I know,' said Alleyn.

'How about having a pop at Mr Liversidge, sir?'

'Who, me?'

'That's right. Will you, sir?'

'At your service, Inspector.'

So Cass was dispatched to the wardrobe-room and returned with Mr Frank Liversidge, who came in looking very beautiful. His black hair was varnished down to his head and resembled an American leather cap. His dinner-jacket, a thought too waisted, his boiled shirt, his rather large tie, were all in perfect order, and so was Mr Liversidge. As soon as he saw Alleyn he uttered a musical laugh and advanced with manly frankness.

'Well, well, well,' said Mr Liversidge, in a dreadfully synthetic language that was so very nearly the right thing. 'Who'd have thought it of you? I've maintained that you were an ambassador incog., and Val was all for the Secret Service.'

'Nothing so exciting, I'm afraid,' murmured Alleyn. 'This is Inspector Wade, Mr Liversidge. He has asked me to talk to you about one or two features of this business. Will you sit down?'

'Thanks,' said Liversidge gracefully. 'So the Yard is coming into the show, is it?'

'By courtesy. Now, will you please give us an account of your movements after the final curtain tonight?'

'My movements?' He raised his eyebrows and took out his cigarette-case. All his actions were a little larger than life. Alleyn found himself thinking of them in terms of stage-craft. 'Bus. – L. taps cigarette. Takes lighter from packet. Lights cigarette with deliberation.'

'My movements,' repeated Liversidge, wafting smoke-rings in Alleyn's direction. 'Let me see. Oh, I went to my dressing-room and demolished the war-paint.'

'Immediately after the final curtain?'

'I think so. Yes.'

'You found Mr Vernon and Mr Broadhead there?'

'Did I? Yes, I believe I did. It's a big room. We share it.'

'They were on at the final curtain, of course?'

'We all take the call.'

'But they reached the dressing-room before you did?'

'Marvellous deduction, Inspector! Now I think of it, I was a little late getting there. I stayed off-stage for a minute or two.'

'Why did you do this?'

'Oh, I was talking.'

'To whom?'

'My dear old boy, I don't know. Who was it now? Oh, Valerie Gaynes.'

'I'm sure,' said Alleyn formally, 'you will understand that these questions are not prompted by idle curiosity.'

'My dear old boy!' repeated Liversidge. Alleyn restrained a wince.

'Then perhaps you will not object to telling us what you and Miss Gaynes talked about.'

Liversidge looked from Wade to Cass and back again at Alleyn.

'Well, as a matter of fact, I don't remember.'

'Please try to remember. It's only a couple of hours ago. Where were you standing?'

'Oh, just off-stage somewhere.'

'On the prompt side.'

'Er – yes.'

'Then perhaps Mr Gascoigne will remember. He was there.'

'He was nowhere near us.'

'You remember that,' said Alleyn vaguely.

Liversidge lost a little of his colour.

'As a matter of fact, Alleyn,' he said after a moment, 'our conversation was about a personal matter. I'm afraid I can't repeat it. Nothing that could have the remotest interest to anyone but ourselves. You *do* understand.'

'Oh, rather. How long did it last?'

'Two or three minutes, perhaps.'

'If you were near the prompt entrance you were not far from the steel ladder that goes up into the grid. Did anyone come down that ladder while you were there?'

'Yes,' answered Liversidge readily enough. 'Just as I turned away to go down the dressing-room passage, Alfred Meyer and the head mechanist came down.'

'Did you stay on the stage after that?'

'No. I went on down the passage.'

'Thank you so much,' said Alleyn. 'That, really, was the point we wanted to get at. Now, after the tragedy, when we cleared the stage – where did you go?'

'I stood with all the others by the entrance to the passage. That was while Hailey was shepherding the guests out. Then I went to the dressing-room.'

'Anyone else there when you arrived?'

'Yes. Branny and poor old Court. He felt very shaken. Branny was giving him a nip.'

'Were you among the last to leave the stage?'

'I suppose I was. I think we were the last.'

'Who was with you?'

'Oh – Val Gaynes.'

'Did you have a second conversation?'

'Just about the tragedy,' said Liversidge. 'I left her at her dressing-room door. She went on to the wardrobe-room, I think.'

'Now, Mr Liversidge, can you tell me if anyone remained on the stage after you left it?'

'Hailey Hambledon went back to – to where you were after the guests had gone.'

'Yes, yes, I know. I don't mean the actual stage within the scenery but the area, off-stage. Did anyone stay behind, off-stage?'

'I didn't notice anyone do so,' said Liversidge.

'Right. Now about this scene in the wardrobe-room. Had Master Gordon Palmer spoken to you about his curious theories?'

Liversidge passed his rather coarse and very white hand over his gleaming head.

'He – well, he did say something about it. Sort of mentioned it, don't you know. I was astounded. I simply can't believe it of dear old Court. Simply *can not* credit it.' Mr Liversidge added that Courtney Broadhead was a white man, a phrase that Alleyn had never cared for and of which he was heartily tired.

'I wish,' he said, 'that you would repeat as much of the conversation as you can remember. How did it begin?' Liversidge hesitated for some time.

'Never mind,' said Alleyn, 'about getting it quite correct. We can get Gordon Palmer's version too, you know.'

This was far from having a reassuring effect on Mr Liversidge. He darted a glance full of the liveliest distaste at Alleyn, made several false starts, and finally bent forward with an air of taking them into his confidence.

'Now look, Inspector,' he said earnestly, 'this is damned awkward for me. You see someone had said something about Val's money to both Gordon and me, and Gordon afterwards asked me what I thought was the true story. That was just after poor old Court had paid up. Well, I said – not meaning Gordon to take it up seriously – just a joke – I mean I never dreamt he'd think for a moment—' Mr Liversidge waved his hands.

'Yes?' said Alleyn.

'Gad, I wouldn't have had it happen for the world. I said – laughing – something about – "Well – Court's suddenly flush – p'raps he's the dirty-dog." Something like that. I mean, never dreaming—'

'Did you pursue this joke?' asked Alleyn.

'Well, don't you know, chaffingly,' explained Liversidge. 'What!'

129

'My God,' thought Alleyn, 'it's supposed to be Oxford, that language.' Aloud he said: 'Did you also talk about the attempt on Mr Meyer in the train?'

'In point of fact – yes. It was all meant for comedy, you know. I just said, all laughingly, that perhaps Alfred Meyer had caught him at it, and so he'd tried to tip him overboard. Well, I mean to say! When I heard Gordon tonight! Well, of course! I was flabbergasted!'

'Did you have any further joking references tonight – after the fatality?' inquired Alleyn, evenly.

'My dear Mr Alleyn!' expostulated Liversidge, greatly shocked.

'No reference of any sort?'

'Actually, do you know, Gordon did say something to me in the passage. I don't remember what it was. I was too shocked and grieved to pay attention. I think he just said something about, did I remember what we had talked about.'

'I see,' said Alleyn. 'Mr Liversidge, do you know at what time during our train journey the attempt on Mr Meyer was made?'

'Eh. Let me see, let me see. Do I remember? Yes – it was sometime before we got to that place where we stopped for refreshments. Isn't that right? I remember the dear old governor telling us about it. Poor old governor! It's hard to realise—'

'Frightfully hard, isn't it! Now before we reached that station – Ohakune – the guard came through the train chanting an announcement.'

'So he did.'

'Were you awake or did he wake you?'

'He woke me.'

'Had you been asleep for long?'

'Ages. I dropped off soon after Val went along to her sleeper.'

'Do you remember that you were disturbed by anyone getting up and leaving the carriage before the guard went through?'

'Didn't Court Broadhead go out to the platform? I seem to remember – good God, old man, I don't mean – you can't mean—!'

'I don't mean anything at all, Mr Liversidge,' said Alleyn. 'Nobody else?'

'I don't think so. No.'

'Thank you. Now about the greenstone tiki. We are anxious to trace it if possible. Miss Dacres has lost it.'

'Is it valuable?'

'It is rather, I imagine.'

'Well, you ought to know,' said Liversidge.

'Quite so. Do you remember handling it?'

'Certainly,' said Liversidge with huffy dignity. 'I also remember returning it.'

'To whom?'

'To – to Branny, I think. Yes, it was to Branny. And he gave it to Carolyn and she put it on the table. I remember that quite well.'

'Whereabouts on the table?'

'At the end on the OP side. It was before we sat down. Funny me remembering.'

'Do you remember anyone picking it up from the table?'

'No. No, I don't.'

'Have you any theory,' asked Alleyn abruptly, 'about the disappearance of Miss Gaynes's money?'

'I? Lord, no! I should think very likely a steward pinched it.'

'It's happened before,' agreed Alleyn. 'She seems to have been pretty casual about her cash.'

'Casual! God, she's hopeless. Fancy leaving a packet of tenners in an open suitcase. Well, of course!'

'All in tenners, was it?' asked Alleyn absently.

'I think so. She told me so.'

Wade cleared his throat.

'I seem to remember,' continued Alleyn vaguely, 'that she said something about paying you a tenner she'd lost at poker. When did she do that?'

'On the last night we were in the ship. After we'd finished playing. Actually it was about one o'clock in the morning.'

'She still had her money then, evidently.'

'Yes.'

'She got this tenner from the hoard in the suitcase, did she?'

'I – I think so. Yes, she did.'

'You saw her, did you, Mr Liversidge?'

'Well – not exactly. I walked along to her cabin and waited outside in the corridor. She came out and gave me the tenner. I didn't know, then, where she got it from.'

'You couldn't see her?'

'No, I couldn't. Damn it all, Alleyn, what's the idea of all this?'

'No offence in the world. Goodnight, Mr Liversidge.'

'Eh?'

'Goodnight,' repeated Alleyn cheerfully.

Liversidge stared uncomfortably at him and then got to his feet. Wade made a movement and was checked by a glint in Alleyn's eye.

'Well, so long,' said Mr Liversidge and went away.

'Let him go,' said Alleyn when the door had slammed. 'Let him go. He's *so* uncomfortable and fidgety. You can get him again when he's spent a beastly night. He'll do very nicely for the time being. Let him go.'

CHAPTER 13

Miss Gaynes Goes Up-stage

'Now, Miss Gaynes,' said Alleyn patiently, 'it's a very simple question. Why not let us have the answer to it?'

Valerie Gaynes lay back in the office arm-chair and stared at him like a frightened kitten. At the beginning of the interview she had been in good histrionic form and, it seemed to Alleyn, thoroughly enjoying herself. She had accounted for her whereabouts during the two crucial periods, she had taken the tiki in her stride, with many exclamations as to its ill-omened significance, she had discoursed at large on the subject of her own temperament, and she had made use of every conceivable piece of theatrical jargon that she could haul into the conversation in order to show them how professional she was. Alleyn had found all this inexpressibly tedious and quite barren of useful information, but he had listened with an air of polite interest, chosen his moment, and put the question that had so greatly disconcerted her:

'What did you and Mr Liversidge talk about before you left the stage after the final curtain?'

He could have sworn that under her make-up she turned white. Her enormous brown eyes blinked twice exactly as though he had offered to hit her. Her small red mouth opened and literally her whole body shrank back into the chair. Even after he had spoken again, she made no attempt to answer him, but lay there gaping at him.

'Come along,' said Alleyn.

When she did at last muster up her voice it was almost comically changed.

'Why – nothing in particular,' said Miss Gaynes.

'May we just hear what it was?'

She moistened her lips.

'Didn't Frankie tell you? What did he say?'

133

'That's the sort of question we particularly never ask a policeman,' said Alleyn. 'I want *you* to tell me.'

'But – it was just about poor Mr Meyer – nothing else.'

'Nothing else?'

'I tell you I don't remember. It was nothing.'

'It wasn't something very private and personal – between you and Mr Liversidge?'

'No. Of course not. We haven't anything – like that – to say.'

'Funny!' said Alleyn. 'Mr Liversidge told us you had.'

Miss Gaynes burst into tears.

'Look here,' said Alleyn after a pause, 'I'm going to give you a very hackneyed bit of advice, Miss Gaynes. It's extremely good advice and you may land yourself in a very uncomfortable position if you don't take it. Here it is. Don't lie to the police when there's a murder charge brewing. Nobody else can make things quite as awkward for you as they can. *Nobody.* If you don't want to answer my question you can refuse to do so. But don't lie.'

'I – I'm frightened.'

'Would you rather refuse to give us your answer?'

'But if I do that you'll think – you'll suspect – terrible things.'

'We shall merely note that you decline—'

'No. No. What are you thinking? You're suspecting *me!* I wish I was out of it all. I wish I'd never told him. I wish I'd never met him. I don't know *what* to do.'

'What do you wish you'd never told him?'

'That I knew – who it was.'

Wade uttered a sort of strangled grunt. Cass looked up from his notes and opened his mouth. Alleyn raised an eyebrow and stared thoughtfully at Valerie Gaynes.

'You knew – who it was who did *what?*'

'You know what. You've known all the time, haven't you? Why did you ask me what we talked about if you didn't know?'

'You mean that Mr Liversidge is responsible for this business tonight?'

'Tonight!' She almost screamed it at him. 'I didn't say that. You can't say I said that.'

'Good heavens,' said Alleyn. 'This is becoming altogether too difficult. We seem unable to understand each other, Miss Gaynes. Please let us tidy up this conversation. Will you tell us in so many words, what is this matter between you and Mr Liversidge? You suspect him of something, obviously. Apparently it is not murder. What is it?'

'I – I don't want to tell you.'

'Very well,' said Alleyn coldly. He stood up. 'We must leave it at that and go elsewhere for our information.'

She made no attempt to get up. She sat there staring at him, her fingers at her lips and her face disfigured with tears. She looked genuinely terrified.

'I'll have to tell you,' she whispered at last.

'I think it would be wiser,' said Alleyn, and sat down again.

'It's the money,' said Miss Gaynes. 'I think Frankie took my money. I didn't believe it at first when Mr Meyer spoke to me about it.'

'Lummy!' thought Alleyn. 'Now we're getting it.' He began to question her systematically and carefully, taking pains not to alarm her too much, so that gradually she became more composed, and out of her disjointed half-phrases an intelligible sequence of events began to appear. It seemed that on the last evening in the ship, when she paid her poker debts, Liversidge actually went into her cabin with her. She took the money from her suitcase while he was there, and gave him the ten pounds she owed him. At the same time she took out a ten-pound note which she subsequently changed at the first saloon bar and paid out in tips. Liversidge told her that she was a fool to leave her money in an unlocked suitcase. She told him she had lost the key of the suitcase and said she was not going to bother about it now, at the end of the voyage. He repeated his warning and left her. Next morning, when she returned from breakfast to pack her luggage, she prodded the leather notecase, felt the thick wad of paper, and fastened the suitcase without making any further investigation. It was not until she opened the notecase in the train that she knew she had been robbed. It was then that she paid her dramatic call on the Meyers and found Alleyn in their sleeper.

'And you suspected Mr Liversidge when you began to tell us about paying your debt to him?'

She said yes. The thought of Liversidge's possible complicity occurred to her at that moment. The next morning Meyer had taken her aside and questioned her closely about the money.

'He seemed to suspect Frankie – I don't know why – but he seemed to suspect him.'

It was then that Meyer had insisted on paying her the amount that had been stolen. He had not made any definite accusation against Liversidge but had warned her against forming any attachment that she might afterward regret.

'Did Miss Dacres speak to you about Mr Liversidge?'

But it appeared Carolyn had said nothing definite, though Miss Gaynes had received an impression that Carolyn, too, had something up her sleeve.

'And have you yourself said anything about this matter to Mr Liversidge?'

Here a renewed display of emotion threatened to appear. Alleyn steered her off it and got her back to the conversation that took place off-stage. She said that, guessing at Meyer's view of the theft, 'all sorts of dreadful thoughts' came into her mind when he was killed.

'Then you thought, at the outset, that it was a case of murder?'

Only, it seemed, because Gascoigne kept saying that there must have been some hanky-panky with the gear. After a great many tedious false starts she at last told

136

Alleyn that, when they were all hustled away from the scene of the disaster, she had blurted out a single question to Liversidge: 'Has this got anything to do with my money?' and he had answered: 'For God's sake don't be a bloody little fool. Keep quiet about your money.' Then he had kept her back and had said hurriedly that for Courtney Broadhead's sake she had better not mention the theft. 'I'd never thought of Court until then,' said Miss Gaynes, 'but after that I got all muddled and of course I remembered how hard-up Court was and then I began to wonder. And now – now I – I simply don't know where I am, honestly I don't. If Frankie was trying to help Court and I've – I've betrayed him—'

'Nonsense,' said Alleyn very crisply. 'There's no question of betrayal. You have done the only possible thing. Tell me, please, Miss Gaynes, are you engaged to Mr Liversidge?'

She flushed at that and for the first time showed a little honest indignation.

'You've no business to ask me that.'

'I can assure you I am not prompted by idle curiosity,' said Alleyn equitably. 'The question is relevant. I still ask it.'

'Very well, then, I'm not actually engaged.'

'There is an understanding of some sort, perhaps?'

'I simply haven't made up my mind.' A trace of complacency crept into her voice. Alleyn thought: 'She is the type of young woman who always represents herself as a fugitive before the eager male. She would never admit lack of drawing-power in herself.'

'But now—' she was saying, 'I wish we had never thought of it. I want to get away from all this. It's all so hateful – I want to get away from it. I'm going to cable to Daddy and ask him to send for me. I want to go home.'

'As a preliminary step,' said Alleyn cheerfully, 'I am going to send you off to your hotel. You are tired and distressed. Things won't seem so bad in the morning, you know. Goodnight.'

He shut the door after her and turned to the two New Zealanders.

'Silly young woman,' said Alleyn mildly.

But Wade was greatly excited.

'I reckon this changes the whole outfit,' he said loudly. 'I reckon it does. If Liversidge stole the cash, it changes the whole show. By crikey, sir, you caught them out nicely. By crikey, it was a corker! He tells you one story about this conversation with the girl Gaynes, and you get the other tale from her and then face her up with it. By gee, it was a beauty!'

'My dear Inspector,' said Alleyn uncomfortably, 'you are giving me far too much encouragement.'

'It wasn't so much the line taken,' continued Wade, explaining Alleyn to Cass, 'as the manner of taking it. I don't say I wouldn't have gone on the same lines myself. It was indicated, you might say, but I wouldn't have got in the fine work like the chief inspector. The girl Gaynes would have turned dumb on us very, very easy, but the chief just trotted her along quietly and got the whole tale. You seemed to guess there was something crook about this Liversidge from the kick-off, sir. What put you on to that, if I might ask?'

'In the first instance, Miss Gaynes herself. That night in the train she was full of the theft until she began to account for the money she had spent. She mentioned Francis Liversidge, suddenly looked scared, and then shut up like an oyster. Tonight Mr Liversidge's gallantry in defending young Broadhead seemed to be as bogus as the rest of his behaviour.'

'Including the queenie voice,' agreed Wade. 'Sounds as if he'd swallowed the kitchen sink.'

'I fancy,' continued Alleyn, 'that Miss Dacres also doubts the integrity of our Mr Liversidge. I fancy she does. She has made one or two very cryptic remarks on the subject.'

'The girl Gaynes never said just *why* she reckoned he

looked suspicious. Was it simply because he'd been in the cabin and seen where she kept the money?'

'That, perhaps; and also, don't you think, because of whatever Mr Alfred Meyer said to her on the subject?'

'*Cert-ain-ly,*' agreed Wade, with much emphasis. 'And if deceased knew Liversidge pinched the money and let the Gaynes woman see he knew, maybe she put in the good word to Liversidge and he thought: "That's quite enough from you, Mr Meyer," and fixed it accordingly.'

'In which case,' said Alleyn, offering Wade a cigarette, 'we have two murderous gentlemen instead of one?'

'Uh?'

'The first attempt on his life was made in the train before the theft was discovered.'

'Aw, hell!' said Inspector Wade wearily. After a moment's thought he brightened a little. 'Suppose Liversidge had found out by some other means that the deceased knew he had taken the money? Suppose he knew the deceased was on to his little game before they left the ship?'

'By jove, yes,' said Alleyn, 'that'd do it, certainly. But look here, Wade, does one man murder another simply because he's been found out in a theft?'

'Well, sir, when you put it like that—'

'No,' interrupted Alleyn, 'you're quite right. It's possible. Meyer would give him the sack, of course, and make the whole thing public. That would ruin Liversidge's career as an actor, no doubt. If he could kill Meyer before he spoke – Yes, it's possible, but – but I don't know. We'll have to see Miss Dacres and George Mason again, Wade. If Meyer confided in anyone, it would be his wife or his partner. But there's one catch in your theory.'

'What's that, sir?'

'It's rather nebulous perhaps, but when the little man told me about the assault in the train he was obviously at a complete loss to account for it. Now, if he'd already let Liversidge see he suspected the theft, he would have

139

thought of him as a possible enemy. But he told me he was on terms of loving kindness and all the rest of it with his entire company, and I think he meant it.'

'It's a fair cow, that's what it is,' grunted Wade.

'Beg pardon, Inspector,' said the silent Cass after a pause, 'but if I might make a suggestion – it's just an idea, like.'

'Go ahead,' commanded Wade graciously.

'Well, sir, say this Mr Liversidge knew the deceased gentleman had seen him take the money, without deceased having let on that he saw, if you understand me, sir.'

'Well done, Sergeant,' said Alleyn quietly.

'Yes, but how?' objected Wade.

'Mr Liversidge might have overheard deceased say something to his wife or somebody, sir.' Cass took a deep breath and fixed his eyes on the opposite wall. 'What I mean to say,' he said doggedly, 'Mr Meyer saw Mr Liversidge take the money. Mr Liversidge knew Mr Meyer saw him. Mr Meyer thought Mr Liversidge didn't know he saw him.'

'And there,' concluded Alleyn, 'would be the motive without Mr Meyer realising it. He's quite right. You're fortunate, Inspector. An intelligent staff is not always given to us.'

Cass turned purple in the face, squared his enormous shoulders, and glared at the ceiling.

'There you are, Cass!' said Wade good-humouredly. 'Now buzz off and get us another of these actors.'

CHAPTER 14

Variation on a Police Whistle

Old Brandon Vernon looked a little the worse for wear. The hollows under his cheek bones and the lines round his eyes seemed to have made one of those grim encroachments to which middle-aged faces are so cruelly subject. A faint hint of a rimy stubble broke the smooth pallor of his chin; his eyes, in spite of their look of sardonic impertinence, were lack-lustre and tired. Yet when he spoke one forgot his age, for his voice was quite beautiful; deep, and exquisitely modulated. He was one of that company of old actors that are only found in the West End of London. They still believe in using their voices as instruments, they speak without affectation, and they are indeed actors.

'Well, Inspector,' he said to Alleyn, you know how to delay an entrance. It was very effective business, coming out in your true colours like this.'

'I found it rather uncomfortable, Mr Vernon,' answered Alleyn. 'Do sit down, won't you, and have a smoke? Cigarette?'

'I'll have my comforter, if you don't mind.' And Vernon pulled out a pipe and pouch. 'Well,' he said, 'I'm not sorry to leave the wardrobe-room. That young cub's sulking and the other fellow has about as much conversation as a vegetable marrow. Dull.' He filled his pipe and gripped it between his teeth.

'We're sorry to have kept you waiting so long,' said Alleyn.

'Don't apologise. Used to it in this business. Half an actor's life is spent waiting. Bad show this. Was Alfred murdered?'

'It looks rather like it, I'm afraid.'

'Um,' rumbled old Vernon. 'I wonder why.'

141

'To be frank, so do we.'

'And I suppose we're all suspect. Lord, I've played in a good many mystery dramas but I never expected to appear in the genuine thing. Let me see, I suppose you're going to ask me what I was doing before and after the crime, eh?'

'That's the idea,' sighed Alleyn, smiling.

'Fire ahead, then,' said old Vernon.

Alleyn put the now familiar questions to him. He corroborated the account Liversidge and Broadhead had given of his movements. At the close of the play and after the catastrophe, he had gone straight to his dressing-room, where the other two afterwards joined him.

'I don't know if that constitutes an alibi,' he said, rolling his eyes round at Wade. 'If it doesn't I understand I am almost certain to be innocent.'

'So the detective books tell us,' said Alleyn, 'and they ought to know. As a matter of fact I think it does give you a pretty well cast-iron alibi.'

Vernon grimaced. 'Not so good. I must watch my step.'

'You've been with the firm of Incorporated Playhouses a good time, haven't you, Mr Vernon?'

'Let me see. I started with *Double Knock* at the old Curtain. Before that I was with Tree and afterwards with du Maurier.' He pondered. 'Ten years. Ten years with Inky-P. Long time to work with one management, ten years.'

'You must be the senior member of the club?'

'Pretty well. Susie runs me close, but she left us for *The Rat and the Beaver,* two years ago.'

'Ah, yes. You must have known Mr Meyer very well?'

'Yes, I did. As well as an actor ever knows his manager, and that's very thoroughly in some ways and not at all in others.'

'Did you like him?'

'Yes, I did. He was honest. Very fair with his actors. Never paid colossal salaries – not as they go nowadays – but you always got good money.'

'Mr Vernon, do you know of any incident in the past or present that could throw any light on this business?'

'I don't.'

'The Firm is all right, I suppose? Financially, I mean?'

'I believe so,' answered Vernon. There was an overtone in his voice that suggested a kind of guardedness.

'Any doubts at all about that?' asked Alleyn.

'There are always rumours about managements like ours. I have heard a certain amount of gossip about some of the touring companies. They are supposed to have dropped money for the Firm. Then there was *Time Payment*. That did a flop. Still, Inky-P has stood a flop or two in its time.'

'Were all Mr Meyer's interests bound up in the Firm, do you know?'

'I don't know anything about it. George Mason could tell you that, probably. Alfred was a very shrewd business man and he and Carolyn are not the social spotlight hunters that most of 'em are nowadays. They lived very quietly. The theatre before everything. I should say Alfred had saved money. Only a guess, you know.'

'I know. It'll all appear now, of course.'

'What puzzles me, Mr Alleyn, is who on earth would want to do in Alfred Meyer. None of us, you'd have thought. Shops aren't found so easily that we can afford to kill off the managers.' He paused and rolled his eyes round. 'I wonder,' he said, 'if that accident on Friday morning gave anybody the big idea.'

'What accident?' asked Alleyn sharply.

'The morning we got here. Didn't you hear about it? One of the staff was up in the flies fixing the weight for the mast. The head mechanist and Ted Gascoigne were down below on the stage, having an argument. Suddenly the gentleman in the flies got all careless and dropped the weight. It fell plum between the two men and crashed half through the stage. Ted Gascoigne raved at the poor swine for about ten minutes, and Fred – the head mechanist – nearly ate him. We all rushed out to see the fun. God, they were a sight!

143

White as paper and making faces at each other.'

'Good lord!' said Alleyn.

'Yes. It would have laid him out for keeps if it had hit one of 'em. Great leaden thing like an enormous sash-weight and as heavy—'

'As heavy, very nearly, as a jeroboam of champagne,' finished Alleyn. 'It was used, afterwards, as a counterweight for the bottle.'

'Was it really!' exclaimed Vernon.

'Didn't you know how they fixed the gear for the bottle?'

'I heard poor old Alfred holding forth on the subject, of course, but I'm afraid I didn't pay much attention.'

'You all knew about the mishap with the counterweight?'

'Oh God, yes. Everyone came out helter-skelter. It shook the building. George ran along from the office, Val Gaynes flew out of her dressing-room in a pair of cami-knicks. The two Australians nearly threw in their parts and returned to Sydney. It was a nine days' wonder.'

'I see,' said Alleyn. He turned to Wade. 'Anything else you'd like to ask Mr Vernon, Inspector?'

'Well now,' said Wade genially, 'I don't know that there's much left to ask, sir. I *was* wondering, Mr Vernon, you having been so long with the company, if you could give us a little idea about the domestic side of the picture, as you might say.'

Old Vernon swung round in his chair and looked at Wade without enthusiasm.

'Afraid I don't follow you,' he said.

'Well now, Mr Vernon, you'll understand we have to make certain inquiries in our line. You might say we have to get a bit curious. It's our job, you understand, and we may fancy it as little as other folk do, but we've got to do it. Now, Mr Vernon, would you describe Mr and Mrs Meyer as being a happy couple, if you know what I mean?'

'I can understand most common words of one or two

144

syllables,' said Vernon, 'and I do know what you mean. Yes, I should.'

'No differences of any sort?'

'None.'

'Good-oh, sir. That's straight enough. So I suppose all this talk about her and Mr Hambledon is so much hot air?'

'All what talk? Who's been talking?'

'Now don't you worry about that, Mr Vernon. That'll be quite all right, sir.'

'What the hell d'you mean? What'll be quite all right? Who's been talking about Miss Dacres and Mr Hambledon?'

'Now never you mind about that, sir. We just want to hear—'

'If it's that damned little footpath comedian,' continued Vernon, glaring angrily at Wade, 'you can take it from me he's about as dependable as a cockroach. He's a very nasty little person, is Mr St John Ackroyd, *né* Albert Biggs, a thoroughly unpleasant piece of bluff and brass. And *what* a naughty actor!'

'*Né* Biggs?' murmured Alleyn.

'Certainly. And the sooner he goes back to his hairdresser's shop in St Helens the better for all concerned.'

'I gather,' said Alleyn mildly, 'that he has already spoken to you about the conversation he overheard in his dressing-room.'

'*Oh*, yes,' said old Vernon, with a particular air of elaborate irony that Alleyn had begun to associate with actors' conversation. '*Oh*, yes. I was told *all* about it as soon as he had a chance to speak his bit. Mr Ackroyd came in *well* on his cue with the old bit of dirt, you may be *quite* sure.'

Alleyn smiled: 'And it's as true as most gossip of that sort, I suppose?'

'I don't know what Ackroyd told you, but I'd swear till it snowed pink that Carolyn Dacres hasn't gone in for the funny business. Hailey *may* have talked a bit wildly. He

145

may be very attracted. I don't say anything about that, but on her side – well, I can't believe it. She's one of the rare samples of the sort that stay put.'

And Vernon puffed out his cheeks and uttered a low growl.

'That's just what we wanted to know,' said Wade. 'Just wanted your opinion, you see, sir.'

'Well, you've got it. And the same opinion goes for anything Mr Ackroyd may have told you, including his little bit of dirt about George Mason. Anything else?'

'We'll get you to sign a statement about your own movements later on, if you don't mind,' said Wade.

'Ugh!'

'And that will be all.'

'Has the footpath comedian signed his pretty little rigmarole?'

'Not yet, Mr Vernon.'

'Not yet. No doubt he will,' said Vernon bitterly. He shook hands with Alleyn. 'Lucky you're here, Mr Alleyn. I shall now go to my home away from home. The bed is the undulating sort and I toboggan all night. The mattress appears to have been stuffed with the landlady's apple dumplings of which there are always plenty left over. Talk of counterweights! My God! Matthew, Mark, Luke and John, bless the bed that I lie on. Goodnight. Goodnight, Inspector Wade.'

'What is the name of your hotel, sir?'

'The Wenderby, Inspector. It is a perfect sample of the Jack's Come Home.'

'I've always heard it was very comfortable,' said Wade, with all the colonial's defensiveness. 'The landlady—'

'Oh, you must be a lover of your landlady's daughter,
    Or you don't get a second piece of pie,'

sang old Vernon surprisingly in a wheezy bass:

'Piece of pie, piece of pie, piece of pie, piece of pie,
    Or you don't get a second piece of pie.'

He cocked his eyebrow, turned up the collar of his overcoat, clapped his hat on one side of his head and marched out.

'Aw, he's mad,' said Wade disgustedly.

Alleyn lay back in his chair and laughed heartily.

'But he's perfect, Wade. The real old actor. Almost too good to be true.'

'Making out he's sorry deceased has gone and two minutes afterwards acting the fool. Our hotels are as good as you'd find anywhere,' grumbled Wade. 'What's he mean by a Jack's Come Home, anyway?'

'I fancy it's a professional term noting a slap-dash and carefree attitude on the part of the proprietress.'

'He's mad,' repeated Wade. 'Get the kid, Cass. Young Palmer.'

When Cass had gone, Wade got up and stamped about the office.

'It's chilly,' he said.

The room was both cold and stuffy. The fire had gone out and the small electric heater was quite unequal to the thin draughts of night air that came in under the door and through the ill-fitting window-frame. The place was rank with tobacco smoke and with an indefinable smell of dust and varnish. Somewhere outside in the sleeping town a clock struck two.

'Good lord!' said Alleyn involuntarily.

'Like to turn it up for tonight, sir?' asked Wade.

'No, no.'

'Good-oh, then. Look, sir. On what we've got, who do you reckon are the possibles? Just on the face of it?'

'I'm afraid it'd be quicker to tick off the unlikelies,' said Alleyn.

'Well, take it that way.'

Alleyn did not reply immediately and Wade answered himself.

'Well, sir, I've got their names here and I'll tick off the outsiders. Old Miss Max. No motive or opportunity. That

147

old looney who's just wafted away, Brandon Vernon. Same for him. Gascoigne, the stage-manager. Same for him on the evidence we've got so far. The funny little bloke, St John Ackroyd, alias Biggs, according to Vernon. He may be a bit of a nosy but he doesn't look like a murderer. Besides, his movements are pretty well taped. The girl Gaynes. Well, I suppose you might say, if she's going with Liversidge and knew Meyer was in the position to finish his career for him, that there's a motive there, but I don't see that silly little tart fixing counterweights and working out the machinery for a job of this sort. Do you?'

'The imagination does rather boggle,' agreed Alleyn.

'Yes. Well, now we get into shaky country. Hambledon. Let's look at Mr Hailey Hambledon. He's after the wood. They none of them deny that. Seems as if he's been kind of keen for a long while. Now if Ackroyd's story is right, she said she'd marry him if Meyer was dead and not unless. There's the motive. Now for opportunity. Hambledon could have gone aloft the first time and taken away the weight. He says he went to his dressing-room and took the muck off his dial. Maybe, but he told the dresser he wasn't wanted, and he could have gone back on the stage, climbed aloft and done it. After the murder he went as far as her dressing-room with the Dacres woman – with deceased's wife. She said she wanted to be alone and then sent for him, some time later. During the interval he may have gone up and put the weight back. That right?'

'Yes,' said Alleyn.

'Then there's Carolyn Dacres. Same motive. Same opportunity. She was the last to appear for the party and she asked to be left alone after the fatality. I don't know whether she'd be up to thinking out the mechanics of the thing but—'

'One should also remember,' said Alleyn, 'that she was the one member of the party from whom the champagne stunt had been kept a secret.'

'By gum, yes. Unless she'd got wind of it somehow.

Ye-ers. Well, that's her. Now George Mason. Motive – he comes in for a fortune if the money's still there. Opportunity – not so good. Before the show he was in this room. The stage-doorkeeper remembers Mason running out and warning him about the guests and returning here. Te Pokiha saw him here. You remember him coming out when you arrived. To get behind, between those times, he'd have had to pass the doorkeeper and would have been seen by anybody who happened to be about.'

'Is there a pass-door through the proscenium from the stalls?'

'Eh? No. No, there's not. No, I don't see how he could have done it. After the murder he came back with Te Pokiha and I saw him in the office here as I passed the door. We'll check up just when Te Pokiha left him, but it doesn't look too likely.'

'It does not. It looks impossible, Wade.'

'I hate to say so,' admitted Wade. 'Next comes young Courtney Broadhead. If he stole the money and Meyer knew, that's motive. Or if he doped it out he'd say Meyer had lent it to him – that's another motive. There's that business on the train—'

'Always remembering,' said Alleyn, 'that the train attempt took place before Miss Gaynes discovered the theft of the money.'

'Aw, blast!' said Wade. 'It just won't make sense. Well – Liversidge. Motive. If he took the money and Meyer knew, and he knew Meyer knew – good enough. Opportunity. Each time he was the last to leave the stage. He could have done it. There you are, and where the bloody hell are you?'

'I weep with you,' said Alleyn. 'I deeply sympathise. Isn't Master Palmer taking rather a long time?'

He had scarcely asked his question before the most extraordinary rumpus broke out in the yard. There was a sudden scurry of running feet on asphalt, a startled bellow, and a crash, followed by a burst of lurid invective.

Alleyn, with Wade behind him, ran to the door, threw it

149

open, and darted out into the yard. A full moon shone upon cold roofs and damp pavements, and upon the posterior view of Detective-Sergeant Cass. His head and shoulders were lost in shadow and he seemed, to their astonished eyes, to be attempting to batter his brains out against the wall of a bicycle shed. He was also kicking backwards with the brisk action of a terrier, this impression being enhanced by spurts of earth and gravel which shot out from beneath his flying boots.

'Here, 'ere, 'ere,' said Wade, 'what's all this?'

'Catch him!' implored a strangely muffled voice while Cass redoubled his activities. 'Go after the . . . little . . . Get me out of this! Gawd! Get me out of it.'

Alleyn and Wade flew to the demented creature. Wade produced a torch, and by its light they saw what ailed the sergeant. His head and his enormous shoulders were wedged between the wall of the bicycle shed and that of a closely adjoining building. His helmet had slipped over his face like a sort of extinguisher, his fat arms were clamped to his side. He could neither go forward nor back and he had already begun to swell.

'Get me out,' he ordered. 'Leave me alone. Go after 'im. Go after the . . . ! Gawd, get me out!'

'Go after who?' asked Wade. 'What sort of game do you think you're up to, Sergeant Cass?'

'Never mind what I'm up to, Mr Wade. That young bleeder's run orf behind this shed and it's that narrer I can't foller. Gawd knows where he is by this time!'

'By cripey, you're a corker, you are,' said Wade hotly. 'Here!'

He seized the sergeant's belt and turned to Alleyn.

'Do you mind giving a hand, sir?'

Alleyn was doubled up in ecstasy of silent laughter, but he managed to pull himself together and, after a closer look at the prisoner, he hunted in the wooden shed, unearthed a length of timber which they jammed between the two walls and thus eased the pressure a little. Cass was pried and hauled out, sweating vigorously. Alleyn slipped into the passage and round to the rear of the shed. Here he found another path running back towards the theatre. He darted along this alley between a ramshackle fence and the brick wall of the property-room. The path led to the rear of the theatre, past a closed door, and finally to a narrow back street. Here Alleyn paused. Back in the stage-door yard he could hear one of the distracted officials blowing a police whistle. The little street was quite deserted, but in a moment or two a police officer appeared from the far end. Alleyn shouted to him and he broke into a run.

'What's all this? Who's blowing that whistle?'

'Inspector Wade and Sergeant Cass,' said Alleyn. 'They're in the theatre yard. Has a young man in evening dress passed you during the last few minutes?'

'Yes. Up at the corner. What about him?'

'He's given us the slip. Which way?'

'Towards the Middleton Hotel. Here, you hold steady, sir. Where are you off to? You wait a bit.'

'Ask Wade,' said Alleyn. He sidestepped neatly and sprinted down the street.

It led him into a main thoroughfare. In the distance he recognised the familiar bulk of the Middleton Hotel. Three minutes later he was talking to the night porter.

'Has Mr Gordon Palmer returned yet?'

'Yes, sir. He came in a minute ago and went up to his room – No. 51. Anything wrong, sir?' asked the night porter, gazing at Alleyn's filthy shirtfront.

'Nothing in the wide world. I shall follow his example.'

He left the man gaping and ran upstairs. No. 51 was on the second landing. Alleyn tapped at the door. There was no answer, so he walked in and turned up the light.

Gordon Palmer sat on the edge of his bed. He was still dressed. In his hand was a tumbler.

'Drinking in the dark?' asked Alleyn.

Gordon opened his mouth once or twice but failed to speak.

151

'Really,' said Alleyn, 'you are altogether too much of a fool. Do you *want* to get yourself locked up?'

'You get to hell out of this.'

'I shall certainly go as quickly as I can. You reek of whisky, and you look revolting. Now listen to me. As you've heard already, I'm an officer of Scotland Yard. I shall be taking over certain matters in connection with this case. One of my duties will be to write to your father. Precisely what I put in my letters depends on our subsequent conversation. It's much too late and we're too busy to talk to you now. So I shall lock you in your room and leave you to think out a reasonable attitude. There's a fifty-foot drop from your window to the pavement. Good morning.'

CHAPTER 15

Six a.m. First Act Curtain

Alleyn longed for his bed. He was dirty and tired, and a dull lugging pain reminded him that he was supposed to be taking things easily after a big operation. He went into his room, washed, and changed quickly into grey flannels and a sweater. Then he went downstairs.

The night porter gazed reproachfully and suspiciously at him.

'Are you going out again, sir?'

'Oh yes, rather. It's my night to howl.'

'Beg pardon, sir?'

'You'll hear all about it,' said Alleyn, 'very shortly. There's something to keep out the cold.'

Back at the theatre he found Wade and Cass closeted with Mr Geoffrey Weston. There was an enormous tear in Cass's tunic and a grimy smudge across his face. He sat at the desk taking notes. Evidently his uncomfortable predicament had upset his digestion for he rumbled lamentably and at each uncontrollable gurgitation he assumed an air of huffy grandeur. Wade appeared to be irritable and Weston stolid. The office looked inexpressibly squalid and smelt beastly.

'I thought I'd better come back and report,' said Alleyn. 'I've locked up your darling little imp for what's left of the night, Mr Weston.'

'So he did go back to the pub,' grunted Weston disinterestedly. 'I told you he would, you know.'

'That's right, Mr Weston,' said Wade.

'I suppose the PC I met in the lane told you what I was up to,' said Alleyn.

'Yes, sir, he did, and very surprised he was when he heard who you were. I sent him after you, Mr Alleyn, and he saw you go into the Middleton so we left you to it. I've just been

153

asking Mr Weston if he could give us an idea why Mr Palmer slipped up on us.' And Wade glanced uncomfortably at Weston, edged round behind him, and made an eloquent grimace at Alleyn.

Alleyn thought he had never seen any face that expressed as little as Geoffrey Weston's. It was an example of the dead norm in faces. It was neither good-looking nor plain, it had no distinguishing feature and no marked characteristic. It would be impossible to remember it with any degree of sharpness. It was simply a face.

'And why did he bolt, do you suppose?' asked Alleyn.

'Because he's a fool,' said Mr Weston.

'Oh, rather,' agreed Alleyn. 'No end of a fool; but even fools have motives. Why did he bolt? What was he afraid of?'

'He's run away from disagreeable duties,' said Weston, with unexpected emphasis, 'ever since he could toddle. He ran away from three schools. He's got no guts.'

'He displayed a good deal of mistaken effrontery in the wardrobe-room, when he as good as accused Courtney Broadhead of theft.'

'Egged on,' said Weston.

'By Liversidge?'

'Of course.'

'Do you believe the story about Broadhead, Mr Weston?'

'Not interested.'

'Did you speak of it to Mr Palmer?'

'Yes.'

'When?'

'In the wardrobe-room, after you'd gone.'

'You must have been very quiet about it.'

'I was.'

'What did you say?' pursued Alleyn, and to himself he murmured: 'Oyster, oyster, oyster; Open you *shall*.'

'Told him he'd be locked up for defamation of character.'

'Splendid. Did it frighten him?'

'Yes.'

'Do you think he bolted to avoid further questioning?'

'Yes.'

'It's all so simple,' said Alleyn pleasantly, 'when you understand.'

Weston merely stared at his boots.

'I suppose,' continued Alleyn, 'that you had heard all about the arrangements for the champagne business?'

'Knew nothing about it.'

'Mr Palmer?'

'No.'

'Can you help us about the missing tiki?'

'Afraid I can't.'

'Ah, well,' said Alleyn, that's about all, I fancy. Unless you've anything further, Inspector?'

'No, sir, I have not,' said Wade, with a certain amount of emphasis. 'We'll see the young gentleman in the morning.'

'That all?' asked Weston, getting to his feet.

'Yes, thank you, Mr Weston.'

'I'll push off. Goodnight.'

He walked out and they heard his footsteps die away before any of them spoke.

'He's a fair nark, that chap,' said Wade. 'Close! Gosh!'

'Not exactly come-toish,' agreed Alleyn.

'Blooming oyster! Well, that's the whole boiling of 'em now, sir.'

'Yes,' said Alleyn thankfully.

But they stayed on talking. A kind of perverseness kept them wedded to this discomfort. They grew more and more wakeful and their ideas seemed to grow sharper. Their thoughts cleared. Alleyn spoke for a long time and the other two listened to him eagerly. Quite suddenly he stopped and shivered. The virtue went out of them. They felt dirty, and dog-tired. Wade began to gather up his papers.

'I reckon that finishes us for tonight. We'll lock up this show and turn it up till tomorrow. There'll be the inquest next. Cripey, what a life!'

Alleyn had strolled over to the door in the back wall and was peering at a very murky framed drawing that hung beside it. He wiped the glass with his handkerchief.

'Plan of the theatre,' he said. 'All fine and handy. I think I'll just make a rough copy. It won't take a moment.'

He got a writing-pad from the desk and worked rapidly.

'Here we go,' he murmured. Stage-door. Footlights. Dressing-room passage here. Prompt-side ladder to the grid, about here. Back-stage one here. There's a back door there, you see. I noticed it when I was in full cry after Master Gordon. We'll have a look at it by the light of day. Now the front of the house. Stalls. Circle. No pass-door through the proscenium. Here's this office. Door into box-office. Door to yard. The bicycle shed isn't in their plan, but it begins just beyond this office. The shed comes forward like that. The yard widens out after you pass the sheds. Packing-cases. Then there's this affair – a garage, isn't it? – and the other shed here. And there's Master Gordon's getaway.'

'Need we mark that?' asked Wade, yawning horribly.

'I'm sure Cass thinks it worthy of record,' said Alleyn, smiling. 'How wide are you, Cass?'

'Twenty-four inches across the shoulders, sir,' said Cass, and was shaken by a stupendous belch. 'Pardon,' he added morosely.

'Then the space between the two buildings is certainly less,' murmured Alleyn. 'Of course, Master Gordon is a mere stripling. Tell me, Cass, how did it all happen?'

'He was coming along as quiet as you please, sir,' began Cass angrily, and instantly interrupted himself with a perfectly deafening rumble, ' – as quiet as you please, when he suddenly lets out a sort of squeak and bolts down that gap like a bloody rabbit. I never stops to *think*, you see, sir. I tears into it good-oh, and I come at it that determined-like I swept all before me, as you might say, for the first six inches, and then it kind of shut down on me.'

'It did indeed,' said Alleyn.

'By gum, yes, sir, it did so. And I was doubled up like as I was saying to Mr Wade, sir, and I hadn't got no purchase.' He belched violently. 'Pardon. It's gone crook on my digestion. Being doubled up.'

'We can hear that for ourselves,' said Wade unsympathetically. 'You looked a big simp, Cass. Get your helmet. Gather up that stuff and bring it along to the station. I'll shut up here.'

'Yes, sir.'

'Finished your plan, Mr Alleyn?'

'Yes, thank you,' answered Alleyn.

He came out of the office and walked past the bicycle shed to the stage-door. Here he found Sergeant Packer.

'Hullo, Packer, are you here for the rest of the night?'

Packer came smartly to attention.

'Yessir. At least, I'll be relieved in half an hour, sir.'

'None too soon, I should imagine. It's cold.'

'It is too, sir,' agreed Packer. There's snow in the back-country.'

'Snow in the back-country!' exclaimed Alleyn, and suddenly he was aware of a new world. The experiences of the night slipped away and became insignificant. He was awake in a sleeping town and not far away there were mountains with snow on them and long tracts of hills with strange soft names.

'Are you a country-bred man?' he asked Packer.

'Yessir. I come from Omarama in the Mackenzie Country. That's in the South Island, sir. Very high sheep country, beyond Lake Pukaki.'

'I've heard of it. You go through a mountain pass, don't you?'

'That's right, sir. Burke's Pass in the north and the Lindis in the south. Still very cold at nights, this time of year, in the Mackenzie, but you get the sun all day.'

'I shall go there,' said Alleyn. Suddenly he felt a great distaste for the position in which he found himself. He had not crossed half a world of ocean to mess about over a

157

squalid and tedious crime. He felt that he had been a fool. He was on a holiday in a new country and he knew that at the back of all his thoughts there lay a kind of delicious excitement which he would not savour until long after he had gone away again.

The office door banged and Wade and Cass stamped out into the yard, beyond the bicycle shed.

'Are you there, Chief Inspector?' called Cass.

'Here! Goodnight, Packer, or rather good morning, isn't it?'

'Yes, sir, it'll be getting light soon. Good morning, sir.'

Alleyn joined the other two, and together they left the theatre and turned into the main thoroughfare.

Their footsteps rang coldly on the asphalt pavement. Somewhere, a long way off, a dog barked. Then, still farther away, a cock crew and was echoed away into nothingness by other cocks. The moon had set but the darkness was thinning and the street lamps already looked wan.

At the second corner Wade and Cass stopped.

'We turn off here,' said Wade. 'It'll be light in half an hour. If I may, sir, I'll call in at the hotel sometime tomorrow.'

'Do,' said Alleyn cordially.

'It's been a great pleasure, sir, having you with us.'

'You've been damn' pleasant about it, Inspector. Hope you're none the worse, Cass.'

Cass saluted. Solemnly and rather ridiculously they both shook hands with Alleyn and tramped off.

The street ran uphill towards the hotel. At the far end there was a clean lightness of sky and, as Alleyn watched, it grew still lighter. Between the end of the street and the sky was the head of a faraway mountain. Its flowing margin was sharp against the dawn. Its base was drenched in a colder and more immaculate blue than Alleyn had ever before seen. And as Packer had told him, this mountain was crested white and the little cold wind that touched Alleyn's face came from those remote slopes. Alleyn paused outside his hotel, still looking up the street to the mountain and wondering at the line traced by its margin against the sky. He thought: 'It is like the outline of a lovely body. All beautiful edges are convex. Though the general sweep may be inward, to attain beauty, the line must be formed of outward curves.' Before he had completed this thought, the peak of the mountain was flooded with thin rose colour, too austere to be theatrical, but so vivid that its beauty was painful. He felt that kind of impatience and disquietude that sudden beauty brings. He could not stand and watch the flood of warmth flow down the flanks of the mountain nor the intolerable transfiguration of the sky. He rang the night bell and was admitted by the porter.

The clocks in the hotel, and the clocks outside in the town, all began to strike six as he got into bed, and when the last clock had struck, the vague rumour of innumerable cockcrows rang in his head. And as he fell asleep he heard the first chatter of waking birds.

CHAPTER 16

Entr'acte

Extract from a letter written by Chief Inspector Alleyn to Detective-Inspector Fox of the Criminal Investigation Department, New Scotland Yard:–

—so you will agree, my dear Fox, it really is a bit of a teaser. I see you wag your head and I know you think what a fool I was not to make my statement and my exit as rapidly as possible. I confess I am surprised at myself and can only suppose that I must *like* teckery – an amazing discovery. You will have got my cable and I shall have received your answer long before this letter reaches you, even if I go a terrific bust and send it by Air Mail. Of course, unless Alfred Meyer made a later will, as far as money goes, George Mason has the strongest motive, but on the evidence before us he could never have got up into the flies to put back the weight. I've told you the whole story and I have outlined my tentative theory which, as you will see, hinges on this one incontrovertible point. Mason was with me on the stage after the murder, and he went with Te Pokiha to the office. I've rung Te Pokiha up and he says he stayed in the office with Mason until he heard the police arrive, and left Mason there when he, Te Pokiha, returned to the stage. To put the thing beyond all argument, it now appears that after the police had come, the doorkeeper went along the yard, saw Mason sitting in the office sipping his whisky, and stayed talking to him until Mason went to the wardrobe-room. By that time the weight was back again. I have laboured this point because I know Wade is going to try and break Mason's alibi for this period and I am satisfied that he cannot do it. Then there's this grim little tiki – I wish you could see it – it's a tiny squint-eyed effigy with a lolling head and curled-up rudimentary limbs. The resemblance to the human embryo is obvious. It's leering at me now from the blotting paper. They tried it for prints and it was smothered with them. Well, it's reasonable to suppose that whoever put the weight back, dropped the tiki on the floor of the grid platform. Mason is ruled out. We have Hambledon, Carolyn Dacres, Liversidge, Ackroyd and the girl, Valerie Gaynes. These four could, I believe, have gone aloft, unnoticed, at both the vital times. At the risk of boring you to tears, my poor Fox, I now append a timetable for the two visits to the grid. I include the entire cast of characters, even our old friend Susan Max. Here it is. You will notice that I have marked the names without alibis. XA or XB stands for no alibi during the first or second vital periods, and XX (Guinness is *good* for you) for no alibi at either of these times. I've also noted the alleged motives.

As regards the attempt on the train (if it was an attempt and not a playful gambol on the part of a homing rugger expert), I regard any attempt to link it up with the theft – an attempt which Wade longs to make – as a likely pitfall. At that time the theft had not been discovered by Miss Gaynes. If Meyer had seen the thief on the job and had tackled him about it, why had he not forced him to return the money before the loss was known? Or, conversely, why had he not made the business public? As he did neither of these things, why should the thief try to murder him? Sergeant Cass intelligently suggests that perhaps the thief knew Meyer had twigged his little game, that Meyer was unaware of this, and that the thief struck before Meyer could take action, missed his pot on the train, and had a more successful go at the theatre. This does not explain Meyer's delay in tackling the matter in the first

	A	B	Motive
	After the show. Before the party. 1st visit to Grid. Weight removed. Pulley shifted. Approx. 10.30–11.	After the murder. 2nd visit to Grid. Weight replaced. Pulley replaced. Approx. 11.15–11.30	
Susan Max	In her dressing-room with Carolyn Dacres's maid.	Went with Carolyn Dacres to latter's dressing-room. Moved to her own room with maid. Returned later to Carolyn Dacres. Left on my arrival. Then to wardrobe-room.	None known.
Courtney Broad-head XB	Went to dressing-room with Brandon Vernon.	Went alone to dressing-room. Found Vernon there. Had a drink. Went to wardrobe-room.	Suggested by Palmer (prompted by Liversidge) that he stole Valerie Gaynes's money, said he'd been lent it by Meyer and killed latter to avoid discovery.
Brandon Vernon XB	In dressing-room with Courtney Broadhead.	Went alone to dressing-room where he was joined by Broadhead and Liversidge. Then went to wardrobe-room.	None known.
Francis Liversidge XX	Last to leave stage and go to dressing-room. Spoke on stage to Valerie Gaynes.	Last to leave stage. Spoke to Valerie Gaynes at entrance of passage. Then went to dressing-room, then wardrobe-room.	Suggested by Valerie Gaynes that he stole her money. If Meyer was aware of this and Liversidge knew it, he might kill Meyer to save his reputation and career.
George Mason ?XA	In office. Door-keeper spoke to him and watched him go back. I met him in yard and went with him to stage.	On stage with us. Went to office with Pokiha. Remained in office talking to doorkeeper. Went to wardrobe-room.	Gets the money.
George Gascoigne ?	On stage. Working with staff.	On stage.	None known.

	A	B	Motive
Valerie Gaynes XX	Left stage after conversation with Liversidge. Went to dressing-room.	Left stage after second conversation with Liversidge. Went to dressing-room then to wardrobe-room.	None, unless to protect person who stole her money. If Liversidge is the thief, this is just possible.
St John Ackroyd ?X ?X	Alone in dressing-room but says that he called out at intervals to the others.	Ditto, and then to wardrobe-room.	None known. NB Vernon says Carolyn Dacres snubbed his advances. Obviously bears Carolyn Dacres and Hambledon a grudge.
Hailey Hamble-don XX	Alone in his dressing-room. Dismissed his dresser. Then on stage.	Says he took Carolyn Dacres to her dressing-room. Then went to his dressing-room. Returned to her. Fetched me from stage. Returned with me to her room. Fetched brandy. Went to wardrobe-room.	Rumoured to be in love with Carolyn Dacres. Ackroyd says he overheard Hambledon ask her if she'd marry him if Meyer was dead. She is reported to have said that she would.
Carolyn Dacres (Mrs Meyer) XX	Alone in dressing-room. Dismissed her dresser who went to Susan Max.	Hambledon took her to her dressing-room. She sent him away. Also sent dresser away. The latter went to Susan Max and later returned to Carolyn Dacres who sent for Susan. Hambledon returned and was sent for me.	Comes in for money but her salary must be enormous. Ackroyd says she refused to consider a divorce on account of being Roman Catholic. Seems hardly likely she would strain at divorce and swallow murder. (More possible that she would shield Hambledon if he did it).
Gordon Palmer	Came in among other guests. Joined party. Made a fuss about not being allowed to visit Carolyn Dacres's room.	Went with others to wardrobe-room.	None, unless calf-love.
Geoffrey Weston	With Palmer. Ditto throughout.		None.

instance. The force is now hunting up the train passengers, to try and let a little more light into the affair. I still incline to the view that the theft is a sideline, put in by the gods to make it more difficult. But what god dropped the little green tiki into this puzzle? I have seen some of the Maori deities in the local museum. Wild grimacing abortions, with thrust-out tongues and glinting eyes. They seem to fascinate me. One seems to smell old New Zealand in them – a kind of dark wet smell like the native forest. Before this case came along I hired a car and make a trip into the country north of this town where a tract of native bush is preserved. On the way there are Maori villages – pas they call them – composed for the most part of horrid little modern cottages. The Maoris themselves wear European clothes with occasional native embell-ishments, among the older people. They have a talent for arranging themselves in pleasant groups and seem to be very lighthearted. The aristocrats among them are magnificent. Te Pokiha is an Oxford man. He is extremely good-looking, courteous, and most dig-nified. I am to dine with him and he is to tell me something of their folk-lore. When, as I have already described, the men handed the little tiki round and Meyer made merry, I felt that he was guilty of the grossest error in taste. Te Pokiha was very cool and well-bred about it. What an idea for a fantastic solution – he killed Meyer because of the insult to the tiki and left the tiki up there as a token of his vengeance. 'Cut it out,' as Inspector Wade would say. The local force is very polite to me. I am to meet the superintendent this morning. They might well have been a bit sticky over me and indeed, to begin with, I sensed a sort of defensiveness on Wade's part. It was a curious mixture of 'How about this for a genuine New Zealand (they say "New Zillund") welcome?' and 'Treat us fair and we'll treat you fair, but none of your bloody superiority stuff.' They are extremely nice fellows and good policemen, and I hope I shan't get on their nerves. One has to keep up a sort of strenuous heartiness, which I find a little fatiguing. The idiom is a bit puzzling but 'corker' seems to be the general adjective of approbation. 'Crook' means 'ill', 'angry', or 'unscrupulous' according to the context; and 'a fair nark', or, more emphatically, 'a fair cow', is anything inexpressibly tedious or baffling. The average working man – such as the railway porter and taxi driver (especially the older type) speaks much better English than his English contemporary. One notices the accent in polite circles, but Lor' bless you, what of it? My poor Fox, I maunder at you. I hope you have enjoyed looking up the affairs of Mason and Meyer's Incorporated Playhouses, and of Mr Francis Liversidge. Such fun for you.

I am feeling much better, so you need not put on your scolding air over my police activities. It is so amusing to be unofficial and yet in the game. I feel I may give surmise and conjecture free rein.

Do write me a line when you've time.

Yours ever,
RODERICK ALLEYN

Alleyn sealed and addressed his letter and glanced at the lounge clock. Ten o'clock. Perhaps he had better take another look at Master Gordon Palmer who, at nine o'clock, appeared to be sunk in the very depths of sottish slumber. Alleyn took the lift to the second floor. The unwavering stare of the lift-boy told him that his identity was no longer a secret. He walked to Gordon's room, tapped on the door and walked in.

Gordon was awake but in bed. He looked very unattractive and rather ill.

'Good morning,' said Alleyn. 'Feeling poorly?'

'I feel like death,' said Gordon. He glanced nervously at

the chief inspector, moistened his lips and then said rather sheepishly: 'I say, I'm sorry about last night. Can I have my key back? I want to get up.'

'I unlocked your door an hour ago,' said Alleyn. 'Haven't you noticed?'

'As a matter of fact my head is so frightful I haven't moved yet.'

'I suppose you drank yourself to sleep?'

Gordon was silent.

'How old are you?' asked Alleyn.

'Seventeen.'

'Good God!' exclaimed Alleyn involuntarily. 'What do you suppose you'll look like when you've grown up? An enfeebled old dotard. However, it's your affair.'

Gordon attempted to smile.

'And yet,' continued Alleyn, raising one eyebrow and screwing up his face, you don't look altogether vicious. You're pimply, of course, and your skin's a nauseating colour – that's late hours and alcohol – but if you gave your stomach and your lungs and your nerves a sporting change you might improve enormously.'

'Thanks very much.'

'Rude, you think? I'm twenty-five years older than you. Old gentlemen of forty-two are allowed to be impertinent. Especially when they are policemen. Do you want to get into trouble with the police, by the way?'

'I'm not longing to,' said Gordon, with a faint suggestion of humour.

'Then why, in heaven's name, did you bolt? You have permanently changed the silhouette of Detective-Sergeant Cass. He now presents the contour of a pouter-pigeon.'

'Oh no, does he? How superb!'

'How *superb!*' imitated Alleyn. 'The new inflexion. How *superb* for you, my lad, if you're clapped in durance vile.'

Gordon looked nervous.

'Come on,' continued Alleyn. Why did you bolt? Was it funk?'

'Oh, rather. I was terrified,' said Gordon lightly.

'Of what? Of your position in regard to Courtney Broadhead? Were you afraid the police would press you to restate your theory?'

'It's not my theory.'

'We came to that conclusion. Liversidge filled you up with that tarradiddle, didn't he? Yes, I thought so. Were you afraid we'd find that out?'

'Yes.'

'I see. So you postponed the evil hour by running away?'

'It was pretty bloody waiting in that room. Hour after hour. It was cold.'

His eyes dilated. Suddenly he looked like a frightened schoolboy.

'I've never seen anyone – dead – before,' said Gordon.

Alleyn looked at him thoughtfully.

'Yes,' he said at last, 'it was pretty foul, wasn't it? Give you the horrors?'

Gordon nodded. 'A bit.'

'That is bad luck,' said Alleyn. 'It'll wear off in time. I don't want to nag, you know, but alcohol's no good at all. Makes it worse. So you eluded Mr Cass because you'd got the jim-jams while you were waiting in the wardrobe-room?'

'It was so quiet. And outside there – on the stage – getting cold and stiff—'

'God bless my soul!' exclaimed Alleyn. 'They took him away long before that, you silly fellow. Now tell me, what did Liversidge say to you when you left the scene of the disaster?'

'Frankie?'

'Yes. In the dressing-room passage, before you went to the wardrobe-room?'

'He – he – I think he said something about – did I remember what we'd said.'

'What did he mean?'

'About Courtney and the money.'

167

'Now think carefully and answer me truthfully. It's important. Who made the suggestion that Broadhead might have taken that money – you or Mr Liversidge?'

'He did, of course,' said Gordon at once.

'Ah yes,' said Alleyn.

He sat down on the end of the bed and again he contemplated Gordon. It seemed to him that after all the boy was not so intolerably sophisticated. 'His sophistication is no more than a spurious glaze over his half-baked adolescence,' thought Alleyn. 'Under the stress of this affair it has already begun to crack. Perhaps he may even read detective stories.' And suddenly he asked Gordon:

'Are you at all interested in my sort of job?'

'I *was,* rather, in the abstract,' said Gordon.

'I'm puzzled by your reactions to this affair. Last night you know, you were so very alert and cock-a-hoop. Your attack on Broadhead! It was most determined.'

'I hadn't time to think. It didn't seem real then. None of it seemed real. Just rather exciting.'

'I know. Perhaps you are one of the people that ricochet from a shock, as a bullet does from an impenetrable surface. You fly off at an uncalculated angle, but do not at once lose speed.'

'Perhaps I am,' agreed Gordon, cheered by the delicious promise of self-analysis. 'Yes, I think I am like that. I—'

'It's a very common reaction,' said Alleyn. 'Let us see how the theory may be applied to your case. A man was murdered almost under your nose, and instead of screaming like Miss Gaynes, or being sick like Mr Mason, you found yourself sailing along in a sort of unreal state of stimulation. You felt rather intoxicated and into your mind, with startling insistence, came a little sequence of ideas about Courtney Broadhead. You thought of your discussion with Mr Liversidge and – an additional fillip – he actually reminded you of it in the passage. Still sailing along, you were seized with the idea of bringing off one of those startling coups, which, unfortunately for us, occur more often in fiction than in police investigations. You would confront Broadhead with his infamy and surprise him into betraying himself. It's a typical piece of adolescent behaviourism. Very interesting in its way. A projection of the king-of-the-castle phantasy – I forget the psycho-analytical description.'

He paused. Gordon, very red in the face, was silent.

'Well,' continued Alleyn, 'when that little affair was over you began to lose speed and come to earth. You had time to think. You tell me that as the others went out, one by one, until only you and Mr Weston were left under Packer's eye, you began to get the jim-jams. You got them so badly that when we sent for you, you bolted. I can't help wondering if there was some additional cause for this – if perhaps you had remembered something that seemed to throw a new light on this crime.'

Still watching the boy, Alleyn thought, 'Really, he changes colour like a chameleon. If he goes any whiter he'll faint.'

'What do you mean?' said Gordon.

'I see I am right. You *did* remember something. Will you tell me what it was?'

'I don't even know what you are talking about.'

'Don't you? It doesn't seem very difficult. Well, I had better leave it for the moment and ask a few routine questions. Let me see, you came round the front of the house to the stage as soon as the show was over?'

'Yes.'

'Did you walk straight on to the stage and remain there?'

'Yes.'

'You did not go to any of the dressing-rooms?'

'No. I wanted to go to Carolyn's room but Ted Gascoigne was stupid about it so I didn't.'

'Right. After the disaster, when I suggested that you should wait somewhere with your cousin until the police arrived, did you both keep together?'

'We went to the wardrobe-room. Geoff took me there.'

'Right. Now about this tiki. What were you going to say about that when I questioned Miss Dacres in the wardrobe-room?'

'Nothing.'

'Shall I make another guess? When I asked Miss Dacres where the tiki was, she put her hand up to her dress with that quick, almost involuntary gesture a woman uses when she has something hidden in what used to be called her bodice. You saw that gesture, and a moment afterwards you made an exclamation and then refused to explain it. That was because you remembered that during the supper-party you saw Miss Dacres slip the tiki under the bodice of her dress.'

'How do you know? I – I wasn't sure. I only thought—'

'A moment afterwards, she looked in her bag and then said she did not remember handling the tiki after she had put it down on the table.'

'There's nothing in that,' said Gordon hotly. 'She'd simply forgotten. That's not surprising after what happened. She wasn't trying to tell lies, if that's what you mean. She'd forgotten, I tell you. Why, I only happened to remember because of her hand—'

'I merely wanted to be sure that you'd seen her do it.'

'Well, if I did, what of it?'

'Nothing at all. And now I shall leave you to arise and greet the latter half of the morning. I suggest two aspirins, some black coffee and a brisk walk to the police station where Inspector Wade will be delighted to receive your apologies for your offensive behaviour. I forget what the penalty is for running away from the police in the execution of their duty. Something with a little boiling oil in it, perhaps. I suppose you loathe *The Mikado?*'

'Look here, sir, what'll they do to me?'

'If you tell them, nicely, what you've just told me, I shall try and stay their wrath. Otherwise—'

Alleyn made a portentous grimace and walked out of the room.

CHAPTER 17

Change of Scene

When Alleyn returned to the lounge he found Wade there, waiting for him. They retired to Alleyn's room where he related the gist of his conversation with Gordon.

'I've told him to give you the whole story himself.'

'I still don't see why he cleared out on us,' said Wade.

'I fancy it was partly because he'd worked himself up into a blue funk over the whole business. His nerves are in a lamentable state, silly little creature. And I do think, Wade, that he's in a devil of a twit over this business of the tiki.'

'Yee-es? And why's that, sir?'

Alleyn hesitated for a moment. A curious look of reluctance came into his face. When he spoke his voice was unusually harsh.

'Why? Because he caught Carolyn Dacres lying. Last night when I asked her about the tiki her hand went to her breast. She fingered her dress, expecting to feel the hard little tiki underneath. Then she said she had not handled it since it was left on the table. She looked in her bag. The only honest thing she did was involuntary – that movement of her hand. I've told you young Palmer started to speak, and stopped dead. This morning I trapped him into as good as admitting he'd seen her put the tiki into her dress.'

'But why did he stop? He couldn't have known where we found it, could he?'

'No. The young booby's head over ears in calf-love with her. He sensed the lie, as I did, and wouldn't give her away.'

'I reckon I'll talk to Miss Carolyn Dacres-Meyer before I do another thing. This looks like something, sir. And she could have gone up there. She could have done it all right.'

'Yes. Wade, at the risk of making an intolerable nuisance

of myself, I'm going to ask a favour of you. Will you allow me to speak to her first? I – I've a perfectly legitimate reason for wanting to do this. At least,' said Alleyn with a wry smile, 'I think it's legitimate. It's just possible she may feel less on the defensive with me. You see – I know her.'

'You go to it, sir,' said Wade, with a violent heartiness that may possibly have concealed a feeling of chagrin. 'You do just as you please, and we'll be more than satisfied. That'll be quite OK. As you say, you'll get a lot more out of her than we would, seeing she looks on you as a friend.'

'Thank you,' said Alleyn. He looked rather sick.

'I'll get back to the station, sir. Let young Palmer come to me – better than seeing him here. The super will be calling in shortly, I fancy.'

'Have a drink before you go,' suggested Alleyn.

'Now, sir, I was just going to suggest, if you'd give me the pleasure—'

They went down to the bar and had drinks with each other.

Wade departed, and Alleyn, avoiding the unwavering stare with which everybody in the hotel followed his movements, buried himself behind a newspaper until the arrival of Superintendent Nixon. Nixon turned out to be a pleasant dignified officer with a nice sense of humour. He was cordial without finding any necessity to indulge in Wade's exuberant manifestations of friendliness. Alleyn liked him very much and saw that Nixon really welcomed his suggestions, and wished for his cooperation. They discussed the case fully and Nixon stayed until eleven-thirty when he exclaimed at the length of his visit, invited Alleyn to make full use of the local station and its officials, and accepted an invitation to dine the following evening.

When he had gone Alleyn, with the air of facing an unpleasant task, returned to the writing-desk. There were now nine people in the lounge, all ensconced behind newspapers. Six of them frankly folded their journals and turned their gaze on Alleyn. Two peered round the corners of their papers at him. The last, an old lady, lowered her paper until it masked the bottom part of her face like a yashmak, and glared at him unwinkingly over the top. Alleyn himself stared at a blank sheet of paper for minutes. At last he wrote quickly:

'Will you give me the pleasure of driving you into the country for an hour or so? It will be an improvement on the hotel, I think.' [He paused, frowning, and then added:] 'I hope my job will not make this suggestion intolerable.'

RODERICK ALLEYN

He was about to ring for someone to take this note to Carolyn's room, when he became aware of a sense of release. A rustling and stirring among the nine bold starers informed him of the arrival of a new attraction and, glancing through the glass partition, he saw Hambledon coming downstairs. He went to meet him.

'Hullo, Alleyn. Good morning. I suppose you've been up for hours.'

'Not so many hours.'

'Any of our people down yet?'

'I haven't seen them.'

'Gone to earth,' muttered Hambledon, 'like rabbits. But they'll have to come to light soon. Mason called us for noon at the theatre.'

'I don't think you'll get in there, do you know,' said Alleyn.

'Why? Oh – the police. I see. Well, I suppose it'll be somewhere in the hotel.'

The lift came down and Mason got out of it.

''Morning, Hailey. 'Morning, Mr Alleyn.'

'Hullo, George. Where are we meeting?'

'The people, here, have lent us the smoking-room. My God, Hailey, they're locking us out of our own theatre. Do you know that? Locking us out!'

They gazed palely at each other.

173

'First time in thirty years' experience it's ever happened to me,' said Mason. 'My God, what would Alf have thought! Locked out of our own house. It makes you feel awful, doesn't it?'

'It's all pretty awful, George.'

'Did you sleep?'

'Not remarkably well. Did you?'

'Damn' queer thing, but it's the first night for months that I haven't been racked by dyspepsia – first time for months – and I lay there without a gurgle, thinking about Alf all night.' Mason stared solemnly at both of them. 'That's what you call irony,' he said.

'How will you let everybody know about the call for twelve?' asked Hambledon.

'I've got hold of Ted and he's doing it.'

'Do you want Carolyn?'

'Have you seen her? How is she?'

'I haven't seen her.'

Mason looked surprised.

'Well, run up now, like a good fellow, Hailey, and tell her not to bother about this call if she doesn't feel up to it.'

'All right,' said Hambledon.

'Would you mind giving her this note?' asked Alleyn, suddenly. 'It's just a suggestion that if she'd like to get away from the pub for a bit of fresh air – she'll explain. Thank you so much.'

'Yes – certainly.' Hambledon looked sharply at Alleyn and then made for the lift.

'This is a difficult situation for you, Mr Mason,' said Alleyn.

'Difficult! It's a bit more than difficult. We don't know what's to happen. Here we are with the tour booked up – the advance is down in Wellington and has put all the stuff out. We're due to open there in six days and God knows if the police will let us go, and if they do God knows if Carolyn will be able to play. And without her—!'

'Who's her understudy?'

174

'Gaynes. I ask you! Flop! The Australian kid would have to take Gaynes's bits. Of course if Carolyn does play—'

'But, after this! She's had a terrible shock.'

'It's different in the business,' said Mason. 'Always has been. The show must go on. Doesn't mean we're callous but – well Alf would have felt the same. The show must go on. It's always been like that.'

'I suppose it has. But surely—'

'I've seen people go on who would have been sent off to hospital in any other business. Fact. I was born off-stage twenty minutes after my mother took her last call. It was a costume piece, of course – crinolines. It's a funny old game, ours.'

'Yes,' said Alleyn. Suddenly he was aware of a kind of nostalgia, a feeling of intense sympathy and kinship with the stage. 'A drab enough story to have aroused it,' he thought. 'A theme that has been thrashed to death in every back-stage plot from *Pagliacci* downwards. The show must go on!'

'Of course,' Mason was saying, 'Carolyn may feel differently. I'm not sure about it myself. The public might not like it. Besides suppose it's – one of us. Everybody would be wondering which of the cast is a bloody murderer. That's so, isn't it?'

'I suppose there would be a certain amount of conjecture.'

'Not the sort of advertisement the Firm wants,' said Mason moodily. 'Undignified.'

To this magnificent illustration of a meiosis, Alleyn could only reply: 'Quite so.'

Mason muttered on, unhappily: 'It's damn' difficult and expensive whichever way you look at it. And there's the funeral. I suppose that will be tomorrow. *And* the inquest. The papers will be full of us. Publicity! Poor old Alf! He was always a genius on the publicity side. My God, it's rum, isn't it? Oh well – see you later. You're going to give these fellows a hand, aren't you? Funny, you being a detective. I hear Alf knew all about it. My God, Alleyn, I hope you get him.'

'I hope we shall. Will you have a drink?'

'Me? With my stomach it'd be dynamite. Thanks, all the same. See you later.'

He wandered off, disconsolately.

Alleyn remained in the hall. In a minute or two Hailey Hambledon came down in the lift and joined him.

'Carolyn says she would like to go out. I'm to thank you and say she will be down in ten minutes.'

'I'll order the car at once. She won't want to wait down here.'

'With all these rubbernecks? Heavens, no!'

Alleyn went into the telephone-box and rang up the garage. The car would be sent round at once. When he came out Hambledon was waiting for him.

'It's extraordinarily nice of you, Alleyn, to do this for her.'

'It is a very great pleasure.'

'She's so much upset,' contined Hambledon. He lowered his voice and glanced at the reception clerk who was leaning out of his window and affecting an anxious concern in the activities of the hall porter. The porter was engaged in a close inspection of the carpet within a six-foot radius from Alleyn and Hambledon. He had the air of a person who is looking for a lost jewel of great worth.

'Porter,' said Alleyn.

'Sir?'

'Here is half a crown. Will you be so good as to go out into the street and watch for a car which should arrive for me at any moment? You can continue your treasure hunt when I have gone.'

'Thank you, sir,' said the porter in some confusion, and retired through the revolving doors. Alleyn gazed placidly at the reception clerk who turned away with an abstracted air and picked his teeth.

'Come over here,' suggested Alleyn to Hambledon. 'The

176

occupants of the lounge can gaze their fill but they can't hear you. You were saying—'

'I am sure the shock has been much greater than she realises. As a matter of fact I can't help feeling she would be better to spend the day in bed.'

'Thinking?'

'She'll do that wherever she is. I'm very worried about her, Alleyn. She's altogether too bright and brave – it's not natural. Look here – you won't talk to her about Alf, will you? Keep right off this tragedy if you can. She's in no state to discuss it with anybody. Last night those damn' fellows kept her at it for God knows how long. I know that you, as a Yard man, are anxious to learn what you can, and I hope with all my heart that you get the swine; but – don't worry Carolyn again just yet. She gets quite hysterical at the mention of it. I know I can depend on you?'

'Oh,' said Alleyn vaguely, 'I'm very dependable. Here is Miss Dacres.'

Carolyn stepped out of the lift.

She wore a black dress that he had seen before and a black hat with a brim that came down over her face which, as usual, was beautifully made-up. But underneath the make-up he suspected she was very pale, and there was a darkness about her eyes. Carolyn looked a little older, and Alleyn felt a sudden stab of compassion. 'That won't do,' he thought, and started forward to greet her. He was aware that the old lady with the journalistic yashmak had boldly advanced to the plate-glass partition, and that three of the other occupants of the lounge were making hurriedly for the hall.

'Good morning,' said Carolyn. 'This is very nice of you.'

'Come out to the car,' said Alleyn. 'It is very nice of *you*.'

He and Hambledon walked out on either side of her. The porter, who had been deep in conversation with the mechanic from the garage, flew to open the door of the car. A number of people seemed to be hanging about on the footpath.

'Thank you,' said Alleyn to the mechanic. 'I'm driving myself. Come back at about three, will you? Here you are, Miss Dacres.'

'You're in a great hurry, both of you,' said Carolyn, as Hambledon slammed the door. Then she saw the little knot of loiterers on the footpath. 'I see,' she whispered.

'Goodbye, my dear,' said Hambledon. 'Have a lovely drive.'

'Goodbye, Hailey.'

The car shot forward.

'I suppose the paper is full of it,' said Carolyn.

'Not absolutely full. They don't seem to go in for the nauseating front-page stuff in this country.'

'Wait till the evening papers come out before you're sure of that.'

'Even they,' said Alleyn, 'will probably show a comparative sense of decency. I thought we might drive up to where those mountains begin. They say it's a good road and I got the people in the hotel to put some lunch in the car.'

'You felt sure I would come?' asked Carolyn.

'Oh, no,' said Alleyn lightly. 'I only hoped you would. I've been a fair distance along this road already. It's an uphill grade all the way, though you wouldn't think it, and when we get to the hills it's rather exciting.'

'You needn't bother to make conversation.'

'Needn't I? I rather fancy myself as a conversationalist. It's part of my job.'

'In that case,' said Carolyn loudly, 'you had better go on. You see, dear Mr Alleyn, I do realise this is just a rather expensive and delicate approach to an interrogation.'

'I thought you would.'

'And I must say I do think it's quite charming of you to take so much trouble over the setting. Those mountains *are* grand, aren't they? So very up-stage and magnificent.'

'You should have seen them at 6 a.m.'

'Now you are being a Ruth Draper. They couldn't have been any lovelier than they are at this moment, even with these depressing little bungalows in the foreground.'

'Yes, they were. They were so lovely I couldn't look at them for more than a minute.'

'"Mine eyes dazzle"?'

'Something like that. Why don't you do some of those old things? *The Maid's Tragedy?*'

'Too hopelessly frank and straightforward for the Lord Chamberlain, and not safe enough for the box-office. I did think once of *Millamant,* but Pooh said—' She stopped for a second. 'Alfie thought it wouldn't go.'

'Pity,' said Alleyn.

They drove on in silence for a few minutes. The tram-line ended and the town began to thin out into scattered groups of houses.

'Here's the last of the suburbs,' said Alleyn. 'There are one or two small townships and then we are in the country.'

'And at what stage,' asked Carolyn, 'do we begin the real business of the day? Shall you break down my reserve with precipitous roads, and shake my composure with hairpin bends? And then draw up at the edge of a chasm and snap out a question, before I have time to recover my wits?'

'But why should I do any of these things? I can't believe that my few childish inquiries will prove at all embarrassing. Why should they?'

'I thought all detectives made it their business to dig up one's disreputable past and fling it in one's face.'

'Is your past so disreputable?'

'There you go, you see.'

Alleyn smiled, and again there was a long silence. Alleyn thought Hambledon had been right when he said that Carolyn was too brave to be true. There was a determined and painful brightness about her, her voice was pitched a tone too high, her conversation sounded brittle, and her silences were intensely uncomfortable. 'I'll have to wait,' thought Alleyn.

'Actually,' said Carolyn suddenly, 'my past is quite presentable. Not at all the sort of thing that most people

179

imagine about the actress gay. It began in a parsonage, went on in a stock drama company, then repertory, then London. I went through the mill, you know. All sorts of queer little touring companies where one had to give a hand with the props, help on the stage, almost bring the curtain down on one's own lines.'

'Help on the stage? You don't mean you had to lug that scenery about?'

'Yes, I do. I could run up a box-set as well as most people. Flick the toggle-cords over the hooks, drop the back-cloth – everything. Oh, but how lovely that is! How lovely!'

They had now left all the houses behind them. The road wound upwards through round green hills whose firm margins cut across each other like the curves of a simple design. As Carolyn spoke, they turned a corner, and from behind this sequence of rounded greens rose the mountain, cold and intractable against a brilliant sky. They travelled fast, and the road turned continually, so that the hills and the mountain seemed to march solemnly about in a rhythm too large to be comprehensible. Presently Alleyn and Carolyn came to a narrow bridge and a pleasant little hinterland through which hurried a stream in a wide and stony bend.

'I thought we might stop here,' said Alleyn.

'I should like to do that.'

He drove along a rough track that led down to the river-bed, and stopped in the shadow of thick white flowering manuka shrubs, honey-scented.

They got out of the car and instead of the stuffiness of leather and petrol they found a smooth freshness of air with a tang of snow in it. Carolyn, an incongruous figure in her smart dress, stood with her face raised.

'It smells clean.'

The flat stones were hot in the sun, and a heat-haze wavered above the river-bed. The air was alive with the voice of the stream. They walked over the stones, over springy lichen, and patches of dry grass, to the border of the creek where the grass was greener. Here there were scattered prickly shrubs and sprawling bushes, that farther upstream led into a patch of dark trees.

'It must have been forested at one time,' said Alleyn. 'There are burnt tree stumps all over these hills.'

And from the trees came the voice of a solitary bird, a slow cadence, deeper than any they had ever heard, ringing, remote and cool, above the sound of water. Carolyn stopped to listen. Suddenly Alleyn realised that she was deeply moved and that her eyes had filled with tears.

'I'll go back for the luncheon basket,' he said, 'if you'll find a place for us to sit. Here's the rug.'

When he turned back he saw that she had gone farther up the river-bed and was sitting in shade, close to the stream. She sat very still and it was impossible to guess at her mood from her posture. As he walked towards her, he wondered of what she thought. He saw her hands move up and pull off the black London hat. In a moment she turned her head and waved to him. When he reached her side he saw that she had been crying.

'Well,' said Alleyn, 'how do you feel about lunch? They've given me a billy to make the authentic brew of tea – I thought you would insist on that, but if you're not tourist-minded, there's some sort of white wine. Anyway we'll make a fire because it smells pleasant. Will you unpack the lunch while I attempt to do my great open spaces stuff with sticks and at least three boxes of matches?'

She could not answer, and he knew that at last the sprightly, vague, delightfully artificial Carolyn had failed her, and that she was left alone with herself and with him.

He turned away, but her voice recalled him.

'You won't believe it,' she was saying. 'Nobody will believe it – but I was so fond of my Alfie-pooh.'

181

CHAPTER 18

Duologue

Alleyn did not at once reply. He ws thinking that by a sort of fluke he was about to reach a far deeper layer of Carolyn's personality than was usually revealed. It was as though the top layers of whimsicality and charm and gaiety had become transparent and through them appeared – not perhaps the whole innermost Carolyn but at least a part of her. 'And this because she is unhappy and I have jerked her away from her usual background and brought her to a place where the air is very clear and heady, and there is the sound of a mountain stream and the voice of a bird with a note like a little gong.'

Aloud he said:

'But I can believe it very easily. I thought you seemed fond of him.'

He began to break up a branch of dry driftwood.

'Not romantically in love with him,' continued Carolyn. 'My poor fat Alfie! He was not a romantic husband, but he was so kind and understanding. He never minded whether I was amusing or dull. He thought it impossible that I could be dull. I didn't have to bother about any of that.'

Alleyn laid his twigs between two flat stones and tucked a screw of paper under them.

'I know,' he said. 'There are people to whom one need not show off. It's a great comfort sometimes. I've got one of that kind.'

'Your wife! But I didn't know—'

Alleyn sat back on his heels and laughed. 'No, no. I'm talking about a certain Detective-Inspector Fox. He's large and slow and innocently straightforward. He works with me at the Yard. I never have to show off to old Fox, bless him. Now let's see if it will light. You try, while I fill the billy.'

He went down to the creek and, standing on a boulder, held the billy against the weight of the stream. The water was icy cold and swift-running, and the sound of it among the stones was so loud that it seemed to flow over his senses. Innumerable labials all sounding together with a deep undertone that muttered among the boulders. It was pleasant to lift the brimming billy out of the creek and to turn again towards the bank where Carolyn had lit the fire. A thin spiral of smoke rose from it, pungent and aromatic.

'It's alight – it's going!' cried Carolyn, 'and doesn't it smell good?'

She turned her face up to him. Her eyes were still dimmed with tears, her hair was not quite smooth, her lips parted tremulously. She looked beautiful.

'I would be so happy,' she said, 'if there was nothing but this.'

Alleyn set the can of water on the stones and built up the fire. They moved away from it and lit cigarettes.

'I am glad you do not go into ecstasies over nature,' said Alleyn. 'I was rather afraid you would.'

'I expect I should have – yesterday. Dear Mr Alleyn, will you ask me all your questions now? I would like to get it over, if you don't mind.'

But Alleyn would not ask his questions until they had lunched, saying that he was ravenous. They had white wine with their lunch, and he brewed his billy-tea to take the place of coffee. It was smoky but unexpectedly good. He wondered which of them was dreading most the business that was to come. She helped him to pack up their basket and then suddenly she turned to him:

'Now, please. The interview.'

For perhaps the first time in his life, Alleyn found himself unwilling to carry his case a step further. He had set the stage deliberately, hoping to bring about precisely this attitude in Carolyn. Here she was, taken away from her protective background, vulnerable, and not unfriendly and yet—

He thrust his hand into his pocket and pulled out a little box. He opened it and laid it on the rug between them.

'My first question is about that. You can touch it if you like. It has been "finger-printed".'

Inside the box lay the little green tiki.

'Oh!—' It was an involuntary exclamation, he would have sworn. For a second she was simply surprised. Then she seemed to go very still. 'Why, it's my tiki – you've found it. I'm so glad.' The least fraction of a pause. 'Where was it?'

'Before I tell you where it was, I want to ask you if you remember what you did with it before we sat down at the table.'

'But I have already told you. I don't remember. I think I left it on the table.'

'And if I should tell you that I know you slipped it inside your dress?'

Another long pause. The fire crackled, and above the voice of the stream sounded the note of the solitary bird.

'It is possible. I don't remember.'

'I found it on the floor of the gallery above the stage.'

She was ready for that. Her look of astonishment was beautifully done. With her hands she made a gesture eloquent of bewilderment.

'But I don't understand. In the grid? How did it get there?'

'I suggest that it dropped out of your dress.'

How frightened she was! Cold nightmarish panic was drowning her before his eyes.

'I don't know – what – you – mean.'

'Indeed you do. You can refuse to answer me if you think it wise.' He waited a second. 'My next question is this: Did you go up into the grid before the catastrophe?'

'*Before!*' The relief was too much for her. The single word, with its damning emphasis, was spoken before she could command herself. When it was too late she said quietly: 'No. I did not go up there.'

'But afterwards? Ah, don't try!' cried Alleyn. 'Don't try to patch it up. Don't lie. It will only make matters worse for you and for him.'

'What do you mean? I don't understand.'

'You don't understand! Tell me this. Was that morning in your dressing-room the only time Hambledon asked you if you would marry him, supposing your husband to be dead?'

'Who told you this story? What morning?'

'The morning you arrived in Middleton. Your conversation was overheard. Now, please answer. Believe me I know altogether too much for there to be anything but disaster in your evasion. You will damage yourself and Hambledon, perhaps irrevocably, if you try to hold out.' He paused staring at his own thin hands clasped about his knees. 'You think, of course, that I am trying to trap you, to frighten you into a sort of confession. That may be true, but it is equally true that I am trying to help you. Can you believe that?'

'I don't know. I don't know.'

'The local police have heard the story of your conversation with Hambledon. They know where the tiki was found. They will learn, soon enough, that you had it on your person after the supper-party. And believe me, they will regard any further attempts at evasion with the very greatest suspicion.'

'What have I done!'

'Shall I tell you what I believe you to have done last night? After the catastrophe you went to your dressing-room. At first the shock was too great for you to think at all clearly, but after a minute or two you did begin to think. Hambledon had taken you to your dressing-room. In a minute I would like you to tell me what he said to you. Like everyone in the cast but yourself, he had been told about the champagne bottle, and knew how it was to be worked. Whatever he may have said, you sent him away saying that you wanted to be quite alone. I think that almost at once

185

the suspicion came into your mind, the suspicion that Hambledon may have brought about the catastrophe. I know that as you left the stage you heard Gascoigne repeating that there had been foul play, that it could not have been an accident. You have told me that you are familiar with the mechanics of the stage, that very often you have actually helped with the scenery. I wonder if you thought you would go up to the grid and find out for yourself. Everyone else was in the dressing-rooms except Mason, Gascoigne, Dr Te Pokiha, and myself, and we were still on the stage, hidden behind the walls of the set. Perhaps you were still too shocked and agitated to think very coherently or wisely; but overwhelmed with this dreadful suspicion, scarcely aware of the risk you ran, you may have slipped round to the back of the stage and climbed the ladder to the gallery.'

He paused for a moment, watching her. Her head was bent down and inclined away from him. Her fingers plucked at the fringe of the rug.

'Stop me if I'm wrong,' said Alleyn. 'I fancy you climbed up to the grid and saw the end of the rope close to the pulley, and perhaps tripped over the weights which had been left on the gallery floor. With your knowledge of stage mechanics you at once realised what had been done. The counterweight had been removed and the bottle had fallen unchecked.'

A strand of the woollen fringe broke in her fingers.

'At this moment we had all moved off the stage into the wings. With some distracted notion of trying to make the whole thing look like an accident you hooked a weight to the ring. While you stooped to pick up the weight, the tiki fell from your dress on to the platform, and lodged between the slats where I found it soon afterwards. Am I right?'

'I – I – would rather not answer.'

'That is as you choose. I must tell you that I am bound to lay this theory before the local police. I have perhaps exceeded my duty in talking about it to you. You asked me last night if I was your friend. I told you that I would give you my help if in return you would give me your confidence. I assure you very solemnly that it is as your friend I urge you to tell me the truth and – really it is the only phrase that fits – the whole truth and nothing but the truth.'

'They can't prove any of this,' she said vehemently. 'Why shouldn't this weight have been there all the time? Why shouldn't it have been an accident? If it was too light—'

'But how did you know it was too light?'

She caught in her breath with a sort of sob.

'You see,' said Alleyn gently, 'you are not cut out for this sort of thing. So you knew it was much too light when you hooked it on? That was very quick and very intelligent. How did you know that? I wonder. The whole scheme had been kept a secret from you—'

Suddenly he stopped, resting his elbow on the ground beside her, and looked into her averted face.

'So you knew about the plan all the time?' he said softly.

She was trembling, now, as though she were very cold. He touched her hand lightly, impersonally.

'Poor you,' said Alleyn.

Then she was clinging to his hand and weeping very bitterly.

'I've been wicked – a fool – I ought never – now you'll suspect him more than before – more than if I had done nothing. You'll think I know. I don't know anything. He's innocent. It was only because I was so shocked. I was mad even to dream of it. He couldn't do that – to Alfie. You must believe me – he couldn't. I was mad.'

'We don't suspect Hambledon more than anyone else.'

'Is that true? Is it? *Is it?*'

'Yes.'

'If I hadn't blundered in, perhaps you would never have suspected him? It's my fault—'

187

'Not quite that. But you have made it a bit more complicated; you and your fancy touches.'

'If only you would believe me – if only I could put it right—'

'If Hambledon is innocent you can put a number of things right by answering my questions. There, that's better. Look here, I'm going to give you ten minutes to dry your eyes and powder your nose. Then I'll come back and finish what I've got to say.'

He jumped lightly to his feet, and without another word strode off towards the little gorge where the bush came down to the lip of the stream. He turned uphill, and after a short climb, he entered into the bush. It was all that remained of a tall forest. Boles of giant trees stood like rooted columns among the heavy green underbrush, and rose high above it into tessellated clusters of heavy green. Light and dull green were the tree-ferns, light and dull green the ferns underfoot. There was something primal and earthy about this endless interlacing of greens. It was dark in the bush, and cool, and the only sound there was the sound of trickling water, finding its way downhill to the creek. There was a smell of wet moss, of cold wet earth, and of the sticky sweet gum that sweated out of some of the tree trunks. Alleyn thought it a good smell, clean and pungent. Suddenly, close at hand, the bird called again – a solitary call, startlingly like a bell. Then this unseen bird shook from its throat a phrase of notes in a minor key, each note very round with something human in its quality.

The brief song ended in a comic splutter. There was a sound of twigs. Then the call rang again and was answered from somewhere deep in the bush, and back into the silence came the sound of running water.

To Alleyn, standing there, it suddenly seemed absurd that he should have withdrawn into such a place as this, to think of criminal investigation and to allow a woman time to recover from the effects of her own falsehoods. It was an absurd juxtaposition of opposites. The sort of thing a very modern poet might fancy. 'The Man from the Yard in the Virgin Bush.' 'I should have worn a navy-blue suit, tan boots and a bowler, and I should complete the picture by blowing on a police whistle in answer to that intolerably lovely bird. Mr Rex Whistler would do the accompanying decorations. I'll give her another five minutes to think it over and, if the spell works, she'll come as clean as the week's wash.' He felt in his pocket for his pipe and his fingers encountered the box that held the tiki. He took the squat little monster out. 'This is the right setting for you, only you should hang on a flaxen cord against a thick brown skin like Te Pokiha's. No voluptuous whiteness for you, under black lace, against a jolting heart. That was all wrong. You little monstrosity! Sweaty dark breasts for you, dark fingers, dark savages in a heavy green forest. You've seen a thing or two in your day. Last night was not your first taste of blood, I'll be bound. And now you've got yourself mixed up in a *pakeha* killing. I wish to hell I knew how much you do mean.'

He lit his pipe and leant against the great column of a tree. The stillness of the place was like the expression of some large and simple personality. It seemed to say 'I am' with a kind of vast tranquillity. 'It is quite inhuman,' he thought, 'but it is not unfriendly.' He remembered hearing tales of bushmen who were brought far into the forest to mark trees for sawmills, and who were left to work there for a week but returned in three days, unable to endure the quiet of the forest.

It was easier to think of these things than of the murder of Alfred Meyer, and Alleyn was repopulating the bush with wandering Maoris, when he was startled by the sound of snapping twigs and hurried footsteps.

It was Carolyn, stumbling, in her thin shoes and fine black dress, through the tangled underbrush. She did not see him for several seconds and there was that in her face which made him feel that he must not watch her unseen.

'Hullo!' he called. 'Here I am.'

She turned, saw him, and stumbled towards him.

'I saw you come in here. I couldn't bear to be alone. It's quite true – everything you said. I'll tell you everything, but Hailey is innocent. I'll tell you everything.'

CHAPTER 19

Carolyn Moves Centre

Carolyn told her story as they sat by the sweet-smelling embers of the fire. The sun was bright on the river-bed, but it was still too early in the spring for the day to be unpleasantly hot. As she began to speak, a man came down the gully, followed by three panting sheep-dogs. The man's old felt hat was tilted over his nose. His jacket was slung across his shoulder and his shirt was open at the neck. He carried a long stick and moved with a sort of loose-jointed ease, as though he had been walking for a long time but was not particularly tired. Against the white glare of the shingle his face and arms were vermilion. He gave them 'good day' with a sideways wag of his head. The dogs trotted past with an air of preoccupation, saliva dripping from their quivering tongues.

'I suppose,' thought Alleyn, 'he imagines we are a courting pair and wonders if he has interrupted an amorous scene, instead of—'

'—so I was frightened,' Carolyn went on when the musterer was beyond earshot. 'You see there had been another scene that morning – yesterday morning. I can't believe it was only yesterday – my birthday. Hailey brought me my present. Something I said started him off again. We were alone in my sitting-room. Alfie had just gone out. He – he was all thrilled about his party and he kissed me before he went and was rather possessive. I think that upset Hailey. He was angry and then – violently demonstrative. He said he'd got to the end of his tether – all the old things over again only he was so – so vehement. I wish I was better at explaining myself – I am afraid to tell you exactly what he said because then you may not understand how I can be so certain, now, that Hailey is innocent. You will think I am only *saying* I know he is innocent because there is nothing else left for me to do.'

'Try me,' suggested Alleyn.

'I must try to explain myself first, my own thoughts from the time Hailey left me yesterday morning until after last night. The next thing to tell you is that, in a way, I knew about the champagne. My poor old boy!' Her voice shook for a moment and her lips parted in an uncertain smile. 'He tried so hard to keep it a secret but he was bursting with mysterious hints. I knew there was some plan, and yesterday morning I went down to the theatre and walked in at the stagedoor when they were in the middle of rehearsing the surprise. He and George, and Ted and Hailey, and some of the staff. That – that horrible thing – the champagne – you know – must have been hanging there, but out of sight, and they had the weights on the other end of the cord. There were two weights on it and Alfie said: "That's pounds too much. Take it off." I couldn't think what it was about and I just stood watching. They didn't see me. Ted Gascoigne took one weight off and the other shot up. They just grabbed it in time. It was very funny – seeing them all rush at it. Alfie swore frightfully and I stayed to see, thinking I'd rag him about it afterwards. At last they found the right weight – a single big one. We use three in the first act, you know. The masts and funnels of the yacht are let down with the small ones and the big one is used as a guide for the bridge. They are painted different colours to distinguish them. When they are not in use they are left up above. I heard them say this while I watched. It sounds as though it was a long time but it was only a few moments, I think, before he – my husband – turned and saw me. I said: "What do you funnies think you are up to?" and he became so mysterious, I guessed it was something to do with me. I didn't let them see that I guessed – he would have been so disappointed.'

She paused, compressing her lips. She raised her hand and pressed the palm against her mouth.

'Take it easy,' said Alleyn.

'Yes. When I saw the cord fastened to the table, I guessed it was something to do with all this business with the weights. Then afterwards – afterwards! Mr Alleyn, I think I went a little mad after it had happened. I could only see three things, and I saw them so horribly clearly, like the things one sees in nightmares. Hailey, angry and excited yesterday morning, Hailey, looking on while they fixed the weights, and – and what happened. That last picture. I sent him away from my dressing-room and then I got rid of Susie. I went out to the stage and I could hear Ted say over and over again: "There must have been some funny business." I think he was speaking to you. I thought I must see for myself there and then. In a way my mind was quite clear but it was a sort of delirious clarity. I went round to the back of the stage, took my shoes off, and climbed the ladder. When I reached the top platform I saw at once that the weight had been taken off the hook. I remembered how the smaller weight had shot up, and I thought: "If I put it on, it will look like an accident. It will look as if, in the hurry after the first act, they used the small weight instead of the large one." The stage down below was clear. I was just going to do it when I heard someone climbing the ladder on the prompt-side. That was just after Hailey had left the stage, and I thought it was Hailey. I stayed still but whoever it was—'

'Me,' said Alleyn.

'You? Oh, what a fool I was! I thought it was Hailey. You went away without getting off the ladder. Then I crept along the platform. I could see the stage. Ted had gone to meet the police – I heard him speak to them. No one was on the stage. I hooked on the small weight – I knew it would be ever so much lighter than even the empty bottle. Then I went down. Ted was still speaking to the detectives. They had gone on the stage and you were standing in the first entrance. I slipped round behind a flat into the dressing-room passage. When I got to my room, Hailey was there. He said he had been waiting there for me, and I told him I had been looking for him, and I sent him for Susie, and then for you.'

'Yes,' said Alleyn. 'That all fits. Now will you tell me, please, what made you change your mind. Why are you now so certain that he is innocent?'

'Because – this is what you will find so strange – because of what he said to me last night when we got back to the hotel. He said: "Carolyn, someone has killed Alfred. There's not a possibility of accident. Someoone has altered the weights." We were both quiet for a moment and then he said: "Yesterday – this morning – if I had known he was going to die I would have thought of you and – what I might gain – and now – I can only think of him." As soon as he had spoken it was as though my brain cleared. I cannot describe how it was. I simply knew that he was quite innocent. I was so ashamed that I had ever thought he might be anything else. He stayed a little while, talking quietly about Alfie and our early days together. When he went away he said' – for a moment the deep voice faltered. Then she made an impatient movement with her head. 'He said: "You know I love you, Carolyn, but I am glad now that we did nothing to hurt him."'

There was a long pause. Carolyn seemed to be lost in her own thoughts. She had become much more composed, and Alleyn thought that while she was alone she must have deliberately set in order the events that she had made up her mind to relate. He realised that physically, as well as emotionally, she was exhausted.

'Shall we go back?' he asked gently.

'First tell me: Can you – do you understand how certain I am of Hailey's innocence? Does what I have said count at all?'

'Yes. It has impressed me very deeply. I am quite sure that you have told me what you believe to be the truth.'

'But you – what do you believe?'

'You must remember that I am a policeman. I attach a great deal of importance to what you have told me, but I would like very much to establish an alibi for the period before the supper-party.'

'For Hailey?'

'For Hambledon, certainly.'

He looked at her. 'Has she got no thought at all for herself?' he wondered. 'Can't she see? Or is she, after all, very, very clever?'

'Hailey was in his dressing-room,' said Carolyn. 'It is next to mine. I heard him send his dresser away. Wait! Wait! Let me think. Last night when that detective asked me questions I could only think about the other time. Wait! When he told Bob – that's his dresser – that he could go, I said to Minna, my maid, that I could manage without her. She helped me off with my dress and then she went out, and she and Bob were talking in the passage. I called out to her to hurry and get ready, and she went off, I think to Susie's room. Then – yes, I called out to Hailey through the wall and he answered. He answered.'

'What did you say?'

'Something about – what was it! – Yes. I said: "Hailey – I've just remembered. I've asked the Woods to the party and nobody knows. How awful!" And he called back: "Not Woods – Forrest." I always call people by their wrong names, you see. Then I asked him to go and tell someone about the Forrests and he said he would as soon as he had taken off his make-up. He said he had got grease-paint on his collar and would have to put on a clean one. We had to shout to hear each other. Someone else will have heard. Who is on the other side of Hailey?'

'We'll find out. Go on, please. After that?'

She held her head between her hands.

'After that? Wait. Bob was outside in the passage, whistling. I remember thinking: "It's in the passage so it doesn't matter."'

'But – what do you mean?'

'It's unlucky to whistle in the dressing-room. Bob stood there – he must have been just inside the doorway to the stage, because I heard him call out every now and then to the stage-hands. I remember thinking that he was evidently not going to bother about tidying himself for the party. He is a great "character" and has been with us for years.'

'Yes, yes,' said Alleyn quickly. 'Go on. Let me have the whole story – give me a clear picture of everything. You are all in your rooms, taking off the make-up. Bob is just outside your door, in the entrance from the stage to the passage. You hear him chaffing the stage-hands. How long was he there? Can you tell me that?'

She glanced at him in surprise.

'I don't know. Why – yes – yes – oh!' Suddenly her whole face was flooded with a kind of tragic thankfulness.

'Listen – listen. Bob was still there when Hailey went out. I heard Hailey say something about why wasn't he on the stage with the party. Bob said: "I don't like butting in, sir. Not my place," and I heard Hailey say: "Nonsense, you're all invited. Come along with me, and we'll make an entrance together." That was like Hailey – he's always considerate with the staff, and nice to them. But Bob was shy and hung back. I heard him say he would wait for Minna. He stayed there. So, don't you see, if Hailey had gone out before, and come back, Bob would have seen him, and when he *did* go he asked Bob to go with him? Don't you see it means Hailey could not have thought of going up to the grid? Why didn't I remember it before – oh, why didn't I!'

'I wish very much that you had. Never mind. How much longer did Bob stay there?'

'I heard the others speak to him as they went past. I don't know how many of them. That was before Hailey went out. But that doesn't matter. It's Hailey that matters – he would never have asked Bob to go with him if he meant to go up into the grid, and besides, I am sure it was too late then. If he had done it he would have gone out before, and Bob would have seen him.'

'Was Bob there when you went out?'

196

'I don't think so. Hailey and George and – and Alfie came for me. We met in the passage.'

'Tell me,' said Alleyn, 'why did you stay so long in your room?'

Something – the faintest shadow – of the old mischievous look, returned to Carolyn's face. He was reminded of that night in the train when she had looked out of one eye at him.

'I wanted to come on last,' she said. 'It was my party.'

'You deliberately delayed your entrance?'

'Of course I did. I remember wishing Bob *would* go. I heard Minna come along and they stood there talking. I wanted *everybody* – but *everybody* – to be on the stage.' She stared thoughtfully at Alleyn. 'It seems so incredible now, me waiting there to make a big entrance, but you see I *am* Carolyn Dacres. I don't suppose you understand.'

'Yes, yes, I do,' cried Alleyn with sudden exasperation, 'but can't you see, you divine donkey, that I want to get your alibi established!'

'Mine?' She caught her breath and then said softly: 'Yes, I do see. For a moment I had forgotten to be frightened about – me.'

'I hope that you will have no need to be frightened. I must see Bob, at once. Come on – get up. We're going back.'

He stood up and held out his hands.

She gave him hers and rose lightly to her feet. They stood for a moment facing each other, hand-fasted as though they were lovers. Her fingers tightened round his. He thought:

'Damn! She *is* attractive.'

She said: 'I hope for only one thing, Mr Alleyn – that you will soon believe us innocent and then I shall be able to be sorrowful.'

'I understand that.'

'It is so strange. I keep thinking "Pooh will tell me how to get out of this fix!" I only realise with my mind – not yet with my heart. Perhaps that sounds rather trite and affected but I can't find other words.'

'Indeed, I understand.' She still held his hands.

'Somehow at these sorts of times, after one has had a great shock, I mean, one speaks one's thoughts openly. I do feel, in the most strange way, that we are friends.'

'Yes,' said Alleyn.

She gave him a candid and gentle smile and withdrew her hands.

'Come along then. Let us return to – everything.'

He collected the rug and basket and they walked together to the car, the voice of the creek growing fainter as they drew away from it. The sun was near the edge of the warm hill and soon their little gully would slip in to the shade of afternoon. Carolyn paused and looked back.

'It is a lovely place,' she said. 'In spite of everything I shall think of it with pleasure. The painfulness of all this does not seem to have touched it at all.'

'No,' said Alleyn, 'it is very remote. We were interlopers but vaguely welcome, don't you think?'

'Yes. It is a friendly place, really.'

'Are you very tired?'

'I believe I am.'

'No sleep last night?'

'No.'

They got into the car which smelt of hot leather and petrol, and bumped over the rough up to the road.

On the way home they were both silent, Alleyn thinking to himself: 'I really believe her. I believe her story. I believe she feels just what she said – a kind of friendliness for me, no more. Was she quite unaware that she attracted me so vividly for those few moments, or was she using her charm deliberately? Is she is love with Hambledon? Probably.'

With an effort he screwed his thoughts round to the case. If this story about Bob was true, and if Bob turned out to be an intelligent fellow, they should be able to check the movements of the actors with much more accuracy than Alleyn had thought possible. As soon as he got back, he would look again at his plan of the theatre. He was practically certain that the passage was the only source of

198

exit from the dressing-rooms to the stage, therefore anyone of the company who went from the dressing-rooms to the ladder, would have to go past Bob as he stood in the narrow entry. If Bob could only tell him exactly how long he had stood there!

They passed the musterer, riding a half-clipped, raky-looking horse at a lope along the rough grass at the roadside. The three panting sheep-dogs ran in the shade of the horse. The man again solemnly wagged his head at them and raised a hand as they passed. The folding hills marched about. A party of Maoris, grouped on a ramshackle veranda, grinned and waved. They overtook several cars and met several more. The settlements grew closer together, and at length they came over the brow of the last hill, and looked across the flat to Middleton.

'Last lap,' said Alleyn, breaking a long silence.

Carolyn did not answer. He turned to look at her. Her head was bent down and, as heavily as a mandarin's, nodded with the motion of the car. She was sound asleep. At the next bend she swayed towards him. With an equivocal grimace he raised his left hand and tipped her head against his shoulder. She did not wake until the car drew up outside the hotel.

CHAPTER 20

Exit Liversidge. Enter Bob Parsons (whistling)

As soon as he had put Carolyn into the lift, Alleyn glanced into the writing-room. Should he try and get off a couple of letters for the English mail, or should he look up Wade and give him an account of the interview with Carolyn? He hovered uncertainly in the doorway, and then noticed George Mason, bent over one of the writing-tables, hard at work. Alleyn strolled across and seated himself at a neighbouring desk.

'Oh, hullo,' said Mason abstractedly. 'Have a nice day?'

Without waiting for an answer, he suddenly burst into a recital of his woes.

'I don't know what I'm doing, Alleyn. I'm all anyhow. I don't know what to tell our advance to do – whether to go on with the tour or cancel everything. And there's all the English end to attend to. I'm going crazy just with not knowing. How long do you think they'll keep us here, for God's sake?'

'Things are looking a bit clearer ahead now,' said Alleyn. 'The local men seem to be very efficient.'

'It's awful to be worrying about the business side of it with old Alf – Well, there it is. The whole thing's so damn' beastly. Everybody wondering about everybody else. No use mincing matters. Someone did it. It's this blasted *uncertainty*.'

'I know,' said Alleyn. 'I say, Mason, you know I've taken a hand in it, don't you?'

'Yes. Very glad to hear it.'

'Well, look here, I'm going to ask you a question in confidence.' Mason looked alarmed. 'You needn't answer if you don't want to, but it'd help matters a lot if you could tell me one thing.'

'Can but ask.'

'Right. Did Mr Meyer know who took Miss Gaynes's money?'

Mason stared at him like a dyspeptic owl.

'Matter of fact, he did,' he said at last.

'You know who it was?'

'Alfred told me,' said Mason uncomfortably. 'It was a question of what we'd do. Damned awkward in the beginning of a tour like this.'

'Yes. Will you tell me who it was?'

Mason eyed him unhappily but shrewdly.

'What'll it lead to? Look here, Alleyn, you're not trying to link up the theft and the murder, are you?'

'Personally, I long to disassociate them.'

'By jove!' said Mason slowly. 'I – wonder.'

'When did Mr Meyer guess who took the money?'

'Oh, Lor' – he saw it happen.'

'Did he, indeed! Come now, I'll put it to you, as our learned friends say. I'll put one name to you, and one name only. If I'm wrong, let it drop. I promise not to go on.'

'All right!' agreed Mason, looking rather relieved.

'Liversidge?'

There was a long silence.

'Oh, Lor',' repeated Mason, 'I thought you were going to say Broadhead. After young Palmer's display, you know.'

'How did Mr Meyer come to see it?'

'It was on board – the last night. Alfred was going along the passage to his state-room and passed Val's door. He'd just seen her in the smoke-room. He heard someone moving about in her cabin and thought it was a funny time for the stewardess to be in there. Then he noticed that her light wasn't up – there's a thick glass fanlight, you know. Alfred saw a sort of flicker as if someone had an electric torch going. He was standing there, uncertain what to do, when the door opened a crack. Opposite the door there was a man's lav. with curtains in front of the entrance place. Alfred popped behind them and watched. He thought perhaps one of the stewards was doing the odd spot of pinching. Well, presently the door of Val Gaynes's room opened wider, and out came Mr Frankie Liversidge, very pussyfoot and cautious. Alf said it was just like a scene from one of the old French farces, and of course, he thought the explanation was the same.'

Mason pulled a face, and then rubbed his nose thoughtfully.

'Do go on,' said Alleyn.

'Well, here's the bit that'll sound rather peculiar, I dare say. You'd never have thought it after thirty years in the business, but Alfred was a bit straightlaced. Fact! He wouldn't stand for any funny business in any of his companies. I know it sounds queer,' said Mason apologetically, 'but that's how he was. Well, what did he do but come out through the curtains and fetch up, face-to-face, with Liversidge. He just stood there and stared at Liversidge reproachfully, and was cogitating what he'd say to him about the way nice young girls were to be held in respect or something, when Frankie said: "I've been making an apple-pie bed for Val." Frankie's face was as white as a sheet and he had his hands in his pockets. Alfie didn't say a word, and Frankie gave a kind of laugh and made an exit. What do you think old Alfred did next?'

'Had a look at the bed to see if it was in apple-pie order?'

'Got it in one,' said Mason, opening his eyes very wide. 'And it wasn't. I mean it was. All tidy and undisturbed. Nothing wrong with it. Well, Alfred toddled off to his own room and did a bit of hard thinking. He decided that Liversidge had been waiting there for Val and had changed his mind, for some reason. Alfred thought he'd watch the situation for a bit, and speak a few heavy-father lines to Val, if they seemed to be called for. That was that. Then came the discovery of the theft and Alf put two and two together and made a burglary.'

'When did he tell you about it?'

'The first evening we were here. He told me he'd tackled Liversidge and there was no doubt he'd done it. God knows why. He'd won a lot at poker. He's just a bad 'un. Well, Alfred said he'd pay it back to Val and stop it out of Liversidge's treasury. And of course Liversidge would go as soon as we could get a decent actor from Australia to play the parts. For the sake of the good name of Incorporated Playhouses he wouldn't make it public. I agreed and that was that. Now look, Alleyn, I've told you as much as I know myself but, if you can, keep it to yourself. The Firm—'

'I understand that. If it doesn't belong to the case we won't press it,' said Alleyn at once. He added a word or two to something he had written while Mason was talking.

'There's just one more thing,' he said. 'Did Mr Meyer get the impression that Liversidge knew he hadn't got away with the apple-pie bed story? At the same time, I mean?'

'I see what you mean. Alfred said Liversidge turned very white as soon as he saw him and seemed very uncomfortable. Alfred just stared at him, sort of more in sorrow than in anger. I don't think he made any pretence of believing the story. He said Frankie's face gave him away.'

'I see,' said Alleyn slowly. 'See here, Mr Mason, I'll have to hand this on to Wade, but I'll ask him not to make it public if he can avoid it. It may have no bearing on the case.'

'Damn' fair of you. Though now we've got murder in the Firm, my God, I suppose we can't be too fussy about an odd theft or so.' And Mason buried his face in his hands.

'I'm dead beat,' he said. 'I feel as if I'd got a red-hot cannon-ball in my chest and half a ton of sawdust in my stomach.'

'Can't you do anything about it?'

'I've seen half the men in Harley Street. I wonder if Te Pokiha would know anything? Some of these natives – Are you going?'

'I must get on. I promised I'd look in at the police station. Thank you so much, Mr Mason.'

Alleyn walked up the hill to the police station, where he

found Wade and Superintendent Nixon. He gave them a full account of his interview with Carolyn and with Mason. Wade was inclined to be sceptical about Carolyn, until he heard the story of Liversidge.

'It looks the most promising thing we've got hold of up to date,' he said. 'If he thought Meyer suspected him he'd have the motive before they got on the train. I reckon it's almost good enough for a warrant, Super.'

'What do you think, Mr Alleyn?' asked Nixon.

'I think I'd hold off a bit,' said Alleyn. 'If you both agree I'll look up Liversidge and see if I can get the delicious creature to bare his nasty little soul for me. Perhaps, Mr Nixon, you would prefer to tackle this bit yourself?'

'No, no,' said Nixon quickly, 'we'll be only too pleased if you'll carry on with us, won't we, Wade?'

'Too right, sir. I want to look up old Singleton again. The stage-doorkeeper, Mr Alleyn. He's always boozy, but he's a bit less boozy at this time of day.'

'Why not ring up Liversidge and get him to come round now,' suggested Nixon, 'and we'll make a party of it?'

'Wouldn't that be fun!' said Alleyn grimly. 'All right. Let's.'

Nixon telephoned the hotel and spoke to Liversidge, who said he would 'toddle over' immediately. Alleyn and Nixon occupied the interval with a peaceful discussion on departmental shop. Liversidge arrived, looking too like a not-so-young actor to be credible.

'This is Mr Liversidge, Superintendent Nixon,' said Alleyn.

'Good afternoon,' said Liversidge grandly.

'Good afternoon, Mr Liversidge,' said Nixon. 'Will you take a seat? As you know, Mr Alleyn is very kindly working with us on this case. He has one or two questions he would like to ask you.'

'The indefatigable Mr Alleyn!' said Liversidge, seating himself gracefully. 'And what can I do for Mr Alleyn? Still worrying about what A said to B when the lights went out, Mr Alleyn?'

'Ah well,' answered Alleyn. 'It's my job, you know. As you make your apple-pie bed, so you must lie on it. Or about it, as the case may be.'

'I'm afraid that is too deep for me,' rejoined Mr Liversidge, turning an unlovely parchment colour.

'Haven't you ever made an apple-pie bed, Mr Liversidge?'

'Really!' said Liversidge. 'I didn't come here to discuss practical jokes.'

'You don't enjoy practical jokes?'

'No.'

'Did you take Miss Gaynes's money as a practical joke?'

'I simply don't know what you are talking about.'

'From information received, we learn that you took this money. Wait a moment, Mr Liversidge. I really should not bother to deny it if I were you. Denials of that sort are inclined to look rather the worse for wear in the face of the sort of evidence we have here. However—' He took out his notebook and pen. 'Did you take this money or did you not?'

'I refuse to answer.'

'Right. On the whole the most sensible thing to do. Perhaps I should tell you that after your interview with Mr Meyer on the day you arrived in Middleton, Mr Meyer had another interview with Mr Mason. It was a matter that concerned the Firm, you see.'

'What has Mason—?' Liversidge stopped short.

'What has he told us? Simply the gist of what Mr Meyer told him.'

'It was all a joke. Meyer took it the wrong way. Look here Mr – Mr Nixon—'

'You are speaking to Mr Alleyn, you know,' said Nixon, placidly.

'Yes, but – well then.' He turned, reluctantly, to Alleyn. 'It was this way. You must believe me, I swear I'm telling

205

the truth. I'd been ragging Val about the way she left her money lying about. I said she'd have it pinched. She just laughed. It was when she'd got out some notes to pay her poker debts. I went back to the cabin and I – well, I took out the money and filled up the case with – er – with – er – toilet-paper. Just for a joke to make her more careful. That was all. Honestly. *Honestly!*'

'Why didn't you tell Mr Meyer this?'

'I tried to but he wouldn't listen,' said Liversidge, moistening his lips. 'He'd got no sense of humour.'

'Pity. Why did you prompt young Palmer to accuse Broadhead of the theft?'

'I didn't – I didn't mean it that way. I told you. He took me up all wrong. It was all a joke. Can't you see it was all a joke?'

'I've got no sense of humour, either,' said Alleyn, 'but I dare say a jury would laugh till they cried.'

'A jury! My God—'

'Now, Mr Liversidge,' continued Alleyn, composedly, 'the inquest on this case will be held tomorrow. Mr Mason will, of course, be one of the witnesses. As I expect you know—'

'I don't know anything about inquests,' interrupted Liversidge, in a hurry.

'Then it will be an interesting experience for you. If you like to give us a statement – a true statement – of this affair and we find it has no direct bearing on the murder—'

'The murder! My God, I swear—'

'We may possibly not think it necessary to bring it out in evidence. If, on the other hand, you prefer that the whole thing be left until the inquest—'

'I'll make a statement,' said Liversidge, and did so there and then, signing it, and taking himself off in extreme disorder.

'You gave him a nice thrashing,' said Nixon appreciatively when Liversidge had gone.

'I still think it looks good enough for a warrant,' said

Wade. 'We've got everything, sir; motive, opportunity – everything. Meyer may even have threatened him with exposure.'

'He may,' agreed Alleyn. 'You're quite right, Wade, but all the same I *would* like to look up Hambledon's dresser, Bob Parsons. I can't help feeling his evidence may be very useful. I think we ought to have it before we crystallise on Liversidge.'

'If Liversidge prompted young Palmer to fake this charge against Broadhead,' said Nixon, 'it looks as if he's a more than usual thoroughgoing bad hat.'

'He's all that,' agreed Alleyn, 'but still—'

'Well, if you will, Mr Alleyn, do go and see Parsons,' said Nixon. 'Wade will give you his address.'

Wade produced the address.

Parsons was staying at a boarding-house close to the theatre. Alleyn went there at once, and in an atmosphere of bamboo and aspidistra he had his talk with Hambledon's dresser.

Bob Parsons was a wisp of a creature with a plaintive face that crinkled into a net of lines when he spoke. His forehead was so crossed with wrinkles that it looked as though it had been wrung out and left to dry and was badly in need of an iron. He had thin nondescript hair, a wide mouth, and a pair of very bright eyes. Alleyn liked the look of him and came directly to the point.

'I'm sorry to disturb you, Mr Parsons, but as I expect you will have heard, I am investigating this case in association with the local police. I want to ask you a few questions. I believe you may be able to help us very considerably.'

'Will you sit down, sir?'

'Thank you. Will you please tell me, as accurately as possible, what your movements were after Mr Hambledon told you to go and get ready for the supper-party last night?'

'*My* movements, sir?'

'Yes.'

'I went into the passage, sir, and watched other people working.'

'Just for a change, what? You mean the stage-hands?'

'Correct, sir. I stood in the doorway watching the boys work overtime.'

'You could see most of the stage from the doorway, I suppose?'

'I could, yes.'

'I suppose you've no idea what the time was?'

'Yes. I have so, sir. It was ten-twenty-five.'

'Good lord, how so accurate?'

'Always time the show, sir. I like to know how she runs. We rang down at ten-twenty-five, and I went straight to the dressing-room and Mr Hambledon came straight off and told me to clear out. "You'll want a clean swaller-and-sigh, sir," I said. "You've got No. 9 all over those." "Well, I can do that," he says, "and how about a clean collar and tie for yourself," he says. "What's the time?" So I told him the time – ten-twenty-six – and I went out.'

'How long were you in the passage?'

Bob screwed his face into a labyrinth of lines and thought for a moment.

'Well, sir, I rolled a fag and smoked it and I rolled another.'

'Whistling a bit, in between times?'

'That's the ticket, sir. I'm a great hand at whistling. My old Dad learnt me that forty years ago. He was a vordervil artist, "Pip Parsons, the 'Uman Hedgesparrer," and he trained me for a Child Wonder. Made me whistle for me tucker. All day he kept me at it. "Pipe up," he'd say, "there's only one place where you *can't* rehearse your stuff, and that's the dressing-room." It grew a habit and when I took on this business I had to unlearn it a good deal faster than I got it. Never do, you see, sir. Unlucky. Whistling people out of their jobs. When I first started whistling I was always being sent out to knock and come in again, to break the bad luck.'

'I see. Miss Dacres told me about this superstition.'

'Miss Carolyn's a fair terror on it, sir. Well I usually tunes up when I gets outside the door. Once through "A Bird in a Gilded Cage" while I roll me fag. That's what I did last night with the falsetto encore. Then I lights up.'

'How long does "A Bird in a Gilded Cage" take?'

'Well – can't say exactly, sir.'

'Look here – will you whistle it through now?'

'Pleased to oblige,' said Bob briskly.

Alleyn took out his stop-watch. Bob fixed his eyes on a picture of two horses being struck by lightning, assumed an expression of agonised intensity, moistened and pursed his lips. A singularly sweet roulade, in a high key, came through them.

'Just to tune up. Count it in, sir. Always do it.' His eyes glazed and he broke into the Victorian ballad, saccharine, long drawn out, and embellished with many stylish trills. The refrain was repeated an octave higher, ending on a top note that seemed to impinge on the outer rim of human hearing.

'Three minutes,' said Alleyn. 'Thank you Bob, it's a grand bit of whistling, that.'

'Used to go big in the old days, sir.'

'Yes, I can believe it did. By the time it was finished you had rolled your cigarette, and you lit it, I suppose?'

'Yes, sir.'

'Suppose you repeat the performance.'

Bob took a dilapidated tin from his pocket and from it produced a hand-made cigarette.

'Always keep some by me,' he said, and lit up. Alleyn glanced again at his watch.

'The next thing,' he said, 'is to remember who came past you from the dressing-room to the stage.'

Bob looked him straight in the eyes.

'I get the idea, sir. Watch me step here. If in doubt say so.'

'Exactly.'

'Well, when I first went out, some of them were still on the stage after the last curtain. Mr Hambledon always goes straight to his room. Mr Funny Ackroyd came along first and then old "I-Played-It-Well-Laddie," with young Broadhead.'

'Mr Vernon?'

'Yes, sir. The boys on the staff called him "I-Played-It-Well-Laddie" after his favourite remark. The last two were Mr Liversidge and Miss Gaynes. They stood talking on the stage – couldn't hear what they said – and then went past me to their rooms. I'd got to the falsetto repeat then, I remember.' Bob sucked his teeth meditatively. 'Well, sir, they was all stowed away by that time.'

'Parsons, you're a witness after my own heart. Now for when they came out.'

'Yes. Have to do a bit of thinking now. Take it easy, sir, it's on the way. Yes.' Bob shut his eyes and took a vigorous pull at his cigarette. 'The four gents was first. Mr Comedy Ackroyd, Mr Vernon, Mr Broadhead Mr Liversidge, all come out together and they stands there chaffing me and asking why I wasn't wearing a tailcoat and a white tie. Ackroyd was that funny I nearly burst out crying. Footpath comedian!'

'You don't care for Mr Ackroyd?'

'Not so's you'd make a sky-sign of it. We're human, sir, even if we do earn our treasury dressing up the great "hactors". Mr Ackroyd doesn't seem to have thought that out for himself. I got Mr Ackroyd's number a long while back. So did my gentleman, and my gentleman *is* a gentleman, sir.'

'Mr Hambledon?'

'Ah! The genu-ine ticket. He knows all about Mr Saint John Ackroyd and so did the guv'nor.'

Bob re-lit his cigarette and looked significantly at Alleyn.

'Why?' asked Alleyn. 'How do you mean?'

'It's an old yarn now, sir. Ackroyd forgot 'imself one evening when we was at the Cri. He's very partial to 'is glass of whisky at times, and 'e don't break 'is heart if there's not much water with it. This night he'd just 'ad just that much too much, and he comes into Miss Carolyn's dressing-room without so much as knocking and 'e starts up on the funny business. 'Struth! What a scene! She tells 'im orf a snorter, and then the guv'nor 'e gets wind of it and 'e comes along and 'e tells 'im orf fit to suffercate. Laugh! I was outside the door when 'e comes out, and to see 'is face! Not so blooming comic and as red as a stick of carmine. Laugh! Next day 'e 'as to apologise. 'E'd 'ave got 'is notice if it hadn't been that piece, I do believe, but 'e was playing a big part and 'is understudy was not too classy. So the show went on, but since then Mr Funny Ackroyd 'as blooming well kept 'is place. Well now, where was we? Ah, I've got it. Mr Broadhead and Played-It-Well, and Mr Liversidge and Ackroyd, they all come out in a bunch. They 'as their spot of comedy with yours truly, and then I rather fancy Ackroyd goes orf to the stage-door. Not for long though. 'E comes back and joins the others, and then they all goes on the stage, and froo the Prompt entrance to the set, see? And they never comes orf again while I'm there.'

'Sure of that?'

'Yes, sir. Sure as s'welp me. Tell you for why. I could hear them telling Mr Gascoigne what a lark they'd ad with me and how I was too shy to come to the party. Very funny, they was.'

Bob paused, his face a painful crimson.

'They sound thoroughly objectionable,' said Alleyn.

'Oh, well, there you are,' said Bob, dismissing them. 'Well, sir. After that lot, Miss Valerie Gaynes came out. She was on the look-out for Mr Liversidge as per usual, and I think she heard his voice on the stage. Anyway she made a bee-line for the door and went on. It was about the time the visitors from the front began to come in. I see you come with the guv'nor, sir, and that young Palmer and so forth. Mr Gascoigne stood by the door looking out for them – the door on the set I mean. Then Miss Max came out and stood

211

talking to me for a while. Always got a pleasant word for everybody. Then Minna come along and starts telling me orf for not 'aving changed me clobber. She's a one, old Minna. We chy-ikes a bit and I say I'll come along in me own time, see, and Minna goes back to doll 'erself up. Yes, that's right, that's 'ow she went.'

Bob paused.

'And then you joined the party, perhaps?'

'Nah! I felt kind of awkward, sir, and that's the truth. The boys – the stage-staff, you know, sir – they was all on, be that time, see? They'd been fixing the stage, see? Else I'd 'ave mucked in with them. Well, blimey, sir, it was all posh-like. Wasn't as if there was a door over on the OP. I could of slipped froo on the QT if there had of been, but there was only the one door, see? So I kind of hung fire and made another fag.'

He glanced shyly at Alleyn.

'I know. It's a bit of a facer making an entrance, isn't it?'

'That is right, sir. Then, after a bit, my gentleman comes out – Mr Hambledon – and he says, "Hullo Bob," he says, "waiting for something?" And 'e seems to tip I'm feeling silly-like and 'e says: "Come on," 'e says, "and we'll make a big entrance, Bob," 'e says. Look, 'e's all right, sir, my gentleman. 'E's very nice. But – 'struth, I couldn't go on with 'im, sir. Wouldn't be the right thing would it, now? So I says I'm waiting for Minna, and he smiles and cracks a joke, pleasant-like, and 'e goes across to the door where Mr Gascoigne is still standing. I see him say something to Mr Gascoigne and look across at me, smiling, and then 'e goes in and Mr Gascoigne shuts the door and comes over to me and says: "We're waiting for you and Minna," and then Minna comes along, and I puts out me second fag and we all goes across together and nobody notices nothing. And in about two shakes Miss Carolyn comes in and after you give 'er that 'eathen image we all sits down to supper and – and my Gawd, sir, then we know what happened, don't we?'

'We do indeed. How long is two shakes, Bob?'

'Eh? Oh! See what you mean. Well now, sir. As we goes in everybody was just asking where was Miss Carolyn. So Mr Hambledon and the guv'nor and Mr Mason they went out to get 'er, passing Minna and me in the doorway. And they came back with her almost immediate.'

Alleyn made a sudden brusque movement, leaning forward in his chair.

'Then – Bob, this is important – it's very important. You can tell me how long it was between the time Miss Dacres came out of her dressing-room and the moment of her entrance with the three men.'

'No time at all, sir. Just a jiffy. They must of met 'er in the passage.'

'And Bob! Could you swear that she came straight off the stage and didn't leave her room till she went in to the party?'

'Yes, sir. 'Course I could. Didn't I tell you I was—'

'Yes, yes, I know. It's all perfectly splendid. Now for Mr Hambledon—'

'Same for 'im, sir. Look 'ere, sir, I'm fly to what you're after. You want to know who went up aloft after the guv'nor come down. That's a fact, now, isn't it, sir?'

'It is, Bob.'

'Well, sir, it wasn't Miss Carolyn or Mr Hambledon – physically imposs., sir. They both came straight orf after the curtain call. I *see* them. And they never come out of their rooms till they goes to the party, and they goes *straight* to the party. I'll take me Bible oaf on it, kiss the book, and face the judge. Can't say fairer than that now, can I, sir?'

'No. It's good enough. Is there any way out from the dressing-rooms except past the doorway where you were standing?'

'No fear, sir. Not bloody likely, if you'll excuse the expression, sir. Beats me they don't have the fire inspectors down on them. There's just the two rows of dressing-rooms downstairs, with the wardrobe-room at the end. The two star-rooms and Miss Max's room all open orf the passage.

Then it goes round at right angles with the wardrobe-room on the right and the three other dressing-rooms on the left.'

'Yes, I know.'

'Yes. So that Mr Comedy Ackroyd's room runs behind the two star-rooms and Miss Max's. Suits 'im a fair treat; 'e can do 'is nosy-parkering nice with them wooden walls. I went to 'is room only the day we got 'ere, and there 'e was, standing on the table with 'is shell-like glued to the wall and 'is eyes shut, tuned in to Miss Carolyn and my gentleman what were 'aving a little pass-the-time-o'-day next door. Never saw me, 'e didn't, but when I goes back I call arht to Miss Carolyn they're getting near 'er entrance and she comes away, see? Mr Saint John Ackroyd!'

Alleyn remembered Ackroyd's version of this incident and chuckled appreciatively.

'And there's no door at the far end of this back passage?'

'No, sir. Only a little window. All gummed up with dirt and cobwebs.'

'Big enough for someone to get through?'

''Ave to be very small, sir, and then it'd be a squeeze.'

'I'll have a look at it. Thank you very much, Bob. Nobody ever calls you Mr Parsons, do they?'

'Lord love you, sir, I sometimes forget I got another moniker. Might almost be an iggyliterate if you'll excuse the bit of fun. Going, sir?'

'Yes – I won't keep you any longer. It's after hours so we can't have a drink, but if you'll allow me—'

'Well, sir, that's very kind of you, but I'm sure I don't want anything. If it's a case of my gentleman, and looking after 'im, well I'm used to doing that and it's a pleasure.'

'I'm sure it is, but don't make me feel uncomfortable, Bob. Just to show you bear me no ill-will.'

'If you put it like that, sir – well, thank you very much, sir. Goodnight, sir, and I'm sure I hope you get the bloke. He was a very fair man, was the late guv'nor. Can't fancy 'ow anyone would want to bash 'is nut in, even if it was with liquor, which is a classy way of 'anding in your notice. I always says—'

Alleyn listened to a somewhat discursive reminiscence and at last got away. He had arranged to meet Wade at the theatre and found the inspector waiting for him.

'Well, Mr Alleyn. Any luck with the dresser?'

'Quite a purple patch.'

Alleyn related the gist of the information.

'By cripes!' said Wade. 'That's something to get our teeth into. How did the man strike you, sir? Reliable?'

'I think so. He's a type that will disappear before long, I'm afraid – the real undiluted cockney. Undersized, sharp as they make them, loyal, independent, and violently opinionated. You should hear him on the subject of Ackroyd. We'll be able to check his statements, I think. I timed his cigarette – sixteen minutes – he had to keep re-lighting it. The whistled song took three minutes so that takes us to a quarter to eleven. He made and lit another cigarette, which he put out before joining the party – say three more minutes, which would mean twelve minutes to eleven when he left the passage. Now when everyone started asking for Miss Dacres, Mr Meyer looked at his watch and said: "It's ten to – time she was making an entrance," and about two minutes later she appeared. If Bob Parsons was in the passage all that time, she can't have done it.'

'Unless he's fixing an alibi for her, or for Hambledon.'

'We'll have to check his statement, of course. But if all these people remember talking to him, it'll be good enough. Personally, I was favourably impressed with him.'

Wade stared solemnly at Alleyn and then swore violently.

'Good heavens, Wade, what's the matter?'

'Here!' said Wade. 'If all he said is right, it – Look here, Mr Alleyn, don't you see what it means?'

'Oh, rather, yes. It washes out the whole bang lot of 'em

at one fell swoop. Tiresome for you. Unless of course the little window—'

'We'll go right along and have a look at the little window. By gosh, talk about eliminating! This is a bit too sudden. What about Liversidge?'

'Bang he goes,' said Alleyn.

'Liversidge – with everything pointing that way! Not only that. Liversidge, Broadhead, the wife and Hambledon. Mason tied up with enough alibis to blow holes in a cast-iron case! Come on, sir. Come on. We'll have a damn' good look at this little window.'

CHAPTER 21

Business with Props

But the little window at the back of the dressing-room passage turned out to be exactly as Bob had described it – dirty and gummed up with cobwebs – and Wade turned to Alleyn with an air of disgruntled incredulity.

'It's a case of "where do we go for honey," isn't it, Wade?' asked Alleyn smiling.

'I'll see this Bob Parsons as soon as we get out of this,' said Wade. 'If anyone's squared him I'll shake it out of him if I have to go at it all night.'

'It's possible, of course,' agreed Alleyn, 'but look at it for a minute. Suppose Liversidge is the murderer. Liversidge plans to take off the weight. Instead of slipping round, unseen, to the back ladder after the last curtain, which would have been comparatively easy, he goes first to his dressing-room, knowing that he must come out again almost immediately into the brightly-lit narrow passage, where any of the others may be hanging about. Well, he risks that and comes out to find Parsons directly in his way. He knows that Parsons will see him go up to the back of the stage – knows, in short, that he is a man who can hang him. He decides to risk all this on the chance of bribing or corrupting the man. Do you think he'd do it? I don't. And the same argument applies to Miss Dacres. To all the rest of the cast for that matter. I think when you see Parsons you will agree that he is not a corruptible type. Check his statement by all means, my dear chap, but I feel certain he is speaking the truth. And now let us have a look at the back of the theatre.'

'The *back* of the theatre, sir?'

'Yes. When I chased round on the trail of Master Palmer, I thought of something that may be of interest. Come across the stage, will you?'

He led the way out of the dressing-room passage to the stage. They had turned on the working-lights, two desolate yellow bulbs up in the dusty proscenium, that cast a little dreary light on the tops of the box-set. Nothing had been moved. The door into the set stood open and through it they could see the white cloth, the chairs pushed back from the table, curiously eloquent, the huddle of broken glass and dead flowers, and the enormous bottle lying on the table.

'That can all be cleared away,' said Wade. 'We've gone over every inch of it today.'

'Come round behind the set,' said Alleyn.

They groped their way round. The stage smelt of old glue and dead paint. Alleyn switched on his torch and led Wade to the back wall.

'Here's the back ladder up to the grid. That, I feel sure, is the one that was used. Have you tried it for prints?'

'Yes. It's a fair muck of prints – so far, nothing that's any good to us. The stage-hands used it over and over again.'

'Of course. Well now, see here.'

In the back wall, a little to the left of the ladder, was a door.

'We noticed this on the plan,' said Alleyn, 'and discussed it as a possible entrance for – say Mason.'

'That's right, sir. But it won't wash as far as he is concerned. If Mason had gone through the audience, out at the front, and round the block, he'd have had to come in here. He would have to go aloft, do the job, come down, and sprint round the block again.'

'Ten minutes at the very least and the risk of being seen running like a madman by any number of people on the pavement outside,' said Alleyn. 'No. That cat won't jump. I saw the door last night when your PC was so suspicious of my movements. Have you got a torch? Let's have a good look at it.'

By the light of both their torches they inspected the door.

'Yale lock, with the key inside,' said Alleyn.

'We noted this door last night, Mr Alleyn. It wasn't overlooked.'

'My dear chap, I'm sure it wasn't. What did you make of it?'

'Well, seeing it was locked on the inside it doesn't look as though anyone could have used it for an entrance. And seeing that there's no exit from the dressing-rooms except to the stage, none of them could have used it for a getaway.'

'None of the cast, no.'

'You're still thinking of Mason. It's no go, sir. I wish to hell I could say otherwise, but it's no go. We've thrashed it over – every minute of it – every second of it. He was in the office at the end of the show, and was seen there by the men from the box-office. He ran along to the stage-door and gave old Singleton – the doorkeeper – the message about not letting in uninvited people. Singleton watched him go back to the office and a minute or two later joined him there. Then Dr Te Pokiha looked in. About two minutes later you overtook him yourself, on the way to the stage-door with the doctor.'

'Not with Dr Te Pokiha. He was at the party when Mr Mason and I got in.'

'Makes no odds, as far as Mason is concerned, sir.'

'That's true. Have you tried this key for prints?'

'Can't say we have.'

'It's early days yet,' murmured Alleyn, 'and you've had a lot of stuff to get through. I think if you don't mind—'

He produced an insufflator and a packet of chalk from his overcoat pocket, and by the light of their torches, tested the key for prints.

'None. It's as clean as a whistle.'

'That's funny,' said Wade, reluctantly. 'You'd have thought it would be used fairly frequently.'

'There's no dust,' said Alleyn, 'so presumably it has been wiped clean.'

Wade muttered something under his breath. Alleyn turned the key and opened the door. Outside was a dingy

219

strip of yard, and a low tin fence with a rickety gate.

'This is where I came out on my chase after Master Palmer,' explained Alleyn. 'I met the PC in the street there. This door moves very sweetly.'

He flashed his torch on the hinges.

'Nicely oiled. Commendable attention to detail on the part of the staff – what?'

'Look here, Mr Alleyn, what *are* you getting at?'

'I think we should concentrate on this door, Wade. When we've done here, we'll go and have a look at the plan in the office and I shall propound my unlikely theory.'

He squatted on his heels and peered at the threshold.

'Not much chance here. Fine night and all that. I think it might be profitable to find out who oiled the hinges. Could you try? And the doorkeeper – Singleton is it? I suppose none of the guests went in twice? No, not Mason – anyone else.'

'*Went in twice?*'

'Yes. In at the stage-door. Out by this one. In again at the stage-door. Nothing in it, I dare say.'

'None of the guests has got a motive, though,' said Wade with a certain air of desperate reluctance.

'Not so far as we know. One might advance something rather fantastic. Young Palmer, mad for love, for instance. Far-fetched.'

'Well then—'

'And Gascoigne. He didn't go to the dressing-rooms. He was on the stage. Have you dwelt on Gascoigne, Wade?'

'Thrashed him to death. We can't get it down to what you might call a cast-iron alibi, sir, because he was mucking round on the stage here, but the hands say he never went off the set and we've found out he was there to welcome each of the guests as they came. No motive, far as we know.'

'And he would have no occasion to use this door.'

220

'This "in again, out again, gone again" stuff with the door. Is it probable do you think, Mr Alleyn? Is it possible?'

'Let's consider. Take any one of the guests – young Palmer or Dr Te Pokiha, for instance.'

'Go ahead, sir.'

'Young Palmer comes to the party, passes Singleton, gives his name, and instead of joining the party on the stage, slips round to the back and up the ladder. He takes off the weight, comes down, lets himself out by this door, shins round to the front, comes in again and joins the party.'

'I'm sure Singleton would have noticed it, Mr Alleyn. You see, Mason had warned him about gate-crashing. He was on the look-out. He had the list of guests and he ticked each one off.'

'Yes, that's the great objection,' agreed Alleyn. 'Still, I'd ask him.'

'Certainly, we'll ask him. The other objection is that the deceased was a stranger here, and most of the guests wouldn't have the ghost of a motive. What about Mason, now? Could he have done this door business, after he went in with you?'

'Unfortunately, I know he couldn't,' said Alleyn. 'He came on to the stage with me and we were together until he went to fetch Miss Dacres.'

'Anyway, sir. Think of the risk a man would run, tearing round the block in his evening duds. It'd look pretty crook if anyone saw him, now, wouldn't it?'

'I don't think he would tear round the block, Wade.'

'What's that?'

'Why not follow the Palmer route, in reverse, and come out in the yard?'

'By cripey, yes. Yes, that's so. But he'd have to know about the path behind the sheds, wouldn't he? Which young Palmer seems to have done, seeing the way he took to it afterwards. Is there anything in this business of young Palmer, do you reckon?'

'Not a damn' thing, I should say.'

'Aw, Geeze!' said Wade disgustedly. 'What a case! It's all cockeyed. Did you ever hear anything like this business of Miss Dacres! Owning up she fixed that weight to protect a man that, as far as we can see, couldn't have done it.'

'At least she's saved us the trouble of accounting for everybody's movements after the murder.'

'She's in a nasty hole. Messing about on the scene of the crime,' muttered Wade. 'She's going to find herself in a very, very uncomfortable little pozzy, is Miss Carolyn Dacres Meyer, widow of deceased.'

'I hope not,' said Alleyn. 'I may even try to corrupt the New Zealand force on her behalf. You never know.'

Wade looked doubtfully at him, decided he was attempting to amuse, and broke out into a guffaw.

'Aw, dikkon, Mr Alleyn!' said Wade.

'What did you say?'

'Haven't you heard that one, sir? I suppose it's NZ digger slang. "Dikkon." It's the same as if you'd say "Come off it." Used to hear it on the Peninsula. "Aw dikkon, dig."'

'On Gallipoli? You were in that show, were you, Wade?'

'Too right. Saw it through from the landing to the evacuation.'

'What ages ago it seems.'

Passing Sergeant Packer, who was on duty at the stage-door, they strolled back to the office, talking returned soldiers' shop.

'What do you think, Mr Alleyn? If there's another war will the young chaps come at it, same as we did, thinking it's great? Some party! And get the same jolt? What do you reckon?'

'I'm afraid to speculate,' said Alleyn.

'Same here. And yet you know I often think : well, it was bloody but it wasn't too bad. As long as you didn't think too much it wasn't too bad. There was a kind of feeling among the chaps that was all right. Know what I mean?'

'I do. One has to take that into account. The pacifists won't succeed until they do. You can't overstate the stupidity and squalid frightfulness, but equally you must recognise that there was a sort of – what? – a sort of emotional compensation; comradeship, I suppose, though it's an ill-used word.'

'I often wonder if crooks feel the same.'

'That's a thought.'

'Know what I mean?' continued Wade, encouraged. 'As if they kind of forgot they were crooks and anti-social, and got a kick out of being all together on the same old game.'

'I should think it was quite likely. All the same they're a hopeless lot – the rank and file. Not much honour among thieves in my experience. Don't you agree? That's why homicide cases are specialised work, Wade. We're not dealing with the class we've been trained to understand.'

'Too right. Look at this case, now.'

'Yes. Look at the damn' thing. We're wandering, Wade. We'll have to get back to business. Come into the office and look at this plan. Have a cigarette.'

'Thanks, I don't mind,' said Wade, taking one. They went into the office, more than ever subfusc in the late afternoon light, with dust already lying thick on Alfred Meyer's old desk, and last night's fire dead in the grate. Wade switched on the lamp and Alleyn walked over to the plan on the wall.

'Taking another look at the old lay-out, Mr Alleyn?'

'Yes. I've got together a sort of theory about the case,' said Alleyn, with his usual air of diffidence. 'If I may, I'll go over it with you. It's the result of this rather wholesale elimination of suspects. You'll probably find gaps in it as wide as a church door. I'd be not altogether sorry if you did.'

'Well, sir, let's have it.'

'Right you are. It begins about five minutes after the final curtain last night.'

Wade glanced up at Alleyn who still stood with his hands in his pockets contemplating the plan.

'How about taking the easy chair, sir?' asked Wade.

223

'You'll be seeing that thing in your sleep.'

'I dare say I shall. You see my whole theory is based on this plan. Come over here and I'll tell you why.'

Wade got up and joined him. Alleyn pointed a long finger at the plan and began to explain.

CHAPTER 22

Fourth Appearance of the Tiki

When Alleyn got back to the hotel he found Dr Te Pokiha waiting for him.

'Had you forgotten that you were to dine with me this evening, Mr Alleyn?'

'My dear Te Pokiha, no, I hadn't forgotten, but I had no idea it was so late. Please forgive me. I do hope you haven't been waiting very long.'

'I've only just arrived. Don't worry, we've plenty of time.'

'Then if I may rush up and change—?'

'If you want to. Not a dinner jacket, please. We shall be alone.'

'Right. I shan't be five minutes.'

He was as good as his word. They had a cocktail together and then took the road in Te Pokiha's car.

'We take the north-east road towards Mount Ruapehu,' said Te Pokiha. 'I expect you are tired of hearing about our mountains and thermal districts. I am afraid New Zealanders are too eager to thrust these wonders at visitors, and to demand admiration.'

'I should like very much indeed to hear a Maori speak of them.'

'Really? You mean a real Maori – not a *pakeha*-Maori?'

'Yes.'

'We, too, are strangers in New Zealand, you know. We have only been here for about thirty generations. We brought our culture with us and applied it to the things we found here. Our religion too, and our science, if we may be allowed to call it science.'

Alleyn looked at the magnificent head. Te Pokiha was a pale Maori, straight-nosed, not very full-lipped. He might have been a Greek or an Egyptian. There was an

225

aristocratic flavour about him – a complete absence of anything vulgar or tentative in his voice or his movements. His speech, gravely formal, carefully phrased, suited him and did not seem at all pedantic or affected.

'Where did you come from?' asked Alleyn.

'From Polynesia, and before that from Easter Island. The tohunga and rangitira say that in the beginning it was from Assyria, but I think the *pakeha* anthropologists do not follow us there. Our teaching was not given to everybody. Only the learned and noble classes were permitted to know the history of their race. It was learnt orally and through the medium of the carvings and hieroglyphics. My grandfather was a deeply-instructed rangitira and I learned much from him. He was a survival of the old order and his kind will not be seen much longer.'

'Do you regret the passing of the old order?'

'In some ways. I have a kind of pride of race – shall we say a savage pride? The *pakeha* has altered everything, of course. We have been unable to survive the fierce white light of his civilisation. In trying to follow his example we have forgotten many of our own customs and have been unable wisely to assimilate his. Hygiene and eugenics for example. We have become spiritually and physically obese. That is only my own view. Most of my people are well content, but I see the passing of the old things with a kind of nostalgia. The *pakeha* give their children Maori christian names because they sound pretty. They call their ships and their houses by Maori names. It is perhaps a charming compliment, but to me it seems a little strange. We have become a side-show in the tourist bureau – our dances – our art – everything.'

'Such as the little green tiki? I understand what you mean.'

'Ah – the tiki.'

He paused and Alleyn had the impression that he had been going to say more about the tiki but had stopped himself. It was growing dark. Te Pokiha's head was silhouetted against a background of green hills and very dark blue mountains.

'To the north are Ruapehu and Ngauruhoe,' he said. 'My grandfather would have told you that the volcanic fires of Ngauruhoe were caused by the youngest son of the Earth Mother who lay deep underground with her child at her breast. The fire was given him for comfort by Rakahore, the rock-god.'

They drove on in silence until the mountains were black against the fading sky.

'My house is not very far off now,' said Te Pokiha quietly. And in a minute or two they crossed a clanking cattle-stop and plunged into a dark tunnel where the headlights shone on the stems of tree-ferns.

'I like the smell of the bush,' said Alleyn.

'Yes? Do you know I once did a very foolish thing. It was when I was at the House – my first year at Oxford, and my first year in England. I became very homesick and wrote in my letters of my home-sickness. I said that I longed for the smell of burning bush-wood and begged them to send me some. So my father sent me a case of logs. It was a very expensive business as you may imagine, but I burnt them in my fireplace at the House and the smoke of Te-Ika-a-Maui hung over the famous Dreaming Spires.' He burst out laughing. 'Ridiculous, wasn't it?'

'Did you take your medical degree at home?'

'Yes, at Thomas's. I was a thorough *pakeha* by that time – almost. Here we are.'

They pulled up in a wide open space before the dark shape of a long one-storeyed house. From the centre of the front wall projected a porch with gable roof, and Alleyn saw that this porch was decorated with Maori carvings.

'An affectation on my part,' said Te Pokiha. 'You may question the taste of joining an old-time porch on to a modern building. At least the carving is genuine.'

'I like it.'

'You must see it by daylight. Come in.'

They dined in a pleasant room, waited on by an enormous and elderly Maori woman, who showed a tendency to join in the laughter when Alleyn cracked a modest joke. After dinner they moved into a comfortable living-room with an open fireplace where an aromatic log fire reminded Alleyn of Te Pokiha's story. The furniture was of the solid smoking-room type – very English and non-committal. A mezzotint of Christ Church, Oxford, an undergraduate group or two, and a magnificent feather cloak decorated the walls.

When, after some excellent brandy, they had lit their pipes, Alleyn asked Te Pokiha if his practice was a general one.

'Oh, yes. When I first came back I had some idea of specialising in gynaecology, but I think it is the one branch of my profession in which my race would tell against me. And then, as I settled down, I began to see the terrible inroads made by civilisation in the health of my own people. Tuberculosis, syphilis, typhoid – none of them known in our savage days when ritual and health-giving dances, as well as strict hygienic habits, were enforced. So I came down to earth – brown earth – and decided that I would become a doctor to my own people.'

'I'm not sure you do not regret your choice.'

'No. Though it is depressing to see how quickly a healthy race can degenerate. I am very busy – consulting-room hours in town, and a wide country beat. I am re-learning some of my own race history.'

And he related several stories about his Maori patients, telling them well, without too much emphasis. The time passed pleasantly in this fashion.

At last Alleyn put his hand in his pocket and pulled out the tiki. He put it on the arm of Te Pokiha's chair.

'May we talk about the tiki?' he asked.

Te Pokiha looked at it with surprise.

'Does Miss Dacres not wish to accept it? Has she returned it to you?'

'No. I hope she will still accept it, though she may not wish to do so. At the moment it is by way of being used in evidence.'

'The tiki? What do you mean?'

'It was found in the gallery above the stage on the spot where the murderer must have stood.'

Te Pokiha gazed at him with something like horror in his eyes.

'That is – is most extraordinary. Do you know how it got there?'

'Yes. I believe I do.'

'I see.'

There was relief and something else – could it be disappointment? – in Te Pokiha's voice. Then, suddenly, he leant forward:

'But it's impossible – that lovely creature! No, there must be some mistake. I cannot believe it of her.'

'Of Miss Dacres? Why should you suspect Miss Dacres?'

'Why, because I saw – but I do not suspect her.'

'Because you saw her slip it into her dress?'

'There is something very strange in this,' said Te Pokiha, staring at the tiki. 'May I ask one question, Mr Alleyn. Do you suspect Miss Dacres of murder?'

'No. I believe her to be innocent.'

'Then how did the tiki get there?'

'I'll tell you presently,' said Alleyn. 'It *was* strange, wasn't it? Almost as though the tiki itself had taken a hand, don't you think?'

'You ask a leading question,' said Te Pokiha, smiling. He had regained his poise completely, it seemed. 'Remember I am a materialistic general practitioner.'

'You are also a pure-blooded Maori aristocrat,' answered Alleyn. 'What would your grandfather have thought?'

Te Pokiha put out his thin dark hand as though to take up the tiki. Then he paused and drew back his hand.

'The demi-god Tiki was the father of mankind. These

229

little symbols are named after him. They do not actually represent him but rather the human embryo and the fructifying force in mankind. The ornament and carving is purely phallic. I know something of the history of this tiki – it was *tapu*. Do you know what that means?'

'Sacred? Untouchable?'

'Yes. Long ago it was dropped from the breast of a woman in a very *tapu* place, a meeting-house, and remained there, unnoticed, for a long time. It therefore became *tapu* itself. The meeting-house was burned to the ground and a *pakeha* found and kept the tiki, afterwards telling where he had found it. My grandfather would have said that this in itself was a desecration, a pollution. The *pakeha,* not long afterwards, was drowned in attempting to ford a river. The tiki was found in his pocket and given, by his son, to the father of the man from whom you have bought it. Your man was once a very prosperous run-holder, but lost almost everything during the depression. Hence his desire to sell the tiki.'

'Miss Gaynes has repeatedly expressed her opinion that the tiki is unlucky,' said Alleyn dryly. 'It seems that she is right. What would your grandfather have thought of the reception they gave it last night? Poor little Meyer was very facetious, wasn't he, pretending to say his prayers to it?'

'Not only facetious but ill-bred,' said Te Pokiha quietly.

'I felt rather ashamed of my compatriots, Dr Te Pokiha, and, as I told you at the time, I regretted my impulse.'

'You need not regret it. The tiki is revenged.'

'Very much so. I shall ask Miss Dacres to return it to me, I think.'

Te Pokiha looked at him, hesitated a moment and then said: 'I do not think she need fear it.'

'Tell me,' said Alleyn, 'if it's not an impertinent question, do you yourself feel anything of – well, anything of what your ancestors would have felt in regard to this coincidence?'

There was a long pause.

'Naturally,' said Te Pokiha, at last, 'I do not feel exactly as a European would feel about the tiki. What do your gipsies say? "You have to dig deep to bury your daddy."'

'Yes,' murmured Alleyn, 'I suppose you do.'

'I hear you are working personally on the case,' said Te Pokiha after another silence. 'May one ask if you feel confident that the murderer will be found?'

'Yes, I am confident.'

'That is excellent,' said Te Pokiha, tranquilly.

'It is simply a question of eliminating the impossible. And, by the way, you can help us there.'

'Can I? In what way?'

'We are trying to establish alibis for all these people. Mr Mason's movements are a little more difficult to trace than those of the cast, because he was in his office before the supper-party. Wade says you saw him there.'

'Yes, I did. At the end of the play I made for the exit at the back of the stalls. I noticed that the office door into the box-office was open, and I thought I would look in on Mr Mason before going behind the scenes. He came in just as I did.'

'From the yard?'

'Yes. He had been out to speak to the stage-doorkeeper, he said.'

'That tallies with what we have. How long did you stay in the office? By the way I hope you don't mind me hauling in shop like this?'

'Not in the least. I hoped that we might discuss the case. Let me see. We stayed there for about ten minutes, I think. Mr Mason said that they would not be ready behind the scenes for some little time and suggested we should have a drink. We took off our overcoats and sat down by the fire. I refused the drink, but he had one, and we both smoked. The men from the box-office came in and Mason dealt with them. Someone came in from the bank to take the cash, and the stage-doorkeeper

231

looked in too, I remember. Oh, yes, and Ackroyd, the little comic fellow, you know – he looked in.'

'Did he, now? What for?'

'As far as I remember it was to tell Mason the guests were beginning to arrive. It struck me he was looking for a free drink, but he didn't get it. Mason packed him off in no time.'

'Did you see him go?'

'How do you mean? I saw him go out into the yard. Then someone else looked in, I think. People were going in and out all the time.'

'Yes, I see.'

'I suppose that was a crucial time,' said Te Pokiha. 'I heard about the counterweight from Gascoigne and Mason, last night. They both insisted that there had been interference. Of course there must have been interference. That sort of thing couldn't happen accidentally.'

'Hardly, one would think. Yes, it's an important period that, when you were in the office. You left Mason there?'

'Yes. He was there when I returned, too; still in his chair by the fire.'

'You returned to the office? Why did you return?'

'Didn't I tell you? How stupid of me. When I got to the stage-door I found I had taken Mason's overcoat instead of my own. We had taken them off at the same time and put them down together. I took my own coat, said a word or two more, and left him locking things up in the office. I remember that I had only just gone on to the stage when you and Mason arrived.'

'I met him at the door of the office as I went down the yard.'

'Well, I suppose I have established Mason's alibi for him,' said Te Pokiha, with a smile, 'and my own too I hope, if I needed one.'

'It's always a handy little thing to have beside you.'

'I suppose so – still there's an absence of motive in my case.'

232

'Ah, yes,' murmured Alleyn, 'we must have motive, of course.'

He picked up the tiki, returned it to his pocket, and looked at his watch.

'Good lord, it's eleven o'clock and I haven't so much as rung up for a car.'

'There's no need. I shall drive you back and spend the night at my rooms. I often do that – it's all arranged. You must have a drink before you go.'

'No, really not, thanks. I promised Wade I'd ring him up before eleven-thirty, so if you don't mind—'

'You can telephone from here.'

'It may be rather a lengthy conversation, so perhaps I'd better leave it until I get to Middleton.'

'Come along, then,' rejoined Te Pokiha courteously. 'I mustn't try to keep you, I suppose.'

'It's been a delightful evening.'

'I hope it is not to be the last.'

They drove back in the starlight. To Alleyn it seemed strange that it was only that morning – a short eighteen hours ago – that he had stood in the deserted street to watch dawn break over the mountains. It seemed to be ages ago. So much had happened. Carolyn by the little stream, talking about her husband, the bush bird whistling. 'She was only a bird—' with a wrinkled human face, Gordon Palmer drinking whisky that poured itself out of the neck of a gargantuan champagne bottle. 'Don't do that, it shouldn't be interfered with.' 'But my old dad taught me. It used to go big in vordevil.' And there was Wade running up and down a ladder like a performing monkey and saying: 'Eight minutes for refreshments at the central police station.' 'Don't do that, you'll muddle the prints.' 'It's all right if you sound your horn at the top. This horn is called a beep-beep. Listen – beep-beep—'

'This horn is called a "beep-beep,"' said Te Pokiha. 'It reminds me of the Paris streets.'

'Lord love us, I've been asleep,' said Alleyn.

'If you will allow me to say so, I think you're overtaxing your strength a little. You look tired. Aren't you supposed to be on a holiday?'

'I'll be able to sink back into sloth tomorrow.'

'As soon as that?'

'I hope so. Here we are at the hotel, I see. Well, thank you so much, Te Pokiha. It's been an extremely interesting evening.'

'I'm afraid I've been of little use as far as your case is concerned.'

'On the contrary,' said Alleyn, 'you have given me a piece of exceedingly valuable information.'

'Really? I mustn't ask questions, I suppose. Goodnight.'

'Goodnight.'

CHAPTER 23

Alleyn as Maskelyne

Alleyn slept heavily and dreamlessly until half past nine. He had arranged to meet Wade at ten, and the inspector was waiting for him when he came out of the breakfast-room. They walked down to the theatre together.

'I've fixed it with old Singleton, Mr Alleyn. He'll be there waiting for us. He's a funny old chap. Dismal Joe, the stage-hands call him; quite an old character in his way, he is, with a great gift of the gab. He says he's an old actor and I believe it's a fact, too.'

'Another actor! I remember giving him my name. He seemed rather a rum old article.'

'It's a theatre show this, isn't it, sir?'

They walked on in silence, and then Wade said:

'Well, Mr Alleyn, I hope you're quite satisfied with the work we've done for you.'

'My dear chap, more than satisfied. I've never had such a case. All the routine work done by you fellows, and damn' well done. All I had to do was to pick out the plums.'

'Well sir, as far as we're concerned it's been a pleasure. We very much appreciate the way you've worked with us, Mr Alleyn, taking us into your confidence all along. I must say when you rang up last night I got a bit of a surprise. I don't say we wouldn't have thrashed it out for ourselves and come to the right conclusion, but we wouldn't have come there so quick.'

'I'm sure you'd have got there,' said Alleyn cordially. 'You fixed up the other business all right, I suppose?'

'Yes. I don't think there'll be any trouble. Packer and Cass are there.'

Packer and Cass met them in the theatre yard. Standing just behind them was the doorkeeper to whom Alleyn remembered giving his name on the night of the party. Old

Singleton was an extraordinary figure. He was very tall, very bent, and remarkably dirty. His nose was enormous and gloomily purple, he suffered from asthma, and he smelt of whisky.

"Morning, Packer, 'morning, Cass,' said Alleyn.

'This is Mr Singleton, Chief Inspector,' said Wade.

'Chief Inspector who, Mr Wade?' asked Singleton earnestly, in a rumbling wheeze.

'Alleyn.'

'Of New Scotland Yard, London?'

'Yes, Mr Singleton,' said Alleyn good-humouredly.

'Shake, sir!' exclaimed Mr Singleton, extending a particularly filthy hand. Alleyn shook it.

'From the Dear Old Town!' continued Mr Singleton emotionally. 'The Dear Old Town!'

'You are a Londoner, Mr Singleton?'

'Holborn Empire! Ten years. I was first fiddle, sir.' Mr Singleton went through an elaborate pantomime of drawing a bow across the strings of an imaginary violin. 'You wouldn't think it to look at me now,' he added truthfully. 'I have fallen into the sere and yellow, Chief Inspector. I am declined into the vale of years. I am a fixed figure for the time of scorn to point his slow unmoving finger at. Yurrahumph!' He coughed unpleasantly and spat. 'You would not credit it, Superintendent Alleyn, if I were to tell you I played the Moor for six months to capacity business.'

As Alleyn really could not credit it, he contented himself with making a consolatory noise.

'Shakespeare!' ejaculated Mr Singleton, removing his hat. 'The Swan of Stratford-on-Sea! The Bard!'

'Nobody like him, is there?' said Alleyn cheerfully. 'Well, Mr Singleton, you're about to take the stage again. I want you to tell us all about last night.'

'Last night of all when that same star did entertain her guests. An improvisation, Chief Constable, based on the Bard. Last night. I could a tale unfold would harrow up thy soul, freeze thy young blood. As a matter of fact I am unable to do any such thing. Last night I merely discharged my degrading duties as a doorkeeper in the house of the ungodly, and repaired to my lonely attic.'

He paused and blew his nose on an unspeakable handkerchief. Wade slipped behind him and gave a spirited imitation of someone draining a glass to the dregs.

'You kept a list of the guests, I understand, and checked off the names as they came in.'

Mr Singleton drew a piece of paper from his bosom and handed it to Alleyn with a slight bow.

'To witness if I lie,' he explained grandly.

It was the list. Alleyn glanced at it and returned to the job.

'Did Mr Ackroyd come out some time before the party?'

'Ackroyd, Ackroyd, Ackroyd. Let me see, let me see, let me see. Ackroyd. The comedian. Yes! Ackroyd came out.'

'You did not mention this to Mr Wade.'

'I take my stand on that document!' said Mr Singleton magnificently.

'Quite so. How long was Mr Ackroyd away.'

'He returned in the twinkling of an eye.'

'You're sure of that?'

'I am constant as the northern star,' said Mr Singleton, stifling a slight hiccough. 'Ackroyd eggzited and re-entered immediately. He went to the door of the office. He appeared to address those within. He returned.'

'You watched him?'

'With the very comment of my soul. Would it astonish you to learn that I played the Dane before—'

'Did you really? Mr George Mason came out of the office some time before that, I believe?'

'George Mason, George! The manager. He did. I have already made a statement to this effect, I believe, Mr Wade?'

'That's right, Joe, but Mr Alleyn just wants to check up.'

Mr Singleton inclined his head.

237

'Quite so. The manager, George Mason, came to the stage-door and repeated, gratuitously and un-nesh – uness-essraly, my instructions. I was to be sure to ask of each guest his local habitation and his name.'

'Mr Mason returned to the office?'

'I swear it.'

'You may have to,' said Alleyn. 'How long was Mr Mason away from the office?'

'Let me see. Let me see. While one with moderate haste might tell an hundred. I showed him my list. I convinced him of my incorruptible purpose. I called to mind, I recollect, the coincidence that I had played the part of the porter in *Macbeth,* and of the sentry, Bernardo, in the Dane – that was in my green and salad days, Commissioner. I had scarce embarked on this trifling reminiscence when Mason turned up the collar of his dinner jacket and observing that the air was chilly, turned and ran back to the office.'

Alleyn uttered a slight exclamation, glanced at Wade, and asked Singleton to repeat this statement, which he did at great length but to the same effect.

'Do you remember, now,' said Alleyn, 'if the office door was open on to the yard as it is now?'

'It was open.'

'Ah yes. You know Dr Te Pokiha by sight?'

'The native? Dark-visaged, like the Moor? The Moor was perhaps my greatest role. My favourite role. "Most potent grave—"'

'Wonderful play, that,' interrupted Alleyn. 'Dr Te Pokiha was among the last guests to arrive, I think?'

'True.'

'Did you notice him coming?'

'I marked him come, yes. He too emerged from the office, carrying his mantle. He darted back and reappeared. He approached me and I admitted him, striking out his name as I did so.'

'Now, Mr Singleton, I take it from what you have told me

that you would be prepared to make a sworn statement that once Mr Ackroyd, or Mr Mason, or Dr Te Pokiha had gone in at the stage-door they did not return to the office, and once they had gone to the office, did not return to the stage without your knowledge?'

'I have sworn it, indeed. In common parlance, sir, you can bet your boots and put your shirt on it.'

'Well now, Mr Singleton, I'm going to ask you to help me in a little experiment. Will you do this?'

'Impart! Proceed!'

'I want you to stand here by the stage-door and treat me as though I was Mr Ackroyd, Dr Te Pokiha, or Mr Mason. As soon as I have gone, I want you to wait for five minutes and then walk along to the office. Will you do this?'

'Certainly.'

'Watch the office door,' said Alleyn, 'and Mr Wade will keep the time.' He glanced at Packer and Cass who had listened to the entire conversation with the liveliest interest. 'You look steadily down the alley, you two. Are you keen on conjuring tricks?'

'I remember—' began Mr Singleton; but Alleyn interrupted him.

'Will any gentleman in the audience provide me with a handkerchief? Sergeant Packer? Thank you. You are perfectly certain this is your handkerchief? You see me place it in the right-hand pocket of my jacket? I thank you. Now, Mr Singleton, I am one of those three gentlemen aforesaid. You see me here in the yard. You are standing by the stage-door. I walk along the yard into the office. Got your watch out, Wade? Off we go.'

Singleton and the three officers stood in a group at the stage-door. Alleyn walked briskly down the yard and into the office, leaving the door open.

'What's the idea, Mr Wade?' asked Cass. 'He's a bit of a hard case, isn't he?'

'He'll do me,' said Packer. 'He's a corker.'

'Watch the door into the office,' snapped Wade. 'And the yard.'

The door remained open on the yard. Nobody spoke. The sound of traffic in the street, and footsteps on the pavement outside, broke the silence. One or two people walked past at the end of the yard.

'He hasn't come out, anyway,' said Cass.

'Time,' said Wade. 'Come on, Singleton. Come on, you two.'

They all walked down the yard and into the office. Alleyn was sitting at the desk.

'Well,' said Alleyn brightly. 'Still here, you see.'

'I thought, Superintendent,' said Mr Singleton, 'that you said we were to receive a surprise.'

'And you are disappointed?' He looked from one dubious face to the other. Wade was staring expectantly at him.

'I expect you'd like to know where the laugh and round of applause comes in,' said Alleyn. 'If Sergeant Packer will look at the bottom rung of the back-stage ladder into the grid he will learn something to his advantage.'

'Go on, Packer,' said Wade.

Packer hurried off through the stage-door. There was a short pause and then he came thundering back.

'By cripey, Mr Wade, it's a corker! By gosh, Mr Wade, it's a humdinger!'

He was waving the handkerchief. Cass's eyes opened very wide. Mr Singleton moistened his lips once or twice but, for a marvel, he had nothing to say.

'Tied to the bottom rung it was,' declared Packer. 'Tied to the bottom rung. By gum, it's a beaut!'

'You see it can be done, Wade,' said Alleyn.

'It's good enough,' said Wade delightedly, 'it's good enough.'

'Ah – um – very neat,' said Mr Singleton. He drew the palm of his hand across his mouth. 'I recollect seeing the Great Houdini—'

240

'Mr Singleton,' said Alleyn, 'I'm afraid I've taken up far too much of your time. We mustn't keep you any longer. Will you allow me to quote your favourite author? – "Spend this for me."'

Mr Singleton broke into a loud laugh as his fingers closed on the tip.

'Ah ha, sir, I can have at you again. "I'll be your purse-bearer and leave you for an hour."' He removed his hat, bowed, said, 'Good morning gentlemen,' and hurried away.

'What a fabulous bit of wreckage,' said Alleyn. 'Poor old devil, I wonder if he – Oh, well! I suppose you'd like an explanation of all this.' He turned to Cass and Packer.

'Too right, sir,' said Packer. 'You've got us beat.'

'What I did was this. I came into this office, as you saw. I came out again as you apparently didn't see, and I went round to the back by what I feel should be called Cass's Alley.'

'But look here, sir, we were watching the yard.'

'I know. I left the door open and I sidled along to the street end keeping against the wall. I was hidden so far by the open door. If you go along to the stage-door you will see what I mean. I was just able to keep out of sight.'

'But the entrance at the end! You had to cross there, and I swear I never took my eyes off it,' burst out Cass.

'You saw me walk across, Cass.'

'I never! Pardon me, sir.'

'You didn't recognise your own overcoat and hat? You left them in here.'

Alleyn pointed to where they lay across the desk.

'I ventured to borrow them. As soon as I got in here I slipped them on, and, as I have said, sidled out under cover of the door, turned to the right when I got out to the pavement, and then walked briskly back across the open end of the yard. You did not recognise me. Now, as soon as I got across the entrance to the yard I was hidden by the projecting bicycle shed. I repeated the sidling game on the

241

other side and came back to Cass's Alley. Once in there, I bolted round to the back door, having borrowed the key. All this took less than two minutes. Another half-minute going up the ladder. I allowed a minute to unhook the weight and came down in less than half. I put the key back in the door and returned by Cass's Alley, reversing the process. I just had time to get your hat and coat off, before you came along. D'you see?'

'I don't know that I do, sir, altogether,' confessed Cass, 'but you *did* it, so I reckon it's right.'

'Come and look at the plan here, and you'll see how it fits in.'

Wade, Packer and Cass all stared solemnly at the plan.

'It's a funny thing,' said Wade, 'how easy it is to miss the obvious thing. That alleyway now. You'd have thought we'd have picked it for something straight away.'

'You'd have thought *I* would,' grunted Cass, 'seeing I'm still sore from where I stuck.'

'It widens out as soon as you're round the corner,' said Alleyn.

'It'd need to,' said Cass.

Wade looked at his watch.

'It's time,' he said to Alleyn.

'Ah, yes,' said Alleyn.

They all stood listening. From the street outside came the irregular sound of mid-morning traffic, the whining clamour of trams, the roar of cars in low gear, punctured by intermittent horn notes, and behind it all the patter of feet on asphalt. One pair of feet seemed to separate and come closer.

Someone had turned into the yard.

CHAPTER 24

Dr Te Pokiha Plays to Type. Warn Curtain

But it was only Mr St John Ackroyd. Cass, who had moved into the yard, stopped him. The others could see him through the half-open door. Beside the gigantic Cass, Ackroyd looked a pygmy of a man. He stood there in his rather loud check overcoat and jaunty hat, staring cockily up at Cass.

'Excuse me, sir,' said Cass, 'but were you wanting to go into the theatre?'

'Yes, I was. I want to get to my wardrobe. Haven't a clean shirt to my back.'

'I'm afraid I can't let you in this morning, sir.'

'Oh, God! Why the devil not? Look here, you can come in with me and see I don't muck up the half-chewed cigar at the point marked X. Come on now, old boy, be a sport.'

'Very sorry, sir. I'm under orders and it can't be done.'

'Yes, but look, old boy. Here—'

Mr Ackroyd appeared to make an attempt to place his tiny hand confidingly in Cass's. Cass stepped back a pace.

'No, no, sir. We don't do things that way. Quite out of the question, thank you all the same.'

'Oh, blast! Well, what the hell am I supposed to do? Buy new shirts?'

'If you'll wait a little, sir, I'll inquire—'

'Here, Cass!' called Wade.

'Sir?'

'Just a minute. Come in, Mr Ackroyd, come in.'

The comic face was thrust round the door and distorted into a diverting grimace.

'Hullo, hullo! All the stars in one piece, including the Great Noise from the Yard. Any room for a little one?'

He came in, followed by Cass, and perched on the edge

243

of Alfred Meyer's desk, cocking his hat jauntily over his left eye.

'Well. How's things?' he inquired.

'I'm glad you looked in, Mr Ackroyd,' said Wade. 'There's just one little matter I wanted to see you about.'

'Is there, by gum! Well, there's another little matter I'd like to see you about. I want to get at my wardrobe.'

'In the statement you gave us on the night of the fatality,' continued Wade in a monotonous chant, 'you said that you went from the dressing-rooms to the party.'

'That's right.'

'Remaining on the stage until after the fatality?'

'Yes. What's wrong with that?' demanded Ackroyd.

'You didn't come out into the yard, at all?'

'Eh? – I – how d'you mean?'

'Just that, Mr Ackroyd. You didn't leave the stage before the party and walk along to the office?'

'Oh, God! Look here, old boy, I – I believe I did.'

'You did?'

'Yes. It was only for a minute. Just to tell George people were beginning to come in.'

'Why didn't you tell us this before, Mr Ackroyd?'

'Damn it all, I'd forgotten all about it.'

'But now you state definitely that you did come here?'

'Yes,' said Ackroyd uncomfortably.

'We'll have to get a new statement to that effect,' said Wade. 'Will you tell us exactly what happened, Mr Ackroyd?'

'Just what I said. I came along and stood in the doorway there. I said: "The party's started, George," and George said: "Right you are. I've got a job here and then I'll be along," or something. The job he had seemed to be a perfectly good drink. Well, I passed a remark or two and went back to the party.'

'Was Mr Mason alone?'

'What? No, I rather fancy the black quack was there.'

'Pardon?' asked Wade, genteelly. 'Who did you say?'

'The black quack.'

244

'Can Mr Ackroyd possibly mean Dr Te Pokiha?' asked Alleyn of nobody in particular.

'You'd hardly think so, would you?' said Wade.

'Oh, no offence,' said Ackroyd. 'I forgot there was no colour bar in this country. The light-brown medico was on-stage. That better?'

'You want to be very careful when you make statements, Mr Ackroyd,' said Wade austerely. 'We'll have to get you to sign a new one. Seems funny, you forgetting you came along here.'

'Why the hell!' shouted Ackroyd hotly. 'What's funny about it? Why should I remember? Don't be silly.'

'Did you go straight back to the stage?'

'Yes, I did go straight back, I – hullo George!'

George Mason's unhappy face had appeared round the door.

'Hullo,' he mumbled. 'Can I come in?'

'Come in, Mr Mason,' said Wade. 'Take a seat. You're just the man we wanted to see. Do you remember Mr Ackroyd, here, coming along to the office before the party?'

Mr Mason passed his hand wearily over his forehead and slumped into a chair.

'Do I remember – Yes, I do. Didn't I tell you that? I'm sorry.'

'Quite all right. We just have to check up these little points. I don't think I asked you, definitely. Cass, take Mr Ackroyd along to his dressing-room and let him get anything he wants. Will you call in at the station between two and three this afternoon, Mr Ackroyd? Thank you. Good morning.'

'And that,' said Ackroyd bitterly, 'takes me *right* off. Good morning.'

When he had gone, Mason turned to Wade.

'Is there any mail here for me?' he asked.

'I think there is, Mr Mason. We'll let you have it.'

Mason groaned. 'I suppose you've nothing definite to tell

me, Mr Wade? I've got our advance going nearly crazy in Wellington, not knowing whether he's representing a repertory company or a murder gang.'

'It won't be much longer.' Wade fell back on his stock opening gambit. 'I'm sorry to give you the trouble of coming down this morning but there's just one little matter I'd like to see you about, Mr Mason. We've been talking to old Singleton, the doorkeeper, about the people that were outside, as you might say, before the party.'

'Boozy old devil. Was an actor once. Makes you think, doesn't it? There but for the wrath of God, or whatever it is!'

Alleyn chuckled.

'He's a bit too boozy for our liking,' continued Wade. He's given us one bit of information, and Dr Te Pokiha's given us another that contradicts it point-blank. It's only a silly little thing—'

'Don't talk to me about silly little things,' interjected Mason peevishly. 'I'm sick of the phrase. There's that Gaynes kid making a scene in fifteen different positions every five minutes, and demanding to be sent home to Daddy because she's "a silly little thing" and so, so upset. And I ate some of this native crayfish for dinner last night and it kept me awake till dawn – silly little thing! Ugh!'

'Mr Alleyn knows more about this than I do. He spoke about it to Dr Te Pokiha.'

'Te Pokiha's coming here, by the way. He looked in at the pub and said you wanted him.'

'If Mr Alleyn—?' said Wade with a glance into the corner of the room where Alleyn sat peacefully smoking.

'It's just this,' said Alleyn. 'The old gentleman tells us that when you went out to the stage-door to warn him about asking the guests' names, you were bareheaded and in your dinner jacket.'

'Oh Lor',' groaned Mason, 'what of it? So I was.'

246

'And Dr Te Pokiha says that he came in here just as you returned from the stage-door and you were wearing an overcoat and hat.'

'It's a case of the drunk being right and the sober man wrong, as far as I can remember. I don't think I put on my coat to go out. No, I'm sure I didn't. I recollect old Singleton started one of his interminable reminiscences and I said it was too cold to stand about and made that the excuse to run away. I believe I did slip my coat on after I got back. Probably had it on when the doctor came in.'

'That explains that,' said Alleyn. 'It sounds idiotic, but we have to fiddle about with these things.'

'Well, if it's any help, that's what I think happened. Look here, Alleyn, *are* you any further on with this? I don't want to make a nuisance of myself but this game is literally costing the Firm hundreds. It's driving me silly, honestly it is. What about the affair on the train, can't you get a lead from that?'

Alleyn got up and walked across to the fireplace.

'Wade,' he said, 'I don't know whether you'll approve of this, but I'm going to take Mr Mason into our confidence over the affair on the train.'

'Just as you please, Mr Alleyn,' said Wade, looking rather blank. 'You do just as you think best.'

'It's this,' said Alleyn, turning to Mason. 'You remember that before we got to Ohakune everyone in the carriage was asleep.'

'Well,' said Mason, 'I don't remember because I was asleep myself.'

'As Mr Singleton would say,' grinned Alleyn, 'a very palpable hit. I put it carelessly. Let me amend it. Each of us has admitted that he or she was asleep for some time before we got to Ohakune. I have asked all the others and they agree to this. They also agree that they were all awakened by a terrific jolt as we got on to the thing they call the spiral. Old Miss Max was decanted into my lap. You remember?'

'I do. Poor old Susie! She looked a scream, didn't she?'

'And Ackroyd let out a remarkably blue oath.'

'That's right. Foul-mouthed little devil – I don't like that sort of thing. Common. He will do it.'

'Well now, you remember all this—'

'Of course I do. I thought we'd run into a cow or something.'

'And Mr Meyer thought someone had given him a kick in the seat.'

'By George!' said Mason. 'Why didn't someone think of that?'

'That's what we're always saying to the chief, Mr Mason,' said Wade. 'The trouble is, we don't, and he does.'

There was a knock on the door.

'That'll be the doctor,' said Wade. 'Come in.' Dr Te Pokiha came in, smiling.

'I'm sorry I couldn't get here before. I had to go to the hospital – urgent case. You wanted to see me, Mr Alleyn?'

'We all want to see you, I think,' said Alleyn. 'It's in connection with our conversation last night.'

He repeated the story of Mason and his overcoat. Te Pokiha listened without a word. When Alleyn had finished, there was a pause.

'Well, Doctor, do you think you made a mistake?' said Wade.

'Certainly not. Mr Mason came in at the outside door wearing his coat and hat. He took them off afterwards, when I removed my own coat. I am not in the habit of making misstatements.'

'It's not that,' said Mason peaceably, 'it's just that I came in before you did and put on my coat because I was cold. I've got a weak tummy, Doctor,' he added with an air of giving the medical man a treat.

'You came in after I did,' said Te Pokiha with considerable emphasis. The whites of his eyes seemed to become more noticeable and his heavy brows came together.

'Well, I'm sorry, but I didn't,' said Mason.

'You mean to say I'm a liar.'

248

'Don't be silly, Doctor. You simply made a mistake.'

'I did not make any mistake. This is insufferable. You will please admit at once that I am right.'

'Why the deuce should I when you are obviously wrong,' said Mason irritably.

'Don't repeat that.' Te Pokiha's warm voice thickened. He lips coarsened into a sort of snarl. He showed his teeth like a dog. 'By Jove,' thought Alleyn, 'the odd twenty per cent of pure savage.'

'Oh, don't be a fool,' grunted Mason. 'You don't know what you're talking about.'

'You give me the lie!'

'Shut up. This isn't a Wild West show.'

'You give me the lie!'

'Oh, for God's sake don't go native,' said Mason – and laughed.

Te Pokiha made a sudden leap at him. Mason scuttled behind Packer. 'Keep off, you damn' Nigger!' he screamed.

The next five minutes were occupied in saving Mr Mason's life. Alleyn, Packer and Wade tackled Te Pokiha efficiently and scientifically, but even so it took their combined efforts to subdue him. He fought silently and savagely and only gave up when they had both his arms and one of his legs in chancery.

'Very well,' he said suddenly, and relaxed.

Cass appeared bulkily in the doorway. Ackroyd, clasping an armful of underwear, peered under his arm.

'Here, let me out,' said Mason.

'What's wrong, sir?' asked Cass, not moving.

'I apologise, Mr Alleyn,' said Te Pokiha quietly. 'You can loose your hand.'

'All right, Wade,' said Alleyn.

'Thank you.' He moved away from them, his brown hands at his tie. 'I am deeply ashamed,' he said. 'This man has spoken of my – my colour. It is true I am a "native". I come of a people who do not care for insults but I should

249

not have forgotten that an *ariki*[1] does not lay hands on a *taurekareka*.'[2]

'What's all this?' asked Ackroyd greedily.

'You buzz off, sir,' advised Cass. Ackroyd disappeared.

'I will go now,' said Te Pokiha. 'If you wish to see me again, Mr Alleyn, I shall be at my rooms between one and two. I am very sorry indeed that I forgot myself. Good morning, gentlemen.'

'And with that he swep' off,' said Mason, coming out of cover. 'My God, what a savage. I think if you don't mind I'll go back to the pub. This has upset me. My God. Has he gone? Right, I'm off.'

He went down the yard. Te Pokiha was getting into his car.

'Follow him,' snapped Alleyn to Cass. 'Don't lose sight of him.'

'Who?' said Cass, startled. 'Te Pokiha?'

'No, Mason,' said Alleyn.

[1] Ariki – gentleman – (literally – first-born).
[2] Taurekareka – slave, low-class person.

CHAPTER 25

Alleyn Speaks the Tag

Extract from a letter written by Chief Detective-Inspector Alleyn to Detective-Inspector Fox, CID:

—I've just returned from the arrest which took place immediately after the inquest. Mason gave no trouble. I think he was taken completely by surprise, though he must have felt things were getting dangerous as soon as the overcoat was mentioned. He said that he was innocent and that he would make no statement until he had consulted a lawyer. Psychologically he might be classed with Crippen, a drab everyday little man; but he's not got the excuse of the *crime passionel.* I suspect a stronger motive than the mere acquisition of money. Your cable seems to point to something fishy about the handling of his side of Incorporated Playhouses. I wouldn't mind betting that you find he's been gambling with the Firm's money and needed this bequest to get himself out of a hole. If the story of his leaving a company stranded in America is true, it looks as if we'll find a history of unscrupulousness over money matters.

He is a superb actor, of course. They told me so in the wardrobe-room and, by George, it's true. He got right into the skin of his part – the insignificant little dyspeptic, worrying about what would happen to the show. The dyspepsia is true enough; we've found half a pharmacopoeia of remedies in his room. Somebody ought to write a monograph on the effect of the stomach on the morals.

You will get a solemn letter of thanks from Nixon, I expect. You've been remarkably nippy getting on to the trail, you cunning old devil. The case has interested me very much. It looked so complicated and it was actually so simple, once Bob Parsons had made his statement. Of course Mason had no idea Bob was in a position to provide a cast-iron alibi for the entire company, and no doubt thought that it would look as if any one of them might have dodged out and popped up to the grid. We have been very lucky. If Miss Dacres had not dropped the tiki I don't believe we should have made an arrest. The stage-staff would have sworn it was murder, but everyone else would have thought they had made a mistake over the weights. I can't help wondering if Mason meant, all along, to do just what Miss Dacres did for him. He didn't get a chance, as it happened. I packed him off to the office with Te Pokiha. Really, he planned the thing quite well. His visit to the stage-door established his alibi, and his remark about the cold air drew Singleton's attention to the fact that he was hatless and in his dinner-jacket. He returned to the office, put on his overcoat and hat, slid along the wall under cover of the open door – it's an ill-lit place at night – walked boldly across the open end where there must have been plenty of people coming away from the show, came back along the yard, hidden from Singleton by the projecting bicycle shed, and then doubled round to the back of the theatre, using the back-door key and leaving it on the inside when he returned.

If Te Pokiha had not come in from the box-ofice, I fancy Mason would have opened the door and shown himself, without his overcoat, to the clerks. That five minutes would never have been accounted for. Of course, we are now going over every inch of the path behind the sheds and hope to get something from it. The defence will have a little difficulty in accounting for Mason's vivid recollection of an incident that never took place. Susan Max was not projected into my lap in the train, nor did Ackroyd utter any oaths.

Mason, of course, thought this little diversion must have occurred when he was out on the platform taking a place kick at Meyer's behind, and did not dare say he had not remembered it. He couldn't say he had slept through it, as he's always talking about being a light sleeper. Broadhead remembers someone coming back from the head of the carriage and sitting somewhere behind him. This, I believe, was Mason returning from his attempt. I fancy he got his idea for the second and successful attempt from the accident of the falling weight.

I've asked Nixon and Wade to give a miss to Carolyn Dacres's performance as a weight-lifter. They are willing enough as it would very much confuse the issue in the minds of a jury. I shall be called and shall give an account of the condition found on my first visit to the grid, when the weight was still missing. Ticklish and possibly rather hot, but quite honest in the last analysis.

I think the verdict will go against him, but there is a Labour Government in power here with anti-capital punishment leanings, so I fancy it will be a life-sentence. Miss Dacres insists on paying the cast a retaining salary for as long as they have to remain in this country. Hamledon and Gascoigne are trying to deal with affairs for her. I suppose she'll marry Hambledon one of these days. He's a nice fellow – Hambledon. I don't think he knows she ever suspected him and I hope she doesn't tell him. Liversidge is sweating blood and shaking in his fancy socks. He is a nasty bit of work and ought to be jugged. He's also rather a fool. I fancy his only idea in letting fall ambiguous remarks about Broadhead and the money was to try and divert suspicion of theft from himself, though, of course, he was terrified we'd find out about his conversation with Meyer and look upon it as a strong indication of motive to murder. He's such a skunk that I suppose he'd have used Broadhead or anyone else as a red herring. The parents of young Palmer and of Valerie Gaynes have cabled for their respective offspring but won't get 'em yet awhile. Young Palmer is not entirely porcine and may turn into a presentable citizen one day. Miss Gaynes is, beyond all hope, abominable, and I hope they don't give her the satisfaction of trying to be an actress in the witness-box. Ackroyd is chastened, old Brandon Vernon philosophical, and Gascoigne worried to death. Our old friend Miss Max shakes her head and keeps a friendly eye on Carolyn Dacres. Young Broadhead seems to be in a state of bewildered relief.

As you will see by this notepaper I am staying with Dr Te Pokiha. I am learning something of his people. He has apologised seven times, up to date, for losing his temper with Mason, and tells me all members of his family hate being called liars. I hope he doesn't fly into a rage with defending counsel, who is almost certain to question his veracity. He's an extraordinarily interesting fellow and, in spite of the temper, he has the most exquisite manners.

I've been asked to stay by several of the surrounding station-holders, so I shall see something of the North Island. They're an amazingly hospitable people, these New Zealanders, very anxious that one should admire their country, rather on the defensive about it, but once they accept you, extremely friendly. I am asked, embarrassingly and repeatedly, about 'the accent' and don't know how to answer. The intelligentsia, who seem to be a gentle distillation of the Press and the universities, speak a queerly careful language and tell funny stories with the most meticulous regard for the *mot juste*. Their views are blamelessly liberal. What a damn' superior ass I sound, talking like this about them. After this case is cleared up I go south to a high plateau encircled by

254

mountains. I have fallen in love with the sound of this place, and indeed, with the country altogether. The air really *is* like wine, balmy and exciting. The colour is clear and everything is exquisitely defined – no pretty smudging.

Well, my old Fox, all this is a long cry from the case. There's no more to say except that I await your air-mail letter with composure and confidence. I shall end this letter by running my pen round the little greenstone tiki so that you have an idea of his shape and size. He will not appear in evidence, I hope, but you will see that in his own way he has played a not inconsiderable part in the affair. Carolyn Dacres tells me she still wants to have him. May he bring her better luck.

Goodbye, you old devil. It must be so exciting to be a detective.

Yours ever,

RODERICK ALLEYN

Epilogue

On an evening three months after the close of the case Alleyn, stretched luxuriously on a widely-spread tussock, looked across Lake Pukaki to where Aeorangi, the cloud-piercer, shone immaculate against the darkening sky. He would smoke one pipe before turning back to the little wooden hotel. With a sigh he put his hand in his pocket and took out three letters with English stamps on the envelopes. His holiday was nearly over, and here was old Fox saying how glad they would be at the Yard to see him again. The second was from his Assistant Commissioner – very cordial. He dropped them on the warm, lichen-surfaced earth, and once again he read the final paragraph in the third letter.

I felt I should like to tell you that Hailey and I think we shall be married in a year's time. Please give us your blessing, dear Mr Alleyn. One other thing. There will be a step-child for Hailey. So you see that the greenstone tiki has fulfilled its purpose and I shall have the best possible remembrance of my dear Alfie-Pooh.

September 16th, 1936.